Man of the World

LAYNE MAHEU

Man of the World

[signature: Layne Maheu]

LAYNE MAHEU

CHATWIN BOOKS

SEATTLE

2021

To my mom,
who ran outside
to the patio
to wave
up to the sky

And to my dad
who tilted the wings
of the rent-a-plane
side to side
and waved back

Hubert Latham, when asked by Armand Fallières, President of France, what he did before flying aeroplanes, replied, *"Monsieur le Président,* I am a Man of the World."

Book I

Aeroship from Across the Sea

Almost every evening a crowd of two or three thousand people comes to see if I will make a flight, and goes home disappointed if I do not. Some of them have come twenty, forty or even sixty miles on bicycles and a few from foreign countries. One old man of 70 living about 30 miles away made the round trip on a bicycle every day for nearly a week.

—Wilbur Wright to his father, Bishop Milton Wright,
Le Mans, France, September 13, 1908

SAINT-MARS-LA-BRIÈRE

THE WIND THAT RIPS THROUGH our valley has a name.

From the time before the Roman and Gaul, la Galerne has swept in from the hills and blasted the thick canopy of leaves from the poplars and dwarf fruit trees. Many a farm boy before my time has climbed up the belfry's ladder, when la Galerne came too early, to pull on the rope with all his might. As you jump and heave and the rope hauls you up, the church bell echoes in your skull with a desperate, white-hot ecstasy. It gives warning to the witches who steer the storm clouds through the sky. It drives off the hail and thunderstorms that threaten the crop. They say the old cloche *can summon the Virgin to our woods, along with lightning, which struck my uncle once up in the belfry and left him blind for three days.*

Eventually, though, the wind leaves us nothing more than the bare branches of winter, and soon after, the soft turmoil of the overcast that quenches the green leaves' thirst each spring. In this way, la Galerne gives its regular, continuous drama of the clouds, as furious or as gentle as it may be at each day's end, like a call to vespers.

Then, one day in the summer of my seventeenth year, la Galerne blew in over the hills and changed my life in an instant. The timeline of my days can be sharply drawn into those that came before, and those that came thereafter.

1.

THIS HAPPENED TO ME back in the August of 1908, on a gray Saturday morning still damp from the rains of the night before. Emerging from the darkened animal air of the barn, I beheld a strange and most wonderful sight.

A passenger balloon came sailing in low over the fields—fat, unwieldy, apparently helpless—about twice the height of the tree line, the treetops of our very own farm. I did not doubt my own eyes, not yet adjusted to the glare of the overcast. I doubted that what I saw was possible. The rounded giant had an unreality to it, as if a village steeple could come unhinged and float above the trees. It approached like an enormous shadow that might collapse at any minute back into the windy ether it came from. Meanwhile, the two figures in the wicker basket below showed complete faith in the unseen forces that kept them sailing through the cloudy gloom. Their swollen ship seemed stationary but gave a little movement, like the lifting of the gills of a fish, as the gusts and riptides pushed it closer and closer toward me.

Surely these two adventurers were lost—blown far off course. Much like the five American Civil War soldiers in Jules Verne's *Mysterious Island*, whose balloon marooned them in the vast regions of the South Pacific. What pilot would ever want to sail above the dwarf fruit trees of our lost hollow? No, these two aeronauts were nearly shipwrecked already. Did they ride in a hot air balloon? Or a ship filled with some rare gaseous mixture produced by scientists in a factory? I'd heard that in the hot air balloon, it is the smoke that lifts the balloon up, a special kind of smoke, the smoke from animal hides. So aeronauts have to burn old shoes and handbags and wasted saddles to get the balloon aloft. The lower their balloon sank, the faster it sailed.

Just when it seemed the two aeronauts' journey was all but over, a burlap sack hanging from the balloon's wicker basket fell to the ground, landing with a thud in the waist-high barley. The pilots let go another bag, which hit near the well with an awful wood-cracking sound. I ran to the sound with dread, only to find the roof above the well had collapsed.

"So sorry, monsieur!" a voice called down. "There is an accident, I see."

I looked up, dazed as in a dream. Were the aeronauts addressing me, or some other hapless creature of the farm? I could not be more disturbed if the very king and queen of Spain were floating there above me. One of the aeronauts especially fit the part of some rare, storied figure; something about his easy leaning posture conveyed that it was only natural he should drop objects on the dwellings of the poor below.

"Don't lead him to us," said his companion.

Up high in their balloon, the two aeronauts continued to argue in hushed tones, distorted by the wind.

"Quick, quick, another bag."

This one landed with a dull thump near the farmhouse.

For a moment the balloon rose, traveling forward as well as up. A thick line dangled from the basket, moving like an ambitious serpent through the trees, then the hedgerow, flattening a square of the herb garden, collapsing a lattice of beans. I had no way of knowing that the three hundred feet of guide rope served as an automatic brake. I naturally assumed that the balloonists were lax. Not only were they destroying the farm, they could not be bothered to pull in their line. More than half its length dragged across the orchard, and while the balloon gained in force, it rose, until a knot in the rope wedged itself into the crook of a dwarf apple tree. And there it snagged. Trees all along the rope bent and shook, and hard little apples came plunking to the ground. The ship—now completely stalled—hung like a kite above the orchard, pulling the rope into a taut, nearly horizontal pitch.

Two more sandbags fell without incident into the windy fields. *"Mon bon monsieur!* Good day. Yes. Would you care to give us some assistance? And perhaps free our balloon."

As I stepped out into an opening through the trees, my agitation grew. Why should I expose myself to the whim of the gods, or worse, these two lesser half-gods, stuck now in limbo, haunted by the frustration of their own reckless passions?

It was here that my first impression of the aeronaut Hubert Latham, who would later come to renown as the most famous pilot in all of France, took shape. It was not favorable. Up high, in his flat, checkered cap, the man in the sky leaned over the rail in the very attitude of outrageous wealth and opportunity that my father held in scorn. And the aristocrat spoke to me from his limited perch as if I were a dullard—simple, slow-witted, and hard of hearing.

"Just a flip or two should do it. If you please. Thank you."

I studied the long line rising from the trees, disbelieving. Severed leaves spun away in the wind.

"Is there anyone you know who can help us?"

The basket's fine fittings and varnished tackle intrigued me as much as the aeronauts' predicament.

After a long pause, I finally answered, having to yell more loudly than I thought. But my voice lacked the authority I had acquired in my two years of boarding school, where my mother had hoped—many years ago—I'd gain the skills to become a clerk in industrial Paris or Rouen. Instead I piped out, weak and boyish, just as I must have appeared to them, like some grasshopper from the farm.

"And what will you do for our farm? In return for the well?"

"We will give you champagne."

"Uncorked by a dancing lady," called the other, leaning eagerly from the basket. "And poured into her shoe."

"What about our well?"

"We offer champagne, and still he wants water."

"We'll repair the well, too."

"How? I'm serious."

"So are we, monsieur. So are we."

"*Are* we?"

"Yes. Of course. You have our word on it."

How I wished for an ax, so that I could chop their line, and they'd be gone from the farm and swept off forever.

"HOW WILL YOU REPAY US FOR THE WELL?"

"At the racecourse. We are on the way there. To watch the demonstration of the flying machine."

"The *what?*"

"The flying machine."

"What do you call what you're flying in?"

"You do realize"—and here the other aeronaut stooped so far over the rail that the basket dipped, and I feared he'd fall overboard—"that the flying machine, as it exists today, is a fixed-wing ship, with a prime mover, or, in other words, an engine, in this case a petroleum-burning combustion engine." I had no idea I was about to receive a lecture, which the wind and turning branches made it impossible to follow. "The balloon acts as an aerostatic sail. A mere envelope filled with gas. There's no moving part about it. It is not a machine."

The aeronaut with the checkered cap brought his black leather gloves together with a satisfying smack. "He's right."

I studied the trembling arms of the ancient apple tree, where the line was caught. "So. There's a flying machine. And you want me to meet you there, at the racecourse?"

"Yes, yes, at this very instant. If you can be bothered to assist us. You know how we can be found. We can't very easily hide, now, can we?"

"Who are you? So I know who to look for?"

"We are, kind sir, members of the *Buontemponi.*"

"The *what?*"

I waited for a different answer.

When none came, I peered up at their enormous aeroship, suspended as if indifferent to the wind, full of the ease of its own inevitable drift, while the dwarf fruit trees cowered and heaved from the tension of the rope.

"*Gentlemen bastards,*" I muttered low, though I doubted they could hear, and took the greasy, mud-colored rope into my hands. "If you do not fix our well," I yelled, "I will cut your balloon into little pieces!"

"As you wish."

To free their line, I had to climb. I'd been climbing the trees of the orchard all my life, and knew every perch and foothold. It was in these branches that I first climbed under the heady spell of Jules Verne's *Village in the Treetops*, with rope bridges that led up to dwellings in the sky, with rooms that floated like boats at the end of a dock. But those lofty huts seemed as impossible to me now, as the balloon did above.

"You don't believe I'll come find you, do you?"

They either agreed or could not hear, as neither answered. Crouching low in the branches, I saw nothing of them but the colossal shadow floating above the canopy of leaves.

"I will! I'll find you out and cut your plaything into pieces!" Even as I yelled, though, I realized that the most difficult part of my revenge would be actually finding them again. And if I should, what would keep them from sailing forever away? How would I ever speak to them? "I'll cut your balloon into pieces and holes so that it will never fly. Do you hear?"

"Monsieur. We will repay you ten times over any reasonable price, as quoted by you. You have our word on it."

Their answer only confirmed my suspicion, but what choice did I have? I grabbed hold of the rope and began to release their knot from the tree.

There was a thrill to the pull on the line, as if I were hauling a whale down from the sky. I hung on for as long as I could. At last, the line took off. It slithered through my hands, it burned them. Lunging for a branch, I missed it completely and hung onto the rope. It jerked me clear up out of the tree, where I dangled, kicking at the bushy treetops and then at nothing but air. In a moment I saw the smallness of my home—thatched roofs, rabbit pen, chickens down on the dung heap—laid out humble and bare below.

"LET! GO!" yelled one of the aeronauts.

"I'm trying!"

"TRY! HARDER!"

Just as the rope laced through the nearing trunks of the poplars, I let go.

⤳⤶

The trees reached out to catch me. Their arms snapped, and I landed on their sharp, bony roots. Wind whooshed thickly through the bearded trees and my head swirled round in the broiling, trying to regain my grip on the rope. Struck with a sudden, inexplicable loss, I watched the rest of the line bounce over the knobby elbows of the trees right before my face. Bound in a dream, doubled over, knocked of breath, I did nothing, as the end of the rope slipped up through the leaves into the sky.

I stood sluggishly and brushed myself off.

The balloon turned with a giant, clumsy splendor over the fields, while the aeronauts were still calling down to me, but what I could not hear.

"I will find you out!" I yelled.

"*We hope so!*" I thought I heard them call from far off, but I could not tell if the words came from the cave of my own brain.

"*Until then!*"

I hurled an apple pitifully into the sky, where the effortless drift of the aeroship still transfixed me. Covered in mesh, with tattered pennants and bunting from better times, it looked all so festive. There was something odd and oblivious, almost optimistic, in the way the ship sailed, untouched by the world. By the time I reached the well—more damaged than I'd thought, broken crankshaft and roof and even rocks and mortar knocked loose—the balloon was just a small, happy speck above the hills.

2.

THE ROAD BEYOND OUR FARM was little more than two deep wheel ruts that the bracken and weeds were taking back. This thoroughfare ran between two rows of poplars, and behind these, the twisted trees of the fruit garden, burdened by choking vines and their own heavy boughs. In this perpetual shade, according to my father, grew a plum so marvelous that in all of France, and all of the world that mattered, none could compare. Everywhere the hard tiny apples and small plums lay on the ground, half rotted. The dusky air was sweet and acrid with their decay. Beyond the road, the hollow fell off into an overgrown patch of woods said to be haunted by spinsters and saints.

A pang of fear gripped me as I considered the highway. In all of my seventeen years, I could count on one hand all the times I had traveled very far beyond the village of Saint-Mars-la-Brière.

Quickly I walked to the barn, where I fetched a mallet, and returned to the well.

With a single blow, I knocked the splintered axle from its broken fitting and heaved the axle free. I unraveled the rope until I had enough of it loose to lower the bucket into the oily dark, where it disappeared, swinging into the gloom. I kept lowering the bucket, hand over hand, until I panicked—somehow the water had dried up. Finally the rope went slack and the bucket made its gulping sound. Then I pulled it back up, pull-by-pull, spilling water back into the dark, so that by the time I retrieved it, I was breathing hard. I poured water over my hands to wash away the dirt wedged into my rope burns and nails. Then, raising the bucket to my face, I smelled the damp root and cold stones of the earth, and drank.

Wondering still over the threatening sky, I heard Odilon and Angèle, the two house servants, walking from the house to the orchard.

"The roof!" Odilon cried. "Auguste, where is your father? There was a horrible, horrible crash." Odilon was a short, thin man, only forty-five. Yet his hair, which he kept long and combed back, was completely silver. "The balloon, my boy! And the calamity."

Never had I seen so much life in him.

Angèle, round and a bit older with a tired, paunchy face, looked at Odilon as if he were ridiculous. "Auguste," she said, "we must find your father. But first, come quick. Look. The house. *Quelle catastrophe!*"

As we followed her to the house, Odilon gave me a few quick jabs, like a fish striking a hook, and pulled me privately aside. He fumbled inside his vest pocket. "Did you see that the balloonists dropped something?"

"Yes, sandbags."

"No. This." He pulled a lump of a handkerchief from his vest pocket and began to unfold it. The cloth bore a monogram, finely stitched, and from it emerged a golden object—a timepiece that Odilon shook and held up to his ear. "Hmm. Still works."

He folded it into the handkerchief again and handed it to me. "There. They said it was for you, in case you couldn't find them. They threw it down after your rough landing. They feared for your well-being."

"How did you learn all this?"

"You mean"—Odilon's face broke open in dismay—"you did not hear? They yelled it down after you. One of them wrapped the watch up and lobbed it down as softly as he could. Yes, quite a gentleman he was, yes."

I unwrapped the watch again. It was finely wrought, with many dials and inlays of seashell, and an equally fine fob. The outside of the lid was inscribed with a short stanza written in a foreign hand. I flipped it open to find another inscription inside, in smaller cursive lettering:

> *To my dearest Hubert,*
> *For good luck in your travels*
> *and return.*
>
> *Love, A*

Intuitively I knew which aeronaut had searched his person and thrown down whatever he could, not only to make good on an accidental debt but to do so with an extravagance he would later, if not immediately, regret. Or perhaps that watch was the only thing within reach, and to ignore his impulse was just—impossible.

I stuffed the unfortunate keepsake into my pocket and followed the house servants around back to the kitchen. There, a shattering light invaded the pantry. The afternoon sky had overwhelmed the cozy gloom that usually hung beneath the crooked beams and smoke-stained walls. On the floor lay heaps and splinters of weather-beaten thatch, blackened by time, soot, and pitch. And there, bursting through an uneven hole in the roof, was the sandbag, suspended over a wide, sagging gap.

I recalled the aeronauts dropping a third sandbag, which seemed suddenly worse, like an insult.

"Chhht-chhht." Angèle clapped at the few brave hens that had wandered into the pantry, pecking away at whatever bugs lay in the heaps of thatch. "*Get, get!* We'll have you back here soon enough."

"The noise," said Odilon. "It was like thunder. I thought the artillery had arrived."

"He ran outside like a general," said Angèle.

"I did." Odilon stood straight and stiff-shouldered, his silver hair in disarray.

"I had them right here." I held open my raw, rope-burned hands. "I helped them. I helped them free."

"*Auguste?*"

Odilon calmed, taking on the grave air of the moral instructor, a tone he'd taken with me ever since I could speak, even though I was old enough now to be on my own. As I began the lengthy explanation of the balloonists and the broken well and so on, my father walked in. He passed beneath the disaster of a roof without ever bothering to look up at it and took his forced, uneven walk over to the cupboard. There he wiped the dust from a tumbler and poured himself a glass of his eau-de-vie, usually reserved for the Sunday meal. Extravagantly, he reached for three additional glasses and, one by one, placed them beside the clear bottle. Odilon alone took him up on the offer. Then, from behind his round spectacles, with a crooked grin, my father blinked.

"To health."

Gusts of wind swayed the hanging knots of onion. Cobwebs in the rafters shook like hair. And rain made a pinging sound upon the clutter—the smoke-blackened pots, the wooden surfaces bowed from the chopping, and the limp-leafed vegetables left in heaps. The chimney drafted poorly, and the usual smells of smoke, soil, sitting milk, and mold seemed even stronger now that the summer rains could come in.

My father rubbed his face, as if trying to rub some sense into it. "It's doubtful the balloonists did it on purpose." He looked at me, finally. "Still, you assist them on their way—without consequence?"

"Well, I didn't *have* them, really. They could have cut the rope, or untied themselves. I figured I'd save them the trouble. They're going to pay us back."

"How? Drop money from the sky?"

Clutching the watch in my pocket, I shot an involuntary look at Odilon, who stepped forward.

"Sir—if I may. Your boy was fierce with them. Fierce and fair. He stood up for the farm. I couldn't have been more proud of him if he were my own."

"That's what I'd expect. Now he should be fair to the farm and stay here, and help us fix the hole in the roof, and the one in the ground. What's he going to do? Chase balloons down from the sky?"

"Yes!"

"What?" My father stared me down.

"At the demonstration for the flying machine. They said I should meet them there."

"Who did?"

"The balloonists."

My father smiled with his usual bemused detachment and looked up through the hole in the roof. He lifted his cap and set it back down. He took a good draw from his tumbler. "So. Would you recognize the balloon if it floated by just now?"

"Father—" I began pacing. "They said they would pay us back ten times over for the well, and that was before we even saw the roof."

"At this demonstration?"

"Yes."

"What day is it, this flying—what? Giant carpet?"

I grew distant with a smoldering resentment and took my pacing from the house out to the barn, where my agitation stirred the old sow to grunt once lowly, interrupting her dreaming in the dense ammonia air. I began clearing the traps and traces away from the saddle. Then my father walked in.

"What are you going to do with *that?*"

"Nothing." I looked down at the saddle, covered with the fine rust-colored dust that settled on everything throughout the barn. "Nothing," I said, and put the saddle back on its hook. I walked to the corner of the barn where I kept my bicycle and began to push it to the door.

"I suppose," said my father with a sly amusement, "I'll start in the kitchen, where we'll need that hammer you left at the well, along with my other tools, and another ladder." He noted the upheaval of tools. "Hmm, what happened here?"

"I had to get the mallet."

"Do you plan on putting anything back?" My father was very slow and deliberate in the way he unhooked the ladder and withdrew it from underneath the rusted tools and planks. The length of it was cumbersome to maneuver in the barn.

"I have to meet the balloonists," I said. "I *told* them I would."

With the lumbering efficiency of a lifetime of work, my father took a few steps back and aimed the ladder through the narrow passageway. "It's a story as old as the rain." He spoke as if to himself, and then in a more muted tone, as if to a more private self, said, "The rich are always pissing on us from their high places." Very pleased with himself, he hoisted the ladder up onto his shoulders and carried it from the barn.

3.

NOT FAR DOWN THE ROAD, THE FIELDS of the neighboring farmer stretch on and on, and in this Norman land, Loiseau's ancient traction engine puffs up its welcome cloud.

Here lies our valley at harvest.

From the black stack of the boiler comes a fantastic circus of smoke—banners and tent tops and spires of smoke rise in a constant panic of soot and ash and collapse then slowly over the fields in a cindery haze. Under this carnival of fumes, the stooped, obscured workers move as if half formed, lost to thought, as their merry-go-round blares out its dull deafening note. The engine's flywheel turns a long leather drive-belt that in turn drives the threshing machine into furious life, and the downcast workers—man, woman, and donkey—move no faster than the din will allow. This scene repeats itself here and there beyond our valley, where the dull, smoldering dust funnels rise like a mechanical dreaming of the hills. Drawing near, you breathe in the sweet reek of spent fuel mixed with the wet, fresh-cut grasses, and if you are from anywhere near to this land, it is impossible to resist the pull of the season's labor.

I did not ask for this stranger's keepsake, nor, if his watch were a mere throwaway, the burden of its failed sentiments. I simply wished to be rid of the burden of choices altogether, to reap and ask for nothing more than to be in this heavy familiar scene of work, and hunger, and more work, until the day was done.

I was pedaling as fast as I could, but the farmer Loiseau saw me. Leaving his team of workers, he walked waist-deep through the wheat to the road. "Look. It's the Tour de France. Off to the races?"

"Business."

"You tell that father of yours, all the business he needs is right here." Loiseau gestured down to his growling engine. For years the shrewd Loiseau had threshed the grain for all the farmers in the valley, with only a few holdouts like my father, who refused the services of his modern machine. "I'll put you to work. I could have used you this morning."

"Sorry. In a hurry."

"It's the flying machine, isn't it? That's your 'business.' "

I stopped short. "What flying machine? How did you hear of a flying machine?"

"You mean one of *les bluffeurs?* The two bicycle makers from America? Who hasn't? And tell that father of yours, I'll thresh his crop—only after I'm done with mine. I'm sure he'll need it."

"I'm sure he will."

"Thataboy—"

Sullenly I began again on my bike.

"Say hello to the birds."

And all over again I felt the guilt of leaving not only in the thick of harvest but while my household dealt with the chaos of a torn roof. But I'd grown used to the needy desire to escape—to leave whenever I could to watch the spectacle of Loiseau's fuming iron monster with its iron wheels with iron teeth, stuck in a gully, or choked silent for no reason. Then I'd help the angry Loiseau drag the engine out, or watch him tinker with its stubborn, greasy parts. More than once he had to leave it in a field overnight and lead out a team of horses the next morning to pull the thing slowly back to the barn. Loiseau would spit out the most venomous language. His heap of iron was somehow animate, but with the patience and indifference of a rock. Afterwards I would lie awake for much of the night, trying to figure what measure would bring Loiseau's traction engine back to life.

Riding off, I looked back once at the valley farmer, and, like my father, envied Loiseau for his gloating.

I soon came to the steep uphill stretch of road, and pedaled as if in a fight against it, moving at nearly the pace of walking. On a horse, the climb would be nothing. But on a bicycle, my thick-soled boots pushed down clumsily on the pedals. I didn't think my legs could do it, but they had to. They had to pedal me in and out of the deep, wide potholes and carriage tracks.

Nearing the top, I stopped the bike and put both feet on the ground and sensed the vast distance of the silence of the woods. From the distance came a wind that twisted the leaves on their spines and caused them to speak in hushed rustling sighs, and go silent, and rise again, trailing off. The trees leaned over the road like a chorus of tall judges, peering down at me in the dissolving noon.

I'd even managed to discover the meaning of the stanza inscribed on the watchcase.

Before I rode off, I'd shown the watch to our house servants' only daughter, Simone, a deaf milkmaid famous in our village for being able to read the newspaper in German at age eleven. She'd once studied with nuns at the Order of the Suffering Silence. Though I knocked on her door, she of course did not hear. I found her sitting at her desk, with an open, startled look at seeing anyone. After finishing her chores for the day, she was rarely seen. She snatched the watch up and opened the case. She turned it this way and that and squinted into its fine engravings until she shrugged. *It's in English*, she wrote on a pad of paper, and gave the impression of needing more time to study it. But when I told her I needed to take it with me, she pushed me down from the stoop of the servants' quarters, moving her arms like someone trying to wave off a boat. She smiled wanly, out of breath. *It's a bit sad, really, if it's a lover's gift.* She began stabbing down urgently as she wrote. *Perhaps he wanted to be rid of it!* Then she hurried me out the door. "*Bon voyage.*" She waved me away as I sat on my bike, looking at her through the window. On the slip of paper in my hands, she'd deciphered the four lines of poetry, or at least written down their gist. Months later, I would learn from the aeronaut himself that they were lines from a poem by an adventuring Englishman named Service:

> *The wind is a mighty roamer;*
> *He bids me keep me free,*
> *Clean from the taint of the gold-lust,*
> *Hardy and pure as he*

Soon I came to the downhill road, the long, fast stretch, so fast I nearly lost control, and thought only of the racecourse I hadn't been to in years, and how I was going to the demonstration of a flying machine, an actual flying machine made by bicycle makers. What if their flying machine looked like a bike? What if they made a bicycle with wings? I'd heard that in Paris they were inventing such a bike. That someday people would pedal and up they would go, up above the road and above the trees.

4.

AT LAST, IN A PARTING THROUGH THE TREES, the balloon appeared, like a dull sun or the morning's moon. It hung, not impossibly high and not too low but with enough altitude to keep sailing forever away, at first above the empty town of Le Mans—eerily empty, except for a stray dog lounging on a sidewalk of raked stones—and then above the grandstands farther off, and then yet farther. I'd hoped I wouldn't see the balloon at all, at the racetrack or anywhere, so that I could turn back around and have the golden timepiece all to myself. I'd possess the wealth of a pirate or a lord, and the curious burden of how to unveil it.

Instead I stood and forced all of my weight down on the bicycle pedals, but gained nothing. The ship sailed on, taunting me with its perfect obliviousness, like a disengaged lightbulb floating above the hills.

At the racetrack I discovered the reason for the strange emptiness in town. Here, not only the grandstands but also the open, sandy areas before the pines were completely overrun. Legs dangled from the garages and trees, where I wished to join them. Then two priests hampered my way, their black robes like solemn shadows trailing behind. Everywhere the people's expectation brimmed, full of the time-old hunger of the crowd. It could have been for a parade, or a dancing bear, or a zebra pulling a rickshaw, or two knuckled boxers beating each other to a quivering pulp.

I was close enough now to see that the balloon carried three occupants, and that their guide rope curved to a stake in the ground. The balloon had been captive all this time, with most likely the best view of all. But even if I could reach it, what was I to do? Yell up at it? Whatever would I say? I had to be where the balloon's rope came down. I had to. I passed by as many Saturday encampments as I could, until the wall of spectators thickened and there was no more stepping past the campstools, baby carriages, and panniers on the spread-out blankets.

I took the aeronaut's watch from my pocket, as if to confirm an imaginary time for an absurd appointment. The golden timepiece gleamed all over, as if coated in sweat. It was just past noon, and the overcast had burned off. Bright, hazy patches of sunlight spread out above the balloon.

One of the aeronauts was aiming a telescope down over the race grounds below, like some venturesome sailor in a crow's nest. Something about his ready posture and the way he posed with the spyglass, as if exploring new lands, confirmed my impression that it was indeed his watch I needed to return. The fine people in the grandstands, the townspeople below, and the pilgrims lined up against the fence, we were all here for his sport—where he likely had a wager on the outcome of the day, though he seemed utterly unconcerned whether the birdman from America would fly or not.

I searched the grandstands for the focus of his attention, skimming over all manner of fashionable bonnets, military caps of high rank, and the rakish hats of gentlemen of means, until my eye caught a pair of opera glasses, aimed upward. Above the glasses rose a hat like the billowing dome of a minaret, all of white, with a white gloved hand supporting the glasses. I could tell little about the woman behind her opera glasses, consumed as she was in the monstrous shadow of her puffed hat. A child sat on the woman's lap and reached up for the glasses. The woman looked away, warily pulling them out of reach of the child before bringing them back up to her face again, intent on the sky. But the only thing there besides the clouds and the sun was the balloon.

Only then did the aeronaut put his telescope down. Together, with their special seeing devices, he and the woman with the glasses seemed to share a secret intimacy that they indulged now only in short bursts, like two adolescents thrillingly oppressed at Sunday school.

I too have looked at life through a telescope. My uncle from Madrid brought one back from his travels aboard a tall steamer on the Arabian Sea, along with exotic wooden masks and the enormous plumes of long-legged birds. Through this telescope I have seen our drab yard birds brought to vibrant color and life. It is a hidden, secret world, seen through the lens. My uncle claimed to have seen the rings of Saturn—a dash of light intersecting a bright star—and the hills of the moon. But also through the lens, perspectives are distorted. Light at the edge blurs. You can see the heat in the air shimmer. And if it is a person, it is as if you stand directly beside the observed, who may have no idea you are so near—a view more stealthy and intimate than spying. How could I have known that the watch in my pocket came from this woman with the glasses? I thought little of it, but when I found out not a few months later that she was the bestower, I was not surprised.

Just then the aeronaut gave off a sudden air of omniscience that shocked me, as if in confirmation of my absurd impressions. Lowering his telescope, he quickly took note of me noting him and stared for quite some time. But then he was far enough away that I couldn't tell if he saw me or not. Could he even make out any one person's features without the assistance of his lens? But he did, he saw, he stared. My face burned. I felt a desperate groveling in my gut, as if *I* were the intruder in his complicated, high-flying affairs with the other aristocrats in their lofty places. Even though he was the one who'd damaged our well and thrown down his burden. Did I imagine he felt his vest pocket where his watch should have been? He looked at me again, this time with his telescope, but for only a second. Then he turned it back to the grand-stands, taking for granted my mundane role as messenger, or watch-bearer, or whatever it might be, as he searched again over the sea of faces.

5.

AT THE FAR END OF THE FIELD, a bugle's call arose in sharp protest. The reveille brought the crowd to its feet.

Then, as if this was a village fair, the local volunteers of the firemen's brigade came to arms, and the rescue, apparently. I'd been so intent upon reaching the balloon, I'd forgotten all about the flying machine from America. Perhaps the delay of the birdman had become unbearable to all. In the field, boys and middle-aged men alike strode with great, vital energy, their sabers and bayonets wobbling with effort, and not all of the company matched. Here a pair of lone red epaulettes wandered from formation. Fighting caps bobbed next to helmets. And smart gray pant legs with a single stripe stepped beside the red of old empire fusiliers. In the defunct issue of the National Guard, the rustic fighters were nearly two dozen strong, held in rank by the loud attentions of their shrill, bespectacled schoolmaster sergeant, whose trained shoulders heaved with each call. A nag pulled an old cannon into place. A booming report split the air. "For Alsace-Lorraine!" called one from the crowd. Never again would these defenders have such purpose. With great precision, they packed the cannon with straw and fired, again! After the third flash of fire and smoke, the show was over. Puffs of black vapor lingered, and I smelled the acrid sweetness of burnt sulfur in the wet air. Now I too begrudged the foreigner his power to make us all wait.

Close to the fence, I could neither sit nor turn around, not with this dense crowd pressing in and choking the motor track further. Amid the grumble of hearsay, I too became an expert on the birdman from America, who sat around all day in a makeshift hut near the garages, just one of the brothers with their miracle flying machine. People wondered if he would ever leave his hut. He couldn't possibly be hiding all this time? Then again, the foreigner was a recluse who had fallen through the ice when he was seventeen, and plunged into a deep depression from which he never recovered. Unfit for university, he became a self-taught genius, just one of his many eccentricities. "And did you know," asked one of my fellow authorities through his bushy, tobacco-stained beard, "that *le monsieur* Wilbur sleeps on a little cot beside his machine? Yes. He eats beans from a can, and won't let the machine out of his sight."

"Well, someone should go and talk with him."

"And?"

"See if he's hungry."

Everywhere country folk lined the outskirts. They climbed wagons, stood on blankets. All for what? To see some magical birdlike machinery sprung from the land of the Wrights, who came from cowboys and Indians.

Finally the makeshift hangar doors swung open. After a long pause, two wide white wings emerged from the shadows—an enormous box kite balanced upon triangular one-wheeled dollies and pushed by workmen.

A file of cavalrymen rode out into the field. The marching band fell silent. And there was a hush as in a ceremony inside a church. I could hear a few low whispers, and the crying of a child. The dense crowd increased the midday heat. The sky had cleared, all except for a thin, milky haze at the horizon. The air still had that mugginess that follows a time of rain. I could not fully make out the shape of the flying machine being shepherded carefully to the field. It was all sticks and wires and long, muslin-covered wings. It looked odd and square, so that I could not tell which part was forward or back, and what part followed what through the sky. It had two long-bladed propellers, which contained the secrets of flight, though they were nothing like the thirty-seven ascension screws on Jules Verne's *Albatross*, reaching up from the deck of the clipper ship on thirty-seven separate masts. What was it like when those propellers stirred the air? Did they leave a visible wake, like the prop wash of a boat? As a motorcar leaves a cloud of dust above the road? Did the props churn the air into bubbles? Did they turn slowly and forcefully, like oars? I had no clue. Did the craft hover dragonfly-like, darting here and there? What about the man inside the contraption? Did he become strangely lighter, hurtling like a bird through the clouds?

It took only a few dragoons to lift the entire aeroplane from its carts and onto the launching track. The cavalrymen were clumsy once off their horses, with their clanking accoutrements and high riding boots. Among all the ungainly coupling of mechanical parts, one man stood out in his dark, modest suit as the bearer of secrets, thin, spare, and solemn. The foreigner tugged on his coat sleeves and walked around his contraption, inspecting a wire, turning a blade. He had in all of his actions the compressed energy of the unwilling performer, the athlete, the escape artist, somewhere between gymnast and shape-shifter, calculating deep within his fantastic schemes. He climbed aboard his contraption and tested the levers, one in each hand, and then worked a control bar with both feet, so that now all four limbs were required to steer the machine. The broad surfaces all around him torqued and twisted, even the large wings that contained him. They warped slightly. There was something about his dark suit and the contained way he moved, so sharp and keen, but also so business-as-usual, as if inside, he was whistling a quiet, unconcerned tune.

Behind him, a line of the dragoons pulled on a rope that lifted a series of weights inside a derrick, and the American braced himself above the wing. His hands and well-shined shoes secured the controls. He then uttered a command in his own language, but everyone knew what he meant. His assistants took their places at the two oarlike propellers, and, at one last word, flung them down in opposite directions. The American just sat there, concentrating on the motor—a surprisingly small one, crouched beside him on the wing. Its four cylinders sputtered to life, unevenly at first, then catching, growing into an angry, popping growl. Even at this distance, I could make out the muted clatter of bicycle chains, turned by their gears and driving the props—bicycle chains of a bicycle maker, who sat still concentrating in his ruminating way. When he increased the throttle, the engine's angry roar increased.

The pilot reached down to a small lever. The weights in the derrick fell. Within seconds, the aeromachine flew from its rails.

An audible breath of satisfaction followed the ungainly box of a Wright Flyer, more engine and thrust than anything bird-like should be. It was a ferocious train in the sky, a steamboat full of fury—but it flew. Immediately the plane took a sudden dip, as if to strike ground, but the American righted the ship. It amazed me how keen and temperamental the steering wings were, out in front. The motor's whine was already fading in the distance when the plane tipped steeply to one side. The crowd gasped, horror-stricken, as the leading wingtip threatened to scrape ground. Then the plane turned in a one-sided descent and gained in force. It pushed against the air in its aggressive, banking angle and turned itself completely around. Now it was so far beyond the racetrack, there was nothing but trees below and nowhere to land. The gleaming white wings came cutting back over the field evenly, about forty feet up, and shouts arose as if the American could hear them. As the angry whirr of the engine diminished again, the crowd quieted too, stunned. The American took his aeroship and repeated the aggressive banking turn in his stately steamboat of the air. There was something altogether beautiful and clumsy in those two muslin-covered wings and all the supports around them as they sliced through the air.

Returning to the lawn before the grandstands, the American landed smoothly, directly between the derrick and the crowd. The skids braked, the engine ceased, and a great cheering arose. Hats were thrown into the air, or held up on the ends of canes. I stood transfigured by the remarkable showmanship of the birdman—ending his show before it practically began—leaving us all euphoric to see more.

In a hurry now to find the aeronauts, I turned. But there was no moving. Behind me stood an old man—not old but with a sandy, sun-raw face and hair completely white, staring out through grave, round spectacles. The lenses were so thick that I doubted the man could have seen a thing. All around him the crowd was in motion, talking loudly, amazed still at the birdman from America. I saw the contained emotion of the pilot as he climbed from the ship. The crowd now must have magnified it—the slight grin—the bow of the shoulders. The old man—his spectacles were so thick they seemed steamed in the sunlight.

"Did you see what I saw?" said the man, still vaguely beholding the sky. I was the only one facing him.

"Yes. Yes, I did."

He pushed up his glasses and wiped at his weepy eyes with a single knuckle. Setting his glasses back onto the crook of his nose, he blinked.

"Sir." He sidestepped, with a slight bow, so that I could pass.

6.

THE CROWD CLOSED IN AROUND THE RACETRACK. The dragoons encircled the Wright Flyer as the American left his ship, himself encircled by a number of dignitaries of great importance. But once the birdman was ushered off, the cavalrymen were completely engulfed by the crowd. We could only gape at the machine—part kite, part motor, and part contraption, the vehicle of science and God. At rest the flyer was quaint and modest. Yet the crowd swarmed round it, awed and ominous, as if something more would happen if they could only get close enough.

My head filled with fiddle music, coarse laughter, and the competing shouts of vendors. I heard the clang of the Angelus up high in the steeple, and from farther off, the joyous reply. The popping of Chinese firecrackers nearly caused a horse to bolt into the crowd. How would I ever get near the balloon?

The racecourse itself was an impossible mess. Over it the silver aeroship of the aristocrats descended slowly with its usual, oblivious splendor, though only a handful of passersby stopped to watch it touching down. Once on the ground, the gasbag continued to collapse, an enormous injured whale lying on its side, sighing its last breaths. Soon the balloonists chased the remaining gases from it and began to fold it as you would a very large blanket. They were younger than I'd thought, which rankled me further.

"Sir ..." I explained my situation to the nearest one, a large, short-haired carrot-top with a gruff manner.

"Me? In the balloon? No sir, you have me mistaken."

"I have reason to believe—" I stopped short. "Look here. It was that balloon there. And one of your sandbags that fell through our roof."

"Roof?"

I reached into my pocket and produced a small section of elegant, tightly bound rope that I'd cut from one of the sandbags. "You have all of France to drop your bags, and you hit not only our well, but our farmhouse too."

"César!" the carrot-haired fellow called to his companion. "We have a gentleman here who claims you dropped ballast on his house."

César was a dark, intense man—quick, with thin whiskers that gave the impression of a physician from the East gone mad. He shot his dark, intense eyes at me, then at the redheaded man, as he answered all of my questions.

"What are we to do? Ride all the way to your farm? What do you mean you aren't *sure* how much damage was done? You *think* it might all be repaired? *Already?* So we can't appraise the damages? The damages couldn't have been that bad, could they, if they are already repaired?"

"I should never have untangled you from the tree. Look. I ride all this way. And you said ten times the repairs. *Ten times.* Not this."

The third aeronaut, the debonair with the checkered cap, walked up to us. He was more than a few years older than me, slight and wan. "César," he said. "Could you please give the gentleman your knife?"

"*What?* And incite homicide?"

"Here, then." With a thoughtful, quizzical expression, he reached deep into his vest pockets, searching for something obviously not there. He squinted, peering far into the vast corners of his imagination. "Here," he said finally, producing a penknife from his coat. "Take mine. You may now cut the balloon into pieces. It is at your disposal."

I stood dumbfounded before the large tarpaulin of silken material, covered in netting, flat against the field.

There was nothing vexed or mocking in the man's manner. Instead his smile welcomed you as an old friend made more familiar by the recollection of a joke that had, over the years, made you both happy. He wore an expression at once likable and good-natured—no, more than good-natured—he beamed with that special knowledge, sensing not only that I had his watch but that now was not the time to unveil it. That there were always greater things in store if only you were as patient as he, and all good things would come about.

In his black leather glove he held out an ivory-handled knife, with fine dark engravings that seemed oriental. "Go ahead. Take a look, if you'd like."

On both sides of the handle was the image of a many-whiskered dragon flying over sharp, cresting waves of a writing too small and beautiful to comprehend.

"It was a gift to me from Prince Tán Sang of Cochinchina," he said. "The prince and I stood for three nights in a row in the jungle, waiting for a tiger to appear. The tiger hunt, you see, is unique in that you do not go after the prize, the prize comes after you. It is the one creature I've hunted that I have yet to see."

I handed him back his knife.

"This is a treasured keepsake." He regarded it with an exaggerated air, turning it this way and that. "But not my favorite."

It was at that moment, just as I figured I'd reveal to him his timepiece, that he gestured with a subtle open palm to calm me. He had a way of turning to the grandstands, as if someone there was keeping a constant watch, pleased with his gestures' silver charm.

He explained the events of the morning to the carrot-top: that it was César who'd panicked and dropped the sandbags without caring where they landed, César who never owned up to incidental property damage, which was not an infrequent expense of ballooning, always at the whim of the winds, and César who at times intentionally named targets and took aim.

César wore a pinched expression as he patted down his coat. From his pockets he produced a single banknote and a few coins.

"Here."

The aeronaut with the checkered cap pulled me aside. "It's going to take him some time to come up with the funds on such a day as this! You were here earlier, were you not?"

"Yes."

"And?" said the aeronaut. "What did you think? What did you think of the birdman?"

"He didn't fly that high." Again I felt like a dolt from the country, thick and slow mannered.

"Not that high?"

"No. Not like… I wanted to see… like the birds. In the clouds. I was expecting him to still be in the sky. Like maybe an aeroship. "

"Like the balloon, perhaps?"

"Well, I didn't know what to expect. My father will not be pleased that I was gone all this time, so close to harvest. And he was right. At least now I can say that I saw you. And that you lied to my face. I've lost the entire day, and more, because of you."

"Sir," said the man in the checkered cap, "when you are an old man, and flying machines are commonplace, you can say that you saw the first one. The world is forever changed."

"And I have to ride back home with what?"

"Why, with a balloon ride, of course. Not home. But in the sky for a short time. While César here goes and fills his coffers. So that he can render unto you what is yours."

"A balloon ride?"

"I know, I know, it's not an aeroplane."

I regarded them with doubt and dread, but I could feel the heft of the watch in my pocket, which made me feel as though I were the unreasonable one.

"No, no. He's too young," said César. "Are you sure you have the courage? Are you? I think not. He seems too young for the rigors, and the dangers, of the treacherous heights." He walked up to the gondola beside the empty balloon. "Aeroship of the *Buontemponi*," he said, clearly perturbed, reading the placard attached to the wicker sides, next to the coat of arms.

"What does that mean?"

"It's Italian," said César. "It means 'Fellows Who Like to Have a Good Time.' We are, of course Italian in ancestry—somehow."

"And he is, of course, having a good time," said the red-haired fellow. "I'm César, at your service and in your debt."

"I'm Marcus," said the carrot-top.

"He's Hubert."

"I'm Auguste."

"Hah! One of us," said César. "Can you believe it?"

"I can," said Latham. "I can. He's better off, though, staying on the ground while you run and get him your debt."

"No. No, I'll go," I said.

"Go where?"

"Go flying. Up in your balloon."

"Good then. So, it's set. Tomorrow. Tomorrow, meet us here after breakfast."

"*Tomorrow?*" I could just hear the voice of my father racking down over my heart, like an old bench vise. "What about now?"

"Now?" Latham gestured. "Just look at our ship. It's empty. It can't fly. Tomorrow. It's tomorrow. Or never."

"Hear, hear."

The *Buontemponi* each raised an imaginary glass.

"To never!"

"Yes, never!"

"Meet us there."

7.

THAT NIGHT I SLEPT BESIDE A HAYSTACK NEAR THE ROAD. On a bed of hay thrown over the sharp stubble, I lay awake in fits of dread and guilt but mostly excitement, unable to picture myself in the small wicker cage of the balloon, carried off into the sky.

And there was the ticking.

From my shirt pocket there came a ticking from the aeronaut's watch. It spread throughout the mound of hay and overwhelmed my every thought. As if it were a seashell, I held the watch up to my ear. Between each tick were smaller ticks and whirrs and echoes. I heard a mechanical music of the spheres contained within that golden case, and found myself in a peculiar state where I could not sleep, nor stay awake, nor dream, nor think clearly, yet I rolled in and out of all of these. I felt tiny insects crawl across my face. In one dream, I held an old screwdriver in my hands—one much too big to fit into the minute golden screw heads that held the watchcase shut. *Go on*, Simone kept urging me. *Open it, will you?* The slip and catch of the gears amplified, to a definite, regular strike. And echo. And strike again. The gears grew large. They became great huge grinding wheels suspended in the dark above my head.

Then the watch fell silent.

And so did the world.

Slowly, I noticed again the sound of crickets, and the scurry of small animals through the shorn field. And a quiet humming beneath it all—the bunching of straw under my weight, or something yet more quiet and mysterious, as in the distant burning of stars or the humming of heaven and earth—and I realized I did not know at all where I was. I could not recognize a thing around me except the stars slipping in and out of the clouds, and I'd never been so far from home.

Fighting the impulse to wind the watch, I let myself sleep. I awoke before daybreak to a light, drowsy rain, and the sky turned windy as I rode my bike to the racing grounds.

❧❧

The field looked like the site of a circus that had picked up and moved on. Wet bunting drooped above the empty grandstands, announcing nothing. A single shoe lay abandoned in the dirt. Why did I believe this was a result of my own doing, as if the very wind and clouds could conspire against me?

Church bells began their deep, doleful tolling for Mass. I stood, listening to the whipping of flags and the repetitive thumping of the rope against the launching derrick, and I realized with even greater defeat that the aeroship of the Impostors Who Liked to Have a Good Time should have been in the field by now, in some stage of being filled, or bouncing on its tether, ready to go. A horse cab stopped along the fence of the track, and the chauffeur leaned down and spoke to the darkly dressed occupants before he shook the reins and drove on. A submerged streak of self-loathing overcame me. From farther away an awkward peasant yelled out, wanting to hear news of a flying machine. But answering would only pain me further, because unlike me, the pilgrim had no elusive hope to keep his stubborn head in the wind.

❧❧

The bell tower tolled for a second Mass. In the middle of the field a group of gloomy seagulls had gathered, puffed up against the weather, some standing on one leg. At the sound of a sharp motor drawing near, they took off reluctantly and circled the sky. From the garages emerged a roadster. It had a long platform in back for the storage of three spare tires. The working tires protruded from all four corners, and the exhaust pipes rattled beneath the louvered bonnet of the hood. Here was a modified version of the Daimler that had won the 1907 Grand Prix, as I would learn later.

As the roadster neared the racetrack, two of the three Buontemponi hopped down from the row of high seats mounted on the gas tank behind the driver. Alone now, the driver gunned the motor, and the chassis rose slightly from its wheels. My heart pressed against my ribs. I'd seen only Loiseau's smoke-belching traction engine, or gentleman motorists tooling gingerly down the road. But here the motor came to a curve and lost all traction, kicking up dirt in the chaos of its drift. Burrowing its way out of the turn, it rose again on its wheels and barreled down the straightaway. Meanwhile, César and Marcus walked into a garage and emerged with the wicker basket of the balloon up on a cart, the silver material folded inside. Nearing them, the motorcar came to a halt, its powerful engine causing the whole car to quake. I walked over to them from the grandstands.

"So sorry, M. Auguste," said César. "For such a miserable day. Worse than the one that sent the sandbags down on your farm."

"Still you went up?"

"Not me," said Marcus, pushing the balloon cart. "And not today."

"Sure, you can go up." César hunched forward, full of delight, carrying the large basket. "But can you come down? And where will you come down? Going up is the easy part, especially in this wind."

"It's only the speed of air," said the racer, killing the engine and stepping down. He kept glancing over at the garages where the flying machine was, as if the birdman from America might still be inside and impressed with his driving skills.

Instead of unfolding the balloon out onto the field, the aeronauts lifted their flight deck up onto the spare tires in back and began to secure it with ropes.

"What?" I said. "We're not flying?" I sensed that Latham was not quite ready to leave either, that he was waiting for the right time for me to offer up his watch.

"I know it doesn't seem like much." César turned to me. "But under this fat, unwieldy whale of a balloon, you are so helpless in skies like this."

"We've gone up in much worse," said Latham.

"We advise against it. If it's compensation you want"—still leaning into the balloon, César patted his coat pockets—"I have it right here."

"But, sirs." I stepped onto the edge of the field where I had expected our balloon ride to begin. "When I am an old man, I will want to say I once flew. I cannot come back here tomorrow."

"Nor will we be here," said Latham. "None of us will." He still had that peculiar manner of forming his thoughts while staring into the rows of the grandstands, though they were empty. He turned to Marcus. "Can he borrow your coat?"

"Coat?" said César.

The three *Buontemponi* stared at each other.

"He's going up?" César eyed me up and down, full of suspicion. Then he reached into the motorcar and grabbed his own coat in a darkened mood. "Come along then. The closer to the gods, the colder it gets."

Soon the *Buontemponi* had the balloon basket free-standing in the middle of the field.

I took hold of a section of the fine silk of the balloon and helped to spread it. The silk in my hands, coursed with equally fine rigging, seemed too light and insubstantial a material to entrust with our lives. The three *Buontemponi* grew grim as César turned a knob on a metal cylinder and the large envelope began slowly to fill with hydrogen, billowing in fat, lazy swells across the ground. All three of them scanned the shifting sky with skepticism, and I was to blame for putting us all in peril.

"Look. I'm sorry. We don't have to go if you don't want to."

The aeronaut Latham looked up from beneath his checkered derby cap.

"Don't worry. We won't plummet. Not before lunch. César has packed a very fine one. I hope you're hungry."

꧁꧂

It was well beyond noon when the ropes of the balloon strained against the pickets, and César, Latham, and I climbed into the wicker basket.

Marcus untied the lines and waved us brusquely off.

Up we went.

The lawn of the racetrack seemed to drop out from beneath us, turning as it fell. The balloon stood motionless against the wind, as if both perfectly still and simultaneously rising. Above us hung the enormous hollow of the envelope, absorbing the light as if the day were suddenly darker and quieter beneath it. What I imagined as the wind dying down was actually the balloon no longer holding fast against it. As the wind moved, so did we.

The racetrack and roof of the grandstands continued to fall away in a slow turning cartwheel. Below us spread out the long lines of the trees, the hills, the farms, the rooftops of town. From one of the farms, I heard the barking of a dog, which from up here sounded mournful. From the hills I heard a train's whistle, and that too seemed mournful and alone. The whole world was engulfed in a strange, far-off melancholy, and I hung on to the lines that ran from the basket to the balloon and looked down with a sudden urge to leap and plunge through the air to the squared-off plots of green and gold. I felt it down in my gut— this involuntary urge to fall, as if a metal weight inside me were being pulled. I clung tighter to the lines. When I looked at Latham, I was sure the aeronaut was smiling at me because he too had often had the same thought of jumping and had grown accustomed to it.

In what seemed like no time at all we were engulfed in a wool-colored fog that soon grew so thick, it seemed you could just walk right out onto it. It became abysmal, there under the balloon, surrounded by solid walls of fur-dark rain. But the rain didn't fall on us. It gathered in the air. It beaded up on the rails and rigging of our ship.

"Shall we?" said César.

Latham shrugged.

César withdrew a knife from its sheath and in one swift, exalted motion did away with one of the sandbags outside the basket. "There."

He bid me to lean over the rail and stare down through the clouds with him. "You're an accomplice."

But this action seemed to have no effect on the balloon or the cloud that contained us. What unlikely forces were at work to hold us captive within a dark cloud mass supposedly in the sky? Every once in a while, the clouds would open up below us to a view surfacing. As if through an eddy in a pool of a stream, I saw a rolling stretch of gray-green land, squared-off fields of crop, a small hamlet of roofs, a winding river, a bridge and the road that led to it. The cloudbanks moved in from below, and our balloon was engulfed again in the great gray deep.

"Where *are* we going?" I asked.

Latham raised his brows at César. "Well?"

"Well what?"

"Where are we going?"

"Where?"

"That's right. I thought you knew."

"Merrily down the stream?"

Latham pulled a compass on a chain from his coat pocket. "Nope."

"North?"

"Wrong again."

"Up? Or down? Who's steering this thing?"

Latham took his barometer from his coat pocket—at first I thought it was his watch—and aimed it at me. "He is. Or King Neptune's ghost. But between you and me, I trust the Potato."

"What?"

"Observe." César pulled a telescope from a leather case attached to the inner rail and aimed it out into the thick element. "You see. You cannot really steer the balloon. You must pray for the favorable winds."

"*Pray?*"

"Well. You can also go up, or down, in search of a wind more to your liking. Before I cut the ballast, we were set to climb fifteen hundred yards. Give or take a thousand. But once you vent away too much gas, or drop all your ballast—you see, your options are very limited. Of course"—César leaned entirely too close to me and paddled with his hands—"we could try to row our way through the sky. Yes, the aerial gondola with oars was invented by the great pioneer of balloon flight, Jean-Pierre de Rozier."

"It was Blanchard," said Latham.

"Yes. You see, this de Blanchard and his colleague, a doctor from America, set out aboard the gondola. It was much different from the basket you ride in now. They were intent on crossing the Channel, setting out from England. They designed four large oars in the shape of fans and attached them to the rail. They had a large propeller that you cranked by hand, and a large rudder too, to help steer."

"Ask him how it went," said Latham, and both of them leaned eagerly toward me.

"Why don't we use paddles now?" I asked, staring into the dense fog beyond the ropes. "At least we could do something." I extended my arm into the cloudbank. It was so thick that the end of my sleeve was nearly lost from sight. The balloon above was a mere gruesome shadow.

"There is nothing out there to push against," said César. "As you push yourself forward, you simultaneously push yourself back. You get nowhere. De Blanchard—."

"There is no 'de,' " said Latham.

"Of course not," said César. "The intrepid aeronaut and the American ended up plowing into the seas aboard their gondola. This was December, now, and the seas were high. But they skirted the ocean for only a short time. They'd long since heaved off all of their ballast, so they threw over the oars. They threw the propeller. And the useless rudder. And all the extensive volumes of research they'd acquired from England—everything, anything that weighed anything. They threw it all into the sea, until eventually they had to cut loose their experimental gondola and crouch along the rigging with nothing but the waves below, and the balloon above. They dumped their coats and even their trousers. They were recovered later that day in the forest, as naked as the winter trees, and taken by carriage and six great horses to the palace in Calais, where de Blazier and the American received great celebrity, honors, and wealth."

"The Frenchman was Blanchard," said Latham. "And the American, Dr. Jeffries. Who was prepared to drown in his clothes, until he saw that they would survive the trip. Then, in an act of bravery, he threw his jacket into the surf. That is how it happened."

"I like your version much better," said César.

"What good are the achievements of past heroes, if they are not celebrated?"

"The names are not as important as the news that the Channel was crossed, and by Frenchmen, and that when you and I crossed it, we were part of the same proud tradition."

"You crossed the Channel?" I asked.

"Now pay attention. You do realize"—here César leered at me—"that the going rate for a two-hour balloon ride in Paris at this time of year is twelve hundred francs."

I turned to Latham, who raised his brows in agreement. Then I glared into the obscurity. I could only hope for a fragment of such a sum for the damages to the farm where I used to live somewhere down below the damp, dark clouds that held us captive. I had the impulse again to leap, or at least take the watch out and chuck it.

"And that is only the beginning of the expenses," said César, reaching out to me like a solemn patriarch. "The honorarium alone is twelve hundred francs."

"Honorarium?" I set myself square against the rail and peered stubbornly.

"Please. Not so quickly. You'll tip the basket. We need a proper distribution of weight. And yes. You must first sign a contract, before ever setting foot inside the basket, to ensure that the balloonist is not responsible for the passenger's life, limb, or mental condition after the balloon ride is complete. The initial ticket is solely for the ride across the sky." César gestured magnificently to the fog and the rigging and the basket and the fittings along the rail. Everything was beginning to drip. The wind took the droplets sideways and sent them into the featureless cloud stuff. "There are the precious gases to consider, and the transportation of the balloon back to Paris, where the balloon is stored. And of course some landings are more expensive than others. If you should ever land in a backward village, the fearful peasants will beat the balloonist with pitchforks and sticks. Science is the hobgoblin of the devil, they believe."

"Then those who ride in balloons must be fools." I spat. "I could never consider such a sum. Why did you bring me up here if it was just to demonstrate our differences?"

Just as I was about to give back to the aeronaut his forsaken watch, Latham spoke up.

"The passenger of the charter balloon also agrees to pay for the protection of life and limb of the balloonists, and any property damage to the actual balloon itself, and to its accessories, *and*"—he put his arm around César and then stepped back in admiration of his friend—"and to the property damage of third parties. *You*"—Latham looked at me—"are the third party in question. You are our guest and victim."

"You are," said César. "We must take care of you. And we must also have lunch."

"But let's get out of this forsaken cloud first."

"Up?" asked César. "Or down?"

"Up. It may be raining."

César took out his splendid knife and held it fast against the cord of yet another bag of ballast. "Who knows how many enemies we create?"

He cut the rope.

"It's up to the fates."

8.

LIKE A BOATMAN DOWN THE NILE, I wanted to row through the sky. I wanted to pole my way down through the whirling wool stuff and find solid enough footing to push us along. I didn't know if the balloon was climbing, sinking, twelve feet above the ground, or above a mountain. When no one spoke, it was altogether still—and quiet—within the cloud. When one of us did speak, the cloud gave our voices a sort of denseness, or echo.

"You'd think some kind of paddle might work," I said.

César peered out from the rigging into the deepening murk. "Yes, you would, wouldn't you? You see, many ideas of propulsion were put forth. They thought that the balloon might be a boat, like a frigate, perhaps. They hung sails from the balloon, as if the balloon itself weren't already a sail. And they tried using cannon. It took an *enormous* balloon to lift even the smallest artillery. They hoped that the recoil would push them forward. They also tried jumping from the balloon, with parachutes, or gliding kites, or umbrellas. One even tried to hang on to birds. He tied little strings around the legs of eagles and pigeons. But agh! To no use. Will we ever get out of this cloud?"

Soon the sun burst through and the clouds turned brilliant. But all you could see was the lighted cloud stuff all around. Then the balloon itself broke through.

I looked out over an endless cloudscape of rolling hills and valleys, snow drifts, sudden abutments of ice. Then I saw them, the far-off fleeting castles of the sky, their snow-clad towers shimmering as if from a childhood storybook, all of it moving, all the same billowy whiteness and the sky above an intense winter blue. The blinding sky was so cold it made everything keener above the shifting arctic landscape that the sun had boiled up so that it all roiled back into itself and was endless. Our balloon was just a small foreign speck above it all. Its shadow, rippling in and out over the chasms, was even smaller, and the rainbow that followed us across the clouds was smaller still.

With a sudden twist of dread, I remembered my farmhouse down there in a valley of that other world. And how I wished I could be there now! How could I ever show my family or the people of my village this? Could Simone ever imagine it? And my hopes stung me through and through, and I was alone just then as César kept speaking a bit impatiently at me—an unkempt, scraggly-haired grasshopper from the farm who was not listening to his stories, which presently involved a balloonist as a goat.

"A what?" I said. "Ahh—I see, a goat."

César rocked on his legs to keep warm, and the clear mucus leaked from his nose as the wind took it flying. He went on to say that perhaps—according to the early pioneers of aerostatics—you could not breathe up here, in the upper regions, in the spheres! "They wondered if, in the rare elements, the ether would poison your lungs and leave you gasping. Perhaps being so close to heaven without dying first would create an intense longing in you, and you would leap from the balloon without ever thinking. Or perhaps you imagined you could fly. So, as safeguards, the first aeronauts were farm animals."

"Every schoolchild in France knows this," said Latham.

I gave a quick involuntary look from one aeronaut to the other as my knees shook from the cold.

Latham bowed his head in deference to the inexhaustible stories of his companion.

César kept on. "The first pilots of the passenger balloon were a goose, a goat, and a rooster. It was a primitive balloon, made of paper, with no one there to stoke the fire. So down they came, less than a half mile away. The only mishap occurred in the loading, when the frightened goat kicked the goose and broke its wing."

"What happened to the balloonist who hung on to the bird legs?" I asked.

"Excuse me?"

"The balloonist who hung on to the birds when he jumped, what happened to him?"

Both aeronauts laughed, and César reached down and handed me Marcus's coat, which had been folded and stored in a corner. Beneath the coat was a valise, from which he extracted a bottle so finely labeled that I had never seen such a thing.

"What do you think happened?" said Latham.

"Well, if he had any success or luck at all, I suppose I would have heard of him, even in my village. I fear the worst."

"Anyone who jumps from a balloon hanging on to little bird legs deserves his fate," said César. "No. The legend has it that the balloonists rigged the birds up to their *balloon*. A remarkable tale. And highly unlikely. Here, Potato. Try this."

César held up a glass full of a lively liquid. The flute of the glass alone was something I had seen only from a distance, while peering into storefronts and at prints in books that Simone kept in her room. Also, from the basket came foodstuffs from the world over—cheeses aged in mountain caves, figs and olives from the shores of the Aegean, and candied pistachios from arid nomad lands. On a plate wrapped in cloth was a browned and quartered hen, preserved in its own jelly. But the most satisfying taste of all was the sharp bite of the sea salt, sprinkled from a wooden jigger onto a hard-boiled egg. "*Fleur de sel*," said César, "from all corners of the seven seas." Then something in my expression caused him to ponder. "Why, one of those seas is only a short train ride away from your valley," he said, then, guessing at the reason for my silence, "So, you've never been to the ocean?"

He must have seen from my staggered look that I had not. He shook his head.

"Ahh—such a pity."

On the egg white, the sea salt was as pure as the coldness of the air. I turned the glass in my hands, feeling light-headed. I thought of my father sneering at the waste and debauchery of the aristocratic classes. I looked at the frozen, icy cloudscape, steaming up and rolling below. A smallish opening presented itself. There were several openings here and there if you looked for them. The clouds that formed the clearing went one way, while the clouds far, far below them—a darker, thinner, whiskery sort of cloud—traveled the other, and somewhere below that was the land. I had a whirling sensation of plunging into the wordless and inescapable, and wondered just how I would ever explain this to Simone, the silent milk maid, with the pens and pad of paper she kept at her nightstand.

"Here," said Latham. "A toast. To our worthy Potato. Who'd have imagined that you'd actually make the trip to meet us?"

"Or go up in the balloon!" said César.

"We gave you every opportunity to sneak away." And Latham brought the elbow patches of his coat up against the railing and stared out in a manner so deliberate as to be contrived.

That's when I could no longer contain myself and took the watch from my pocket and began to unwrap it from the linen.

"What's this?" César grabbed at my arm. "He's nothing but a common swindler."

César swatted at the watch. Instinctively I pulled back. But my elbow hit up against the rigging, and both the watch and the linen flew from my hands. I lunged for them, feeling altogether clumsy in the stranger's ill-fitting jacket, and came up empty-handed. Then all three of us leaned over the rail. Only the white handkerchief with its silver-stitched monogram could be seen, tumbling in a limp-rag way, collapsing and opening and collapsing again, turned by the wind, until it too plunged into the clouds and disappeared without a trace.

"Hubert. Was that really your watch?"

"I believe so," said Latham. "I also believe it is the only reason the Potato is even here—to return it."

I could say nothing, my heart bleeding with the heat of failure. It radiated from my chest and face, despite the sky's arctic cold. Had the watch landed in a small parish graveyard? Or the impenetrable woods?

A swamp? A body of water such as a lake or a pond? It could be in any number of landscapes hidden below the vastness of the clouds.

"Wasn't that something of your father's?" asked César. "A family heirloom?"

"No. Not my father's. Not really," said Latham, lost in the slump of dejection. "Just a watch."

9.

For the longest time we stared without speaking, our faces drawn involuntarily down to the clouds. Nor could I bear to look at either aeronaut. I assumed they stared as I did, as if to stare oneself awake from this horrible dream.

I finally gathered the nerve to step away from the rail and face my hosts, and just then two objects dropped to the basket floor: the watch, and the gold chain just after. Apparently some combination of the watch and chain had pinned itself between my overcoat and the weave of the bulwarks.

Immediately Latham fell to his knees. "That which is lost returns. You found it after all." He clung to the watch as if it were a wiggling fish that might flop itself back into the water, both coddling and strangling the life out of it at once. "There's a divinity that shapes our ends." He was inclined to spout off famous-sounding sayings, especially in English, and, as I later learned, especially those from the prince Hamlet. He quoted the line for me in both the English and a French translation, not like an actor or a sea captain, but different, yet more. He had that belief. Rising to his feet, he looked up at me and in his starchy, deliberate way, said, "Potato. You're a young man of talent, I can tell. The world needs individuals such as yourself."

"But—I didn't find it. Someone on our farm did. My tutor, from childhood."

"Well." Latham composed himself and straightened out his coat sleeves. "Thank your tutor, then. He taught you well."

César reached over and took the watch from Latham's hands. "Where on earth did you get this?" He shot his unbelieving eyes at me, then at the watch, then at me again, not as though I were a thief but more a magician.

"I meant to throw down my barometer," said Latham, "as collateral of some sort. The boy seemed hurt."

But even as he said it, I suspected otherwise—that the throwing of the watch was a test of sorts, not of me but of some superstition I was merely a part of, some greater notion of fate that had Latham ensnared.

César leaned back, suspicious, arms crossed.

"I thought I lobbed down my barometer," said Latham.

"But this is from Antoinette." César flipped the watchcase shut.

"It is."

And Latham took the watch up himself, visibly disturbed, and turned it this way and that, and opened the case up briefly to check the inscription, before pocketing it in his vest. He then buttoned up his jacket with resumed pride.

"Have you talked to her father yet?" asked César. "Will he still put you into an aeroplane?"

"I have not. I have yet to see him. But I do have a wager that I will be the first to fly across the English Channel."

"Who would bet against you?"

"The archdeacon himself."

"You know of an aeroplane maker?" I asked.

" 'Aeroplane maker?' " César mocked. The phrase must have seemed to him naive, as if aeroplanes were not quite made in the practical sense but more conceived or galvanized from some futuristic process too far-fetched and scientific to comprehend. "Are you referring to the engineer of the most advanced, high-speed engines in all of the world? Not only do we know such a man but—do you remember the watch you nearly sent to the clouds?" Before I could reply, César said, "The woman who gave him that watch is the daughter of the investor."

But Latham seemed lost to the vast expanses.

César eyed me with a sympathetic expression. "Potato," he said. "Why the long face?"

"I'm thinking about the harvest. Where I should be right now. I've been gone for two days."

"Two? Only two?" Latham seemed profoundly amused. "A person such as yourself? You should see more of the world, then. And come with us to Paris. To see the aeroplane maker yourself."

"Yes. Perfect. A must," said César. "Are you sorry you left?"

"Left?"

"Left the earth, my boy. Look. Just look at what the gods see."

"I think I have to get home someday."

"And so do I," said Latham. "So do I." He pulled on a cord, releasing some of the buoyant gas through a vent in the balloon. "But first, let's have coffee."

"Shall we?" César produced a thermos of Turkish brew, still warm enough to emit steam.

"Where are we, anyway?" I said.

"The Orient, perhaps," said César.

"I was hoping for the South Pacific. Do you have a fondness for exotic women?" The rumple-suited racer kept hold of the cord.

And the balloon descended, nearing the overcast below.

10.

I RETURNED HOME after a three-day absence. In the early morning, a steam was curling up from the sagging eaves of the farmhouse, still dark from the night's rain. It rose from the poppies and grasses that grew on the roof, and the barn also let loose a moisture, as if from the puffing and sweating of the animals inside. I found my family in the kitchen, stooped over breakfast, beneath a hole in the roof that seemed no different than on the day I had left it. Except now a ladder reached up above our heads, and blankets had been arranged across the floor to soak up the rainwater. My father had hired a few extra croppers, who ate at the end of the long table.

With the promise of fair weather, the new field hands were quick to finish breakfast and head for the fields, as did everyone else. Except my father, who stood deep in deliberation. Slowly he drew himself a basin of water, readied a small mirror, and began to shave. Seeing how I had stayed behind also, he asked our house servant Angèle if she wouldn't mind leaving the kitchen for a bit.

Halfway through my father's shaving, I threw down the purse I'd brought back with me from the balloon ride.

My father put the razor down and grabbed the satchel. He bounced the weight of it in his hands. Across the velvet material were the swirling initials of the *Buontemponi* in gold.

"Very good, son. *Very.* I'm proud of you."

As if it were a beanbag, he tossed it back without looking inside, and turned to walk out the door, but remembered his task—his face still half lathered. He returned to the basin, dipped his razor into the foamy water, and brought it back up to his face.

"As you can see"—he spoke awkwardly into his hands—"the kitchen isn't fixed yet. But I did manage to borrow some mortar from old Loiseau, which you'll use to fix the well."

"But what am I to do in the fields?" I asked. "For harvest?"

My father cupped his hands into the basin and splashed water across his face, once, briskly.

"One other thing," he said. "Until the well's fixed, it's your job to draw water for the field workers. They'll tell you when they're thirsty. They're on their way there. If you'll excuse me."

He began for the door.

❧❦

With each passing harvest I'd been given more and more responsibility, but now I had none. That, and the fixing of the well, were the only consequences of my absence, which included a third day so that a farmer in the far reaches of the Normandy countryside could take us—me, the aeronauts, and the ship of the *Buontemponi*, all folded up and stuffed inside the basket—to the nearest train station. Back at the racecourse, I'd retrieved my bicycle. "Don't be so glum," the aeronauts said. "Come visit us in Paris." They made me promise.

❧❦

The bucket had to be lowered still by hand into the well's dull, answerless dark, and retrieved just as slowly, or slower, heavy now with water that I poured into the wheelbarrow of mortar and aggregate. As I began mixing the mortar with a spade, Simone appeared. She wore the same blue printed kerchief she always wore, in all weathers, and held the kerchief back as if it might come loose and drop into the well. She leaned so far over the well's edge that I feared she'd lose her footing. Calmly studying the fall, she sensed my eyes upon her. She turned and smiled, but it wasn't a smile really. I'd never experienced anything like it. Her unbroken silence lent a purpose and dignity to her every gesture. In early adolescence Simone had emerged from scarlet fever thin and ravaged and very nearly deaf in both ears, while her older sister had died from it. So my father felt obliged to provide for the only surviving child of his house servants by arranging for her to board at a special school for the deaf.

I remember the day Simone first returned to our farm from the Order of the Suffering Silence. She poked her head out of the stagecoach and into a hazy day of spring. A professor picked the twelve-year-old girl up by the armpits and swung her down. She'd grown old enough now to fit into her deceased sister's dresses, and remained rigid while the yellowed material flung about her stockings and knees. She stumbled when she landed, and the professor caught her up. The fever had also affected her balance. Then she and the young professor began to talk, using the frail, quiet gestures of the hands. The nuns too leaned out the window and gestured with the same kind proficiency—gentle, and somehow medicinal, as if they were nurses. Over her sister's dress, the girl wore the same shawl and blue apron as the nuns. She turned and approached her mother, who through a shimmer of tears saw at once both a ghost and a miracle, but a miracle unable to speak. The schoolgirl had the self-sufficient air of a survivor in her every gesture, and looked about her with sleepy eyes at the farm as if she were in a strange land of useless customs. She seemed content only when doing chores.

Two weeks later the carriage returned, and Simone and the nuns began to talk again with the beautiful, fluid movements. Simone was transformed entirely, simply by the use of her hands; she smiled, her eyes smiled, her skin grew flushed. Her hands moved like birds, like someone plucking apples. She was throwing salt, chopping vegetables, holding something precious; then she was gone, back to the school. When she returned to live on the farm for good, she carried around with her an instructional booklet that illustrated the most basic words of the hands. Even these most simple gestures overflowed, harboring a secret, inner eagerness. It was all I could do, back at the age of thirteen, to keep from following her around so that I could speak to her in this new, foreign language.

⁂

"Where is it?" Simone asked, with a giddiness that was unsettling. "I want to study the watch."

She rarely spoke, especially when she was agitated, when the words came out like blather—too loud and painful to hear, with strangely evolved pronunciations. Her voice had all the want of a child freshly awake from a deep and troubled dreaming. Even as she wore a clever grin, the disturbance was there.

"*I'm sorry.*" I shrugged, using my rudimentary gestures. "*I don't know where it is.*"

"*You don't know?*"

"*Well, with the balloonist, I suppose.*" I pointed to the sky.

She looked at me with a keen skepticism.

"*I had to give it back.*"

"*Did he say who the gift was from?*"

"*Oh, he has many gifts, I think.*" And I gestured for Simone to hand me the small notepad and pencil she kept in her apron. I wrote down that even their balloon was a gift, from an Italian nobleman, who had sailed it here from across the Alps.

I squinted significantly into the clouds. After a balloon ride such as mine, I thought I might convey a greater sense of things with just an expression, a certain posture—that I radiated a superior quality. Just as I was trying to figure how I would ever explain to her my balloon ride in the sky, the three field hands drew near, like stray cattle with no particular purpose. So I had to humiliate myself by drawing water for the croppers, even the new one, who stood by with a taunting impatience.

Before leaving, Simone asked, "*Is that where you've been these past three days? Searching for the owner of the watch?*"

"*Yes.*"

"*And he has so many gifts he can just toss them around?*" Then aloud she said, "Even a lover's forget-me-not?"

Before I could answer, she wandered off, and I lowered the bucket again down into the darkness below the fields.

~⁊ ⁊~

Throughout the course of the day I'd exhausted all the excitement of imagining over and over again the strange lands and distant cities beyond the clouds. But someone had to know—I had to describe to someone what our farm might look like from the balloon, and how quiet it was, above the rooftops, above the trees. I had only to look up and was transported again to the open pastures and rooms of the clouds. I felt somehow both enormous and small and also quietly above the hills all at once.

Soon I had nothing to do but wait for the mortar of the well repairs to dry.

Desperate for escape, weary with guilt, I sought out Simone in the fields, hoping she might be thirsty. It was not unusual to find her flat on her belly, drinking from a stream beside the goats and cows, and then she'd stand, with a scattering of leaves on the nun's apron she still wore from her days at the Suffering Silence. That afternoon I found her asleep on a knoll. Sent out to mind the cows, she'd dozed off in the field below the sun. Finding her, who would have the heart to instruct her that napping beneath the sun was wrong? The subtleties would require pen and paper, and by then I'd find myself taken in by her placid wonder in a wordless field close to the animals. Yes, napping midday with the cows was wrong, unless you were Simone, or could speak to her in the language of the hands.

Auguste . . . I am thirsty . . . , came the taunts from the nearby field workers.

They yelled as though they knew I was not far off, caught up in the spell of a girl dreaming on the other side of the trees. Rather than stir her awake, I let her drift farther off, beyond the banks of her wordless, soundless afternoon, knowing I was denied her special paradise.

11.

THAT NIGHT I SLEPT POORLY.

Strange winds rushed in and rattled the curtains the whole house over. Creeping downstairs, I found myself in a wash of blue moonlight that spread throughout the rooms. Chilled winds came in through the ripped-open thatch and blew out the match I'd struck. Once lit, the kerosene lamp revealed the soggy array of blankets and buckets put there to catch the rainwater, where the smell of drenched wood shavings lingered. And there, beneath the sagging hole in the roof, the pantry had been emptied—all the sacks, jars, and root vegetables stacked wherever they would fit. A ladder still leaned up through the hole in the roof, where the repairs were mainly to the rafters and joists.

Then Simone appeared. Or perhaps she'd been there all along, and my lighting of the lamp only discovered her, slowly. By degrees she emerged from the shadows cast by the moon through the roof. In the flickering light, her eyes were fiery with questions, and her mouth drawn tight.

"They say you watched me sleep in the field. Why didn't you wake me? I should keep track of the herd."

Her accusation was hushed, but unnervingly constrained. I tried to shush her, and held my hands out in an open gesture to signify the rest of the household, asleep. To be quieter, we moved to the entrance of the walk-in chimney, beneath huge black pans hung from black ancient hooks.

"*Why didn't you wake me?*" It was difficult to follow her gestures in the near darkness, until my eyes could adjust. "*And how long were you there, just standing there?*" Stepping back, she became an incredulous shadow. "*Watching me? Watching me sleep?*"

"*I wanted to tell you. But you looked so peaceful I did not want to wake you—*"

"*Tell me what?*"

"*You won't believe it. It's so—fantastical. I mean, I hardly believe it myself.*" I wasn't exactly sure of what I said when I used my hands, but I kept at it. "*I haven't told a soul. Because no one would believe me.*"

"*Did you die and come back? Please. If you can't speak plainly, I have no other course but to—*"

She attempted to walk around me. But I stopped her by trying to make the shapes of my balloon ride in the sky. I tried to demonstrate with my hands how I'd floated through the clouds, but I didn't have the words for it. My language of the hands was not so good. I often made up gestures, while Simone watched with a blank look. I began wishing for a pen and paper. "*When I gave the aeronaut back his watch,*" I gestured clumsily, "*they took me up in their balloon.*"

Simone looked on with a frank, animal-eyed suspicion, endlessly kind, but for the most part wary. It was this wordless apprehension that always stirred me. In the cave of the fireplace, her shadowy figure mixed with my memories of trying to learn my first words of the language of the hands. In the shade by a stream, or a cove of trees, or the barn with its midday darkness, she would move her hands through the air. She would draw the same lines over and over again before my face, with an adolescent giddiness. I usually had no idea what she was saying, except that it was an exotic gesture learned from nuns. If I could not re-create it, Simone would reach out and nervously take my hands and show them how to move. In this slow and awkward dance, we withdrew farther into some shadowy, secluded spot, behind a hedge, or the haymow, or inside the chimney, though I didn't know if she was saying "*rain*" or "*thunder*" or "*come follow.*"

❧⚜❧

"Auguste. My boy, is that you?"

My father's voice arrested us in the dark. Then I heard him walk over to the table and pick up the lamp. The kerosene flame came blindingly into the stone mouth of the fireplace, until its burning, golden source was all you could see.

Simone took off like a shadow, while the harsh golden light hardly moved.

Then, from behind his lamp, my father's voice spoke out: "There has been some talk around about you, Auguste." He spoke as if reading my very soul. "If you're even thinking of leaving, I mean striking out on your own, then you'd better make up your mind. If you're going to leave . . ."

My father either grinned or grimaced or both. I could not tell through all of the swimming of the kerosene flame, all the sudden guilt of being discovered sneaking into the fireplace with Simone. My silence gave my father the indisputable authority of the father, and I still a boy under his tutelage.

"Have you seen how extensive the repairs will be?"

Emerging from the chimney, I noticed his tools adding to the kitchen's disarray: the rusty saw, the toothless hammer, the dull chisels, the "farmer's mix"—tins of rusted, bent-out nails, spikes, and lags, all of different sizes, different shapes, most of them pulled from planks that had been in the barn from a time before I was born. He winced, putting the ladder into place.

"Here. Take those wandering eyes of yours up there, if you please."

Upon the ladder, I could not make out all of the work my father had done, just a tangle of jagged shapes in the dark. And there, through the ruptured thatch of the roof, I saw, as if for the first time, the moon, and the spherical quality of the moon. It had never seemed so bright and close, like a great, friendly, glowing orb. The silver clouds too were beautiful, moving high above the rip in the thatch. Not far off, along the road, the poplars bent and swayed in windy indecision, their tall tops disappearing into the dark.

Once back down the ladder, I found my father drinking from a glass. His hair seemed especially thin and flyaway, brought freshly out of sleep. After a good draw from his tumbler, he smacked his lips and looked up through the roof.

"Well. Let's get some sleep, shall we? I could use some extra help in the morning, lifting that beam into place. And let's hope it doesn't rain too much tonight, either. Good night, son."

To my father, the balloon had long ago sailed into the realm of folktales and hearsay. For him, there were no foreign countries, no lands beyond the hills, no place on earth except here, this farm village here, and that indolent, incomprehensible place where lived the foreigner, who might as well be an exotic animal or a ghost. The difference between the Prussian, Parisian, or Turk was not worth considering; they were all invaders. For the simple man who my father talked like, with a deceptive air, there were only these hills, this village, and these folk. The elderly had always been old, and the young ones slowly took their place.

"G'night," I said.

"Yes, it is, isn't it?"

He blew out the gas lamp, and I listened to his slow, crotchety walk through the house and up the creaking steps.

Through the torn roof, the pale, uneven moonlight kept pouring in.

Book II.

The Aeroshow

Any notions that French airmen and designers continued to lag fundamentally behind the United States were dispelled by a seminal event that occurred at the end of 1908: the Premier Salon de l'Aéronautique, held in the Grand Palais in Paris.

—Richard P. Hallion, *Taking Flight*

The Salon was a smashing success. Opening day saw the pavilions so crowded that extra police had to be ordered in to prevent the surging, pushing crowds from hurting one another or damaging the exhibits. This was especially true around the Wrights' airplane, where a cordon of police had to be stationed. ... Nineteen hundred and eight was the year aviation became an industry.

—Dennis Parks, "Paris 1908: The First Aero Trade Show"

12.

In the fall, the aeronaut César summoned me in a letter.

He wrote enthusiastically of an upcoming aeroplane exhibition to be held at the Palace of Machines. Well, not the Palace of Machines exactly, but the Petit and Grand Palais both. The actual Palais des Machines was to host an auxiliary display of boats and other oceangoing vessels—diving bells, ships that ply undersea, and suits that allow you to breathe in the oceanic deep. I was to meet the two aeronauts there, at the nautical exhibits, in the fantastic realms of Captain Nemo, brought to life by a new age of mechanical invention.

César wrote also of new avenues of employment for me, not to mention—though he did anyway—an unofficial invitation to take part in the launching of an aeroplane yet to be flown. He ended the letter on behalf of Latham, who wished I'd attend for the "obvious good luck," and in appreciation for bringing back his watch.

The premier *Salon de l'Aéronautique* was to begin that Christmas Eve.

≈≈

In the slow month of December, my father liked to take his seat at the breakfast table just before the rest of us were done eating. That way he could signal us to begin our winter tasks a little earlier than we might have wished. Then he could luxuriate. Like a magistrate, he took his inventories, calculated his returns, and wrote down official letters, such as the one to the officer of health, adjusting for an error on a receipt. My father was especially satisfied that year, as he had just received an appointment from the firemen's brigade to be second-in-command under the captain, a venerable gentleman in the country who was too far away to respond yet liked to preside, mostly at banquets and parades. My father was still deliberating over the terms of his acceptance.

When our breakfast was nearly finished, and no one had yet left the table, he asked me where I had received my black eye.

"Is it black?"

"All day yesterday. You must have run into something in a hurry. It's all swelled up, my boy, and fresh."

I fell silent and bent my head over my plate, rubbing the bruised part of my brow.

❧❀❧

I had received the black eye two nights before, on the day Simone handed me a note—just a sentence—asking me to come see her.

On the cold nights when *la Galerne* blew, the path to Simone's was a bit longer than I might have wished. I'd forgotten my coat, and the bare winter branches were so thick that the light of the moon and stars could not reach through. It was in this starless black that I crept past our farmhouse and down a path of frozen hedgerow and scrub. What functioned as the servant's quarters had once, generations ago, been the neighboring farmhouse. One of my ancestors had been smitten by the knobby-kneed beauty just over the hedge, and our family's acreage grew. One farmhouse annexed the other, and our little hollow became a tribe all its own.

When I came to Simone's door, I found it locked. I could not knock—nor tap lightly on her window without waking her mother or father instead. Whether she was awake, and sometimes she was, with a glowing light within—no matter, I could not summon her. So

I waited outside a row of three doors to a brick house, one for her, one for her mother, and one for Odilon, all of whom I'd known all my life, all now asleep. I stood, determined but helpless, shivering in the wind that moved the tangle of branches, both high and low, as if it were the unsettled dreaming of the hollow.

Then her door opened.

Reaching to her nightstand, Simone lit a candle sunk deep inside a seat of wax, and sat down in sleepy caution, twisting her elbows within her robe. The mound of wax had something of a geographical shape to it, floes and valleys, tributaries that ran from the dish and broke off. Above the candle a blackened trail of soot rose as straight as a bowstring up the wallpaper. The smoke stain faded and gained again in depth until the smudge hit the ceiling, where the blot of old fumes fanned out in a blackened, star-shaped pattern, radiating and fading out. Beside the candle were a few open books, placed page down.

Simone yawned, as if I'd interrupted her on the verge of sleep. She had breath like warm milk, and her skin was the nicest, smoothest thing I had ever touched. She flinched, though, and moved away when I sat down beside her. Retreating farther, she barely lifted her hands, asking, "*What are you doing here?*"

"*The note?*" I opened my hands, also like a question.

"*But you waited until nightfall, until everyone was asleep.*"

"*My father is always watching me.*"

"*Is he watching now? What I mean to say is, what are you doing back home at all? Why don't you just leave?*"

"*I have to get a few things.*"

"*Oh.*"

Neither of us spoke, staring into the low-burning candle.

"*So you are leaving. Weren't you going to tell me? Weren't you going to say goodbye?*"

"*I haven't left yet.*"

Simone further nursed her bare elbows, facing the wall. Her disturbed breathing scared the cat with no name, and it jumped from the bed and scratched at the door. Simone rose and calmly slipped her wooden clogs over her woolen stockings. She wrapped a shawl around her night robe, opened the door, and followed her pet into the night.

The cat loped away, as proud as any Arabian horse, however tiny, its tail raised to the air. Every time Simone drew near, the cat took off again, but for only a few paces before it looked back around, slightly confused, wondering when this chase would end. Grimly I followed. Beyond the trees, the moonlight was reflected everywhere off the snow, blotting out the stars and exaggerating our breath. Simone's footsteps crunched across the field. Her clogs slipped, and she staggered. Soon there was no cat anywhere, yet I did not wonder why she wandered out into a frozen field of snow-covered stubble.

Then she stopped walking and turned around to face me. She spoke with her arms, but I could not make out what. I reached out for her.

"Don't," she spoke aloud, and yanked herself free, and kept walking.

"*You see me as some sort of monster, don't you?*" She waved in strange, looping gestures. "*Some circus freak.*" She used the same signs she and I had made up when we read *Frankenstein*. "*A changeling. An imp. As everyone else does too.*"

"No—" I reached out for her again, and she heaved herself free. I kept reaching, this time catching her off balance. Then Simone lunged out and lost all footing and came at me—elbows swinging through the dark, elbows so swift I lost all sense. I was bending forward to better see her when she caught me in the face, hard, and kept charging until we both fell over a root. There were voices in the long and twisted limbs, in the air, in the steam of our breath, not voices, more like whisperings, presences, hushed after the blow, and a black and steady flickering, on and then off again, disturbing the snowy flat of the field. I faltered, trying to come to my feet, but could not quite lift myself, as if I'd done this before and was remembering something, as if dreaming and then awakening and still having it feel like a dream. Simone stood above me with slobbering breaths, whimpering in the loud, awkward way of the mute. Then she fell to her knees, horrified at what she'd done, and put her hands to my face. Feeling a numbness in my bones and a throbbing in my head like the rushing of a waterfall, I saw her all the more clearly. She slowed the forceful movement of her hands, until I could nearly understand her.

She was sorry, she was sorry, she was sorry.

She sank down in the snow.

"*I'll come for you,*" I said.

"How? You don't even know where you're going. And you'll be gone for so long. Some girl will fall in love with you. She'll hear your voice. She'll fall in love with your voice. There's always been a part of you that feels so sorry for me."

Of all the voices she could remember, she remembered mine most vividly. She said at times my voice came to her. It sprang into her head and spoke at crucial times with strange or wonderful meanings, or sometimes at random with no meaning at all. Her face was distorted with grief. It poured from her reddened, swollen eyes, which she tried to hide, or slow, until it fairly glistened across her cheeks. She always believed she had a bad heart—the very reason she had been left deaf. She believed her older sister had been taken away out of the purity of her soul, but she had been passed over by the very God of Heaven and returned to a world she'd been partly denied. Unable to hear the world, still she had to live in it, at her sister's expense.

This wasn't so, I tried to tell her, that she'd made it up—

"Don't." The words came out half-formed, soaked and porous, as if through water. "Go now, please," she said aloud. "Please. The sooner, the better."

Standing, she wiped the snow from her blue nun's apron and walked back under the dense trees to her house in the hollow.

❧❧

On the morning I left for the train station, my father gave me a suitable knapsack for a long journey, as well as a shovel, a pickax, and a hoe, tied together at either end with a section of rope burned neatly at the ends so it wouldn't fray.

"Here, take these with you. That way they'll know you're serious, and that you're willing to do anything, wherever you go. And if you need to, you can work your way back."

As I set out, Simone ran from her house. She reached into her apron and pulled out the gift of two picture postcards that she'd bought at the mercantile, as reminders of my upcoming journey. One was of a double-decker tramcar, the other of a fancy café where fine people sat outside and ate pastries.

13.

THE DAY FINALLY ARRIVED. My train ride to Paris. City of cities. Capital of engine vapors, drizzle, and gloom. In my naive farm boy's way, I imagined that all cities must be like this, and, simultaneously, that Paris was the only city in the world. During the morning train ride, I watched as the trees parted and gave way to rows of squat dingy houses, and more dismal homes in double rows, street upon street in a dull industrial fog. Once our train compartment filled, we six passengers stared at each other. I held the three great rusty heads of cropper's tools propped up before my face. Through the awkward shapes of the farmer's tools, I kept searching the upcoming station signs for my destination. The farther the train ride stretched out, so did Paris, without end. Flakes of soot stirred with the snowflakes in the air, leaving a thick black coating along the edge of lampposts and walls. Here stood a chemical factory, tall brick chimneys, and then a timber merchant's yard of soaked and grimy stacks.

The city of my imagination finally took shape, in the far off distance, as the famous tower of the World's Fair appeared above the haze.

∽❧∾

At la Gare Montparnasse, I asked a porter where I could keep my belongings safe. He only looked at my bundle and sneered.

"Believe me. They will be safe." And the agent in his gray, embroidered suit held out his hand and took his fee, storing my cropper's tools behind his counter.

Once beyond the station, I passed beneath a grocer's sign hung above stomped-gray straw, and traffic came to a halt when a brewer's dray and a butcher's cart unloaded at the same time. All manner of horse carts, motors, and even a double-decker omnibus—like a giant, trundling turtle—passed over the sunken trolley rails beneath the cobblestone. Christmas boughs and cedar wreaths draped across doorways and windows, and a man sold bunches of mistletoe hung from a stick he carried over his shoulders. The gray streets became especially bustling as I neared the Grand Palais. The crowd there was threatening, aimless, and unruly, with people stuck in haphazard lines. When I asked which line was for what, I received a variety of surly answers, while the line before the ticket booth did not move, and the booth workers stared through the windows with stern faces and did nothing.

Finally I had it in my hands: one mustard-yellow ticket that radiated its promise. The ticket would be good for today, and only today, and I wondered if the aeronauts would be in attendance as their letter professed. In line at the main gates, I turned and looked back up at the storybook ceiling of the Grand Palais. It was glass, all of glass, with arches and domes and girders of steel. Under the glass peaks, occasionally, the beginnings of a strange bulbous shape would peek up—a balloon, just like the balloon I had ridden in, only smaller. I couldn't be sure if this was my ardent imagination or not—but still, a balloon, free-floating inside the palace. Only the top of it would appear, strung with the rigging needed to tote a basket not yet in view. Then the hint of the aeroship would descend slowly behind the sculpted walls.

⁂

With the rest of the crowd, I handed over my ticket to an usher dressed in a gold-braided uniform fit for an admiral.

In a daze, I entered into any number of Jules Verne's *voyages extra-ordinaires*, at one moment in a floating city, and then on a clipper in the clouds, and then on Propeller Island. A two-hundred-foot behemoth of a dirigible overwhelmed the space beneath the vaulted ceiling of glass, filled with helium and moored to its lines, its four inflated fins drooping enormously over the sea of heads. But the oblivious whale was a killer. Two coal-colored machine guns hung from the dirigible basket, glinting with oil and pointed above the crowd.

Inside the hall of flying machines, I felt a strange haunting, remembering the Wright Flyer from America. I saw all kinds of configurations of muslin, motor, and wood, some suspended from the ceiling by ropes. I saw biplanes and monoplanes and a combination of machinery that turned a large windmill-like paddle above the pilot's head. There was no shortage of French technological superiority on display. To enter the hall you first had to pass below a set of wide-reaching, pointed bat wings. A billboard draped in red theatrical curtains announced that this was a replica of the first true flying machine in the world! Eighteen years ago, back in 1890, France's Clément Ader had sailed his steam-powered ship of bat-wings for over sixty yards at a height of about eight inches. A year later, he claimed to have flown over twice as far, at almost a foot in elevation, but this event was less substantiated. The Wrights' achievement of being first to fly was even further disputed by the flight of the famous Brazilian aeronaut Alberto Santos-Dumont, who, two years ago, flew a machine that looked like a backward box kite at a height of about five yards in a straight line, up and then down again, at a marching grounds just outside of Paris. Highly documented, this was the first true public demonstration of a flying machine in the world. The Wrights had flown only in secrecy up until then. Others claimed the Wright Flyer was nothing more than a glider, as it had to be catapulted into the air, and could not take leave of the earth on its own power.

I left the rumors of history to swirl on their own, however, as I realized how late it was, and how I needed to get to the hall of nautical vessels, or I'd miss my appointment with the aeronauts altogether. But the going was slow. I'd never encountered such a crowd, so thick and meandering.

Beyond the aeroplanes were the balloons, free-floating inside the palace, six in all. The balloons went up, the balloons came down, lifting various important personages and causing a stir of hand waving and calls. The midwinter haze came shining through the shellacked fabric of the flying machines and made clear the framework of wooden struts and ribs, like the configuration of bones as seen through the miracle of the x-ray machine. There was an aspect ghostly and angelic to the winged things, outstretched in the air above our heads. It was a phantasmagoria of strange, new animalesque shapes. Not just flying machines but all manner of machinery that dug, or hauled, or floated, or plied the ocean deep. But most especially that flew. Before our collective faces, upturned, dumbstruck, and vaguely comprehending, the clouds of industrialism gathered.

14.

IN THE HALL OF NAUTICAL VESSELS, I tried to hide my distress. The hour drew late, and the boat portion of the exhibition was so poorly attended that the guests had to speak in hushed, almost apologetic tones, for fear of being overheard. The crowd still swarmed beneath the aeroplanes, but here cigar stubs, nutshells, and discarded programs littered the floor. I searched down the empty rows of pleasure boats, doubting whether the aeronauts would be in attendance as their letter had professed. I doubted whether anyone would wait here through an hour, let alone an entire week, expecting an appointment that had no real set time. But I had to prove to someone—at least myself—that I'd actually gone up in a balloon one rainy day. I saw neither member of the *Buontemponi*, and asked several attendees about a certain motorboat racer, a Monsieur Latham, and where he could be found. No one knew of such a person, or what I was even talking about. Until finally a roundish fellow with bright porcine slits for eyes, a florid beard, and a commodore's cap pointed in the direction of the motorboat at the end of the row.

"That is the vessel of his interest."

"Is he working today?"

The commodore smiled broadly and dismissed me with a bow.

The boat in question was the *Antoinette*, made of dark-stained wood from the Tropic of Capricorn, with a hull of burnished purple heart and rail caps of iron bark. Behind the slender shovelnose, it was long and low and gleaming with lacquer and paint. I marveled at it for so long that it transformed itself into a craft that could sail down only mythic rivers, and none that I knew, for it was too powerful with lightning speed. I walked up and down its length. I read its placard all over again, and loitered for as long as I could, until I realized I was entirely alone.

Nearby, a string quartet played to an empty indoor café. Small unattended tables were bordered by a row of uniform cypress trees in sculpted pots. A fountain spouted. A larger, indoor tree spread its winter arms over the empty scene. It was a place intended to give rise to some forgotten time of antiquity that had most likely never really been. So here was a fitting end to my journey. I would never find the aeronauts, but felt wonderfully unburdened, free to go now, wherever my imagination wandered.

Beyond the motorboats, the vessels turned foreboding, spiny and ironclad, destined for a home altogether inhospitable, under the sea. Here was an inkling of the curiosity that gathered below the flying machines. The spectators gaped idly at a series of small underwater compartments for workers, more confined and hellish than prison, into which oxygen was pumped for the blasting, drilling, and erecting of the bases of enormous span bridges. There was a heavily reinforced diving bell, within which an imaginative philosopher might sit and peer out to contemplate the realms of the fishes and whales. And there were smaller, surprisingly similar orbs, except for the curvature at the base for the shoulders. These were to be worn, over your head, with fittings for an oxygen tube, and small, reinforced glass portals for viewing, a larger one to the front and two smaller ones to either side, through which the diver could see out, pivoting his head. I was standing before a two-man submarine, appearing for all the world like an ironclad mackerel, when I felt a tap on my shoulder.

"M. Potato, I presume."`

I turned, and it was César—César with his sly, ridiculous grin and satyr's beard. He immediately began to lead me by the arm. "I didn't recognize you in such clothes. And also"—he waved his hand through the air, "you are missing that peculiar country air of yours"—he leaned in more closely—"of livestock."

In his excitement to actually have a customer, I believe he'd nearly forgotten who I was, and even now spoke as if I might consider buying this 1904-model racing motor yacht. This was my first experience with a salesman. He spoke of the delicacies of the motor. He spoke of the craftsmanship of the shipwrights who built it. He spoke not to me but to his own eager anticipation, peering far into the ledgers of his recent memory, and as I did nothing to deflect him, he finished his story and we were both the better for it.

But he did not stop there. He climbed up onto the flying bridge. As if he were the pilot, he sat among the heavy varnishes and polished brass and spun the wheel. He crawled down along the short gangway to the engine. He spoke of the brilliance of the designer, a man he simply called Le Père—"A man of great mechanical vision, you'll see." César spoke loudly, as if the motor were throttling into urgent life. The engine casing, along with the entire boat, shone like a jewel, like a many-faceted Fresnel lighthouse lens. Everything was immaculate.

César then came to the boat's history—how the *Antoinette* had once bored through the waves of the coasts of both Normandy and Nice, and how Latham had once sailed this very boat in the great Regatta of Monte Carlo. What? César was shocked. Had I never heard of the first and only boat race of our friend's illustrious career? Under heavy seas, the green helmsman had upset many local favorites, including the sixty-year-old Papagris the Sailor, and the one they call *Le Frère*. But before Latham ever won his trophy, he already had reserved a ticket to set sail on a packet boat bound for the Egyptian port of Alexandria. There he and a small team of two very important government officials-in-training—his cousins, to be more exact—were to deliver the gift of a grandfather clock down the Blue Nile and White Nile, and past the deserts of Khartoum, far into the unmapped territories beyond the source of the great river. The clock was to be a gift to the emperor of the sultans of Abyssinia, an official commission from the French Ministry of Colonial Affairs, among others. The journey would last the better part of two years. Though his two cousins returned early, Latham kept traveling, down through sub-Saharan Africa, across the Indian ocean, and on to Cochinchina.

As I listened, I peered out through a series of small portals at the bow. Three, actually, above the headrest of the main sleeping berth, allowing one to look out as if into a dream. Here was a place one could fall asleep and wake up in a completely foreign setting. My mind had not yet recovered its bearings from the drowsy train ride of the morning—and I could barely believe in all the far-off travels César spoke of—and so through those portals, the hall of nautical vessels transformed itself into a harbor of boats of such vast and fantastical beauty, more opulent than any imaginings of the Orient could conjure. As César's recital kept on, I'm not sure which happened first, the sight of the woman, or the announcement by César that the boat's namesake had arrived.

"Ah yes, the very one whose watch—or gift rather—you returned."

She turned down the corridor of boats, and through those smoky portals I saw not just another dark beauty of the kind I believed existed naturally everywhere throughout Paris, but something else altogether, exotic, austere, and captive. I say captive, but surely it was some suppressed nervous energy. Was this the same woman I had seen in the grandstands during the demonstration of the flying machine from America? I had to wonder, and this bothered me. She had been far enough away that day, and hidden beneath her overflowing hat and the reflective green of her opera glasses. I could see now that she was quite young, and part of a small entourage, very distinguished and intimate with one another, as if all of the same family, huddled beneath their dense winter coats and picture hats.

Cashmere, laces, jeweled eardrops—the woman wore all these things, yet she seemed like a captive of fashion or her circumstances. Even her lace-up boots seemed as if she were sliding down within them. She held her hands clasped before her as if she were cold, and her eyes—severe and watchful, surrounded by raw, dark circles—were either sleep-deprived or tragic. Yet their very color, an alarming sea-gray-green against dark Eastern features, made her all the more a siren. And despite her strained attempts to suppress her unease, she had that careful, watchful presence you could not forget, nor ignore, even as you looked away. She honed all your energies, like a charge that stirs the particles of the air.

César underwent a visible change as he climbed down from the boat to greet the family. He moved all too slowly and deliberately, with a pained, nearly stoic look on his face. The one he called *mon oncle* seemed just past fifty and wore his sideburns long and untrimmed, which gave him an elfish quality, especially when he pulled his monocle from his frock coat.

"I was under the impression," said César, "that your business partner would also attend to his boat at some point. I've been here all week. Does he even know I'm here?"

"I'm surprised anyone is here," said *l'oncle*.

As he and César traded confidences, the very watchful woman caught me staring, and I looked away, flustered. I had the impression that César was trying to arrange an appointment for Latham to fly an aeroplane when *l'oncle* said, "But, he already has a pilot."

"Does his pilot have his own mechanic—from the country?"

L'oncle looked me up and down with his monocle. "I see that."

César turned to me. "Say, what do you know about engines?"

"I only know steam," I said. "A neighboring farmer sends for me when his steam engine is down."

"Perfect. A natural. Like our Latham. So you see. Bring *Le Père* to the party tonight."

"Please. With so many would-be pilots these days, and so few planes, especially of the flying variety . . . Let me talk to him over the winter. Besides"—*l'oncle au monocle* leaned in closely and spoke into the side of César's face—"I'm sure he has not had time yet to talk with his mother . . ."

"He has, that he has." César nodded, and nodded, peering out with a grave air of significance.

"And?"

"And the family is fully prepared to invest in the Antoinette motorworks. She sees it as a way for him to finally settle into—something. So. You'll be at the party." César turned quickly to the woman of the intense bearing. "Will you?"

"Me?" The woman shrank imperiously from any attention. "Why me?"

"Why, the very namesake of this boat"—César raised his hands in a magnificent plea—"and of the very aeroplane we hope to launch into the sky."

She turned to *l'oncle*, who looked by all appearances to be her father. "Couldn't you give the different machines different names?"

Her father looked down with a strained patience. "Everyone knows that Otto Benz has his Mercedes; and the Antoinette motorworks shall have its Antoinette."

The daughter paused, open-mouthed, only to smile thinly and hold her white-gloved hand out to César. "I wish you the best of luck."

Then the young woman whom I'd later come to know as Antoinette was gone, as was the whole family, and César relaxed, casually grandiose. Though he called the exhibit of motorboats tiresome, he smiled, hands in his pockets, disheveled, confident, and modest as ever, as if he were responsible for the entire palace affair. He peered with great importance over the hall and asked if I had ever heard the story of how the famous Antoinette motorworks had received its name. No?

"Well. Let us tell the melancholy tale then, step by step, and in its proper setting."

15.

CÉSAR LOOKED OUT OVER THE HALL OF NAUTICAL VESSELS and, in his grand, expansive manner, began.

It happened, he said—when one considers the course of a lifetime—so many years ago. But like all stories, it happened just the other day. Imagine the green of the Mediterranean: how it shines as it does still today. Imagine the cool, salty air, the calming quality of the breeze. There are four Gastambides out walking on the cliffs with their fine avuncular friend Léon Levavasseur. The eccentric engineer has just received a commission to run Jules Gastambide's electric works in Morocco, but his true lifetime ambition is just then finding voice. He's always been a dreamer. He studied at the Académie des Beaux-Arts in his youth, you know. A short, squat circus bear of a fellow, he works his singular appearance to his advantage. He mentions the cormorants that wheel upon the breeze that day and how inspirational they are. He turns to his lifelong friend, and hopeful investor, Jules Gastambide, and says, "Someday, man should fly even better than the birds."

"Better than the birds?'

Levavasseur stopped walking, so all of the family did too. The engineer knew that many a sound, brilliant mind of his day had been considered crackpot for pursuing the invention of powered flight. Yet there was a confidence about him, an inspiration. It was the dawn of a new century. There were several successful glider experiments at the time, where the pilot steered by shifting his body weight around, kicking his legs, and shimmying this way and that. Léon Levavasseur knew he could build a combustion engine lightweight enough and still powerful enough to lift one of these competent gliders into the air.

"Oh yes. Count on it. And the engines of these flying ships will be the result of the new company just now forming." Here the ever-charming inventor bent down to the red-cheeked face of the daughter of the potential investor, fully aware of the salesmanship of his flattery. "And we shall name these engines 'Antoinette,' after you, my dear, as a symbol of obvious good luck."

Finishing his tale, César gazed meditatively down the hall.

"That hardly seems melancholy," I said.

"Pardon me?"

"You said it was a melancholy tale. But I see a boat here and many aeroplanes that use the Antoinette engine. It seems like a story of good fortune, after all."

César was still staring far off into his reverie. "Precisely," he said, with a jolt, as if I'd just solved the riddle of the sphinx, though I understood no more than before. He enjoyed that vantage of a sage, awaiting the correct moment to enlighten his pupil. I sensed he had something more remarkable yet that he wished to communicate, a puzzle to ponder. He had a curious ability to make things appear more interesting than they probably were. It was a hopeful, optimistic outlook.

But then a chauffeur in a double-breasted navy blue uniform tapped me on the shoulder. In his hands was an invitation.

César snapped it from my hands, confounded. "Why, this is from—" He opened it. "Latham. How on earth did he know?" He stood open-mouthed, peering far beyond the small, flat envelope in his hands.

The invitation was addressed to a certain M. Auguste La Pomme de Terre, in a very formal and mannered hand, begging that monsieur attend a party that evening at Latham's Champs-Élysées address. Also on the invitation was an appointment with a tailor that I should keep along the way.

The chauffeur gave a magisterial look above him and turned his stiff shoulders and gray head of hair down the hall. I assumed that everyone associated with him had, like Latham, traveled far and wide, and this gave the chauffeur his bored, wise, imperturbable face.

"This way, please," he said with an exaggerated formality, and we made our way between the towering bow stems of the boats.

16.

THE CHAUFFEUR DELIVERED ME far too early to the party. Still he motioned me to a dark, dusty portal—painted at one time some bleak forlorn color—and drove off. Though it was a busy street, there was no commerce, and the walled-off estates up and down its length offered no welcome. Each gate seemed to guard a monastic concentration of privacy within, and also the slightest, reluctant hint of grandeur. The pitted lion's head knocker creaked when I reached for it, and the ancient portal swung open after my initial strike. It gave way to a cloistered graveled court overhung by bare winter branches, with three imposing walls of closed-off windows. It could have been the entryway to a convent, if it weren't for the tall old man in dapper coveralls scrubbing away at a fountain, who seemed shocked at my early arrival.

"Are you here for a delivery?"

I held out my invitation.

The old worker appeared flustered, but managed what seemed like a habitual courtesy my way.

He led me through two black, wide-paneled doors, each as tall as two doors alone, and up a winding staircase. There I found a team of servants already in tailcoats, arranging the furniture of endless hallways and rooms. I watched the toting off of a full lounge set of

Empire chairs, and the removal of an entire library wall of books. As if at an invisible command, busy hands had begun to bring in a series of large, grimy crates when who should enter but César, carrying a crowbar as if it were a wand. He pried open the first crate with great ceremony, and from the straw packing he brought forth the feathery pelts of enormous flightless birds and the skins of the most exotic small-game animals, accompanied by carefully detailed drawings of each and a description of the savannah bush where they were shot.

Heavy copper jewelry, wooden masks of deep foreboding, a leather-skinned banjo with a single string—as I helped lift the hand-hewn treasures from the crates, César explained the various rumors of their origins. The two-year Latham/Parmentier expedition had a commission from the National Museum of Paris for the collection of rare specimens of flora and fauna, as well as artifacts of cultural interest. Latham's horsemanship and distinction as a crack shot in the military must have helped. But might there not have been a more clandestine motive—to help chart maps and gather information on the British-held territories beyond the Nile?

"It's not the British we need to worry about—"

"No?"

"No," the servants murmured in hushed alarm.

"The Italians are there too."

"Yes, the Italians and the Germans."

And a hint of dread moved through us at the mention of Germans and of spies.

Soon the drawing room and parlor had been transformed into a tabernacle of sporting pursuits. It was then that, from a long hallway, a thin, spare woman in a spare black dress emerged. A formidable beauty, she had long teeth and a strongly outlined jaw. Her dark hair was flecked with strands of steel wool and bound in black lace, and she kept her thin lips pursed.

César apologized to her for the nearly completed decorative upheaval.

"It's a menagerie," she said, and receded, straight-kneed, floating with her black dress and that awful medieval shadow of hers back into rooms so far off they had a disappearing quality.

This was the same Madame Latham who had spent her years as a young widow ridding the family estate of just such clutter. Her late husband had turned out to be quite a rogue, packing the holds of steamers in the Indian Ocean and the China Seas with cumbersome artworks, impractical furniture, and exotic trophies of surprising beasts. It was from her, though, that her son had received his remarkable forehead—unfurrowed and hiding a remote intellect.

After watching her leave, César informed me that this collection was to be archived by the curators of botany and zoology at the Museum of Natural History, who would begin their appraisal that night. He turned my attention to two smallish, dark carved chests with leather hinges and a leather hasp. In them were very nearly the gifts from the Queen of Sheba. It is said that her retinue from Saba in the heart of eastern Christendom had carried similar amber vessels of perfume and spices, sealed with wooden stoppers and coated in beeswax. The bottom of the chests were lined with sprigs of dried herbs and wildflowers, gathered by Latham himself. Under the cover of nightfall, so as not to raise the suspicions of his porters, Latham had scavenged the crumbling walls of a roofless basilica, where, it was rumored, the ghosts of the queen and King Solomon still wandered. There, by moonlight, Latham managed to find more wildflowers and a few small relics from the temple ruins, interesting-looking stones, really. All of this was bound up in the chests, one of which was to be offered up to his mother, who I had just met.

"And the other?" I asked.

"Here is where the tale turns melancholy," said César. "He does not know how to present the other chest of gifts."

I thought César would explain himself further, but he only turned his critical gaze upon me. "I thought the chauffeur . . . Well. He was instructed to bring you to the department store."

"He did."

"To make your appointment with a tailor."

"He did."

"Yes. Well, all I've seen that you have changed over your existing covering is a new pair of spats over your boots, and a very colorful napkin in your pocket."

With imperturbable gravity, the chauffeur explained, *"Le monsieur* kept wanting to ride up and down the elevators, until I finally convinced him the ride was over." He turned to me. "Where's your new hat? And cane?"

I pulled the bowler hat and cane down from the coat rack and held them up. "Is this not enough?" The cane had a fine duck's-head handle made of brass.

The more dissatisfied César became, the more he seemed to be enjoying himself. "This way, this way." He hurried down yet another long, mysterious hallway and into a wardrobe itself as long as a hall, where suit after padded suit hung in hefty rows of gray, English tweed, and herringbone.

"Hmm." He pulled down one of the nearest and give it a quick once-over. "About your size."

Latham's coat sleeves were a little short, and the neck was tight.

"Perfect," said César. "You know what they say, 'You never know what it's like to be another man until you've walked around in his suit.' Or is it 'No man is a stranger to his tailor'? At any rate."

The jacket smelled faintly of stale tobacco and eau de cologne. And suddenly I was a man of means, proud-shouldered and alert. I stood before a round mirror and pulled a whalebone comb through my hair. On the wall before me, above the sink, was a polished spigot with a bronze handle, which I turned. The miracle of plumbing came hissing out from the narrow spout. Water gathered in a basin and immediately drained into another pipe lower in the wall. I turned the knob again, and this time the water sputtered and stopped with a knock, leaving the basin to drain in silence, as if the legendary cisterns of Rome had been animated by that great writer of scientific romances, Jules Verne. And now I too was more than just a man of means, I was a man of the future. In the hallway, incandescent lamps urged me on, like a string of moths fanning their bright, electric wings, rising with the voices of the guests just now arriving.

17.

THE PARTY SPILLED OUT PAST THE TWO FRONT DOORS and onto the mezzanine, where I paused, at a loss before the feats and inventions of fashion. Knowing no one in all of the glamour and swirl, I took refuge beneath the arabesque dome of an enormous white wire birdcage. There I found myself in the company of a great white parrot of a bird with shocking head feathers it would lower and raise at the guests who leaned in and spoke to it through the wickets. They'd repeat the same worn-out, clever phrase over and over again into its hard kernel eyes, hoping the bird would mimic their nonsense. But the bird would only scratch and ruffle, indifferent, then claw ambitiously across the pickets. Finally it chose a face, a particular woman's face, and flashed its white tiara—fully raised, then half-fluttered in gray afterthought, then up again. Then the bird bobbed furiously at the exposed guest before speaking in a far-off, disembodied voice, the voice of a miniature ghost—"My love, my love, my little cabbage, *mon petit chou*"—and then snipping at the admirer's hat.

"Watch the fingers," said the butler in a tone of command and satisfaction as a tray of sparkling tumblers flew past, fizzing and clacking with ice.

I soon developed many strategies, besides being fascinated by a parrot, to give the impression to anyone watching—though no one was—that I was not alone. On the mezzanine was a door that led to a balcony. There, three stories up, I could lean against the wrought-iron railing and look out over the city. Never had I seen so much busyness at night, aglow in the haze of a dream. Horses cantered back and forth on the avenue with a crazed, nocturnal look in their eyes and steaming mouths, pulling coaches along the same routes as the motors, and I felt the presence of some tireless engine illuminating the city and urging it on.

I walked through the Lathams' library, a narrow affair of high-backed leather chairs and tobacco-stained wainscoting, hung with etchings of English hunting dogs and gentlemen from the country who rode around on horseback. As if Latham's travels to all of those distant lands were not enough, the far-ranging topics and titles of the volumes on the shelves alone spoke of worldly discoveries beyond comprehension. How could that vast warehouse of knowledge be stored in any single brain? It was in these very rooms—as I'd learn later from Latham himself—that he'd once proclaimed himself with a voracity he would never forget.

"I've always known I was meant for this," he'd said when he was just eighteen, as a great roaring sense of destiny rose inside him. He and Antoinette had wandered off alone during a family visit. "To discover an unknown land, or the North Pole for that matter, if it is not yet discovered when it's my time."

Antoinette had only looked at him in horror. "With what will you discover the distant poles of the earth?"

"There was a Swedish explorer," said the young Latham, "who commissioned the largest balloon to ever set sail. But he was held up on a small arctic isle, covered in ice. For some reason, none of his homing pigeons delivered his distress notes, and he froze there."

"I do hope you are more successful," she said.

"Until then I must procrastinate all that relates to my affectionate feelings and keeps me from my purpose. Nor can I endanger another's heart."

The boy's belief in himself stirred her to the very depths, and she turned bravely to the window, rapturous but also a little baffled. "We must all suffer for the advancement of science."

It was then that she had the watch made.

⚞⚟

Latham was not the only one haunted by his father's travels. He also recalled for me his father's art collection, so enthusiastically installed in the family castle at Maillebois before Latham was even born, and maintained by his mother, who, after his father's death, dressed in nothing but black for the remainder of her days. Antoinette told him of her deep, superstitious fear of the collection. She remembered with a thrill of gothic inspiration the carved teak treasure chests and dragons and fierce demon masks.

"There's so much more upstairs," said Latham, "banished, actually, by Maman to the attic." Immediately Antoinette said she must see it. He led her up the steps, without any idea what he was doing, though he did remember acting worldly for age twelve. "We'll need a lamp." He lit one. They found a table centuries old, hewn from old jungle wood that had borne the weight of the banquets of countless generations of an exotic tribe. Carvings of flying nymphs hung from strings. The arrangement of the wood furnishings and other statuary was not artless. Stacks of wooden goblets and bowls and plates were set out on the thick block table, ready for a feast, and chairs arranged around it. One of the three Latham cats hopped down from the table and into the shadows. "They like it when I bring them scraps," said Latham. And they held hands, in the dusty feast of cobwebs for ghosts, not knowing what else to do.

18.

THE MUSICIANS ARRIVE, AND A SHIMMERING intensity fills the air, bright with the chatter of money's constant urge. The maestro throws back his coattails and in a huff takes up his instrument. He and his fellows saw on their strings, tuning up while eyeing suspiciously another group of late-arriving musicians, Left Bankers dressed for Bohemia in patched-up hobnail boots, missing teeth, golden teeth, and golden vests. One has a strange shadow of a beard, dark and comical, as if painted on a clown. They reach down to the buffet with obscene skeletal arms the instant the hors d'oeuvres arrive: strawberries dipped in ether; the green ghosts of absinthe dancing through burning sugar; eaux-de-vie of unimaginable flavors and suggestive colors; roast pigeon, duck, and rabbit browned to an intoxicating glaze; and a charred pig, his sneering, skull-like face all too human.

At first the tunes played by the two groups of musicians clash and jar. But eventually the string ensemble meanders up next to the accordion's café number, like a song with a deepening melody, one that has been going on for a while yet is just now beginning. Here Mademoiselle Daphné de Cassandra—the opera singer of the abundant hair, which falls in thick seaweed tendrils about her head—is free to sing as if still at the Folies-Gobelins, stripped nearly bare to the waist, her face a tragic smear of tears. The guests' utter indifference to the musicians seems both expected and profound. I walk again from room to room, buoyed along on a tide of exclaiming faces, of dresses spread out like frosting on a cake, of cut-glass decanters filled with amber distillations, of steam rising from laden plates. Below us, the floor shifts with the dancers. The room lurches, lifting us gently upward. We turn, as in the balloon, borne away on an updraft of anticipation, moving yet seeming to stand absolutely still.

And underlying every bright and vanishing note of song, and in the lull between each ascending wave of voices, comes also the vague but persistent hint of a tale, of a story as yet unfolding, perhaps of unseen doings, perhaps of a great event about to occur. There's that swelling buzz in the air that speaks of a rare special time in the offing, that all else was only preparation for now, for this, for what will soon begin, or was long ago set in motion, or will end someday in overwhelming triumph, someday when we are shining in our old age, gentle with wisdom, which is the gift of time.

Then every electric lamp goes black. All the musicians stop, all but one violin. And in the echoing rooms the guests cry out with an astonished, ghostly quality. Quickly, here and there, servants begin lighting candelabras. With only a few flames against the smoldering gloom, the music starts up right where it left off, while couples continue to circle in an ongoing dance. Some, embarrassed or estranged by the sudden dark, break off and retreat one from the other, while others twist closer in a slow, tortured embrace. Yes, they dance now in deepening anonymity, beneath the service ladder that the butler climbs to light the tapers of the chandelier. As the match finds the first few candles, it's as if he lights the elaborate antlers of some ancient, sullen beast, hiding enormously in the dark.

19.

"It's the work of some devilish prankster!" A carouser laughed at his own wit, somewhere in the scandalous dark.

In the streets outside, the handiwork of this clever little devil continued. The electricity had vanished there too, causing a commotion of horns, heated name-calling, and threats. Out on the balcony, I looked down at the traffic stuck in the dark limbo below. Then I searched through small strange parlors, past the rustle of a dress, the clack of heels, the laughter, the tryst; I lost my way, despite a whole candle all to myself. I found myself in a mere closet of a room, perhaps a child's nursery, or what used to be one. By the dim flame, I spied a small knit cap, wooden toys, and a pair of baby shoes, all arranged as if on some dusty altar to childhood; and on the wall the most curious keepsake of all—a small, frail watercolor behind a glassed-in frame, painted in the style of a child's storybook illustration. In it, an elephant walks in profile across a dull landscape of uniform hills. Up high on the elephant's back is a tiny hut, much like a pilothouse with curtains, and in the hut rides a small figure wearing a pith helmet. The explorer and the elephant wander alone. Below them, at the base of the watercolor, read the inscription:

"To my young Hubert, when he makes his world tour."
Underneath was a date, March 1884, a time when Latham would have been a toddler. I imagined this was a gift from his father, commissioned after a long absence from just such a travel. And I imagined also the child who had slept here night after night under the painting's powerful spell, haunted by the storybook figure in this spectacular getup on an elephant's back, floating like King Hamlet's ruddy ghost through the young Hubert's nightly dreams. His father had died in a tragic hunting accident before Latham was three. But the absence of Latham at his own party struck me as mysterious and significant, and, as I considered it more, disturbing.

A stranger's voice, dry and languid, startled me with a question: "Where are you wintering these days?" Out of the shadows a figure emerged, or rather one round, cloudy eyeball, and above it a pale forehead. The other eye was completely covered with an eye patch, and both were behind thick owl-eyed spectacles.

"Innsbruck? Salzburg?" The accent was vaguely British. "With the Gastambides? The family still?"

"Wintering?"

"Oh, dear boy." He finally took a good look at me and lifted his glasses and even the eye patch below, as if his eye had phantom sight. "So sorry. I thought you were someone else." And off he walked, inquiring into the dark, "Who on earth dusts such books, up so toweringly high on ridiculous shelves?"

Caught in Latham's inner sanctum while wearing his suit, I felt exposed, a trespasser. Hearing footsteps, I blew out the candle, anxious to move on. I took a narrow staircase that turned constantly through the dark, listening for any noisy hallway that might lead back to the party. The short flights and cramped landings were overrun with fantastical artwork—wooden masks from the Orient, winged nymphs with heated expressions, six feminine arms. Painting after painting floated in the dark, like nighttime ships following me along a crowded horizon. Until above me on the stairs I saw . . . who I expected to see all along, or imagined I would, especially as I was wearing Latham's suit. In the periphery of my imagination, she was always drawing near. It was, after all, a party in her honor—the legendary daughter for whom the engines and flying machines were named—or at least a celebration of the partnership between her family's company and the new pilot. Could it be? She looked as though she were readying to leave, umbrella held out like a cane. The netting of her hat hid her features as she stood in the dark stairwell.

She spoke. "I hear you're pursuing my father's hobby."

She waited for an answer, but I never imagined I would ever speak to her, or that she'd ever have reason to address me, and I could find no words.

"Is it true?" she asked. "Has your mother offered to invest?"

A scant light came in through a small window behind me, and up close, under the shadows of her netting, she was far more beautiful, with a gleaming to her eyes, and her dress spread out in an elaborate masquerade.

"You know it makes no money, don't you? None. I can tell you that as a principal shareholder, it's a terrible investment. Though my household stands to gain, I advise against it." She lifted the skirts of her dress as if to climb up before me, and all her features focused, like the eyes of a cat opening to gather the dark. But the gauzy material of her hat must have hidden my own identity.

"Please," she said. "Are you going to just stand there, and offer no explanation?" Her skirts rustled as she turned in the narrow stairwell to leave, but then she spun back around. "You know, I sent you three letters. And wrote many more, which I hadn't the heart to send. Did you not receive any?"

She walked up to a small lead window on the landing above and stared out. "Charles and I . . . our son is quite the little man now." Her voice had fallen to a remote whisper. "He walks. He talks. He should like to meet you, I suppose. In due time, someday, yes."

There was a great swooshing of fabric above me. She was gone. And I followed, wishing to say, *But I am not him.* But there was no one in the unlit hallways, and the din of guests told me how far away she had traveled.

20.

ALL AT ONCE THE ELECTRIC LIGHTS CAME ON. In the harsh yellow glare, the party seemed to have ended, or at least lost its orchestral glow. But the evening was still young, the party just starting, and it was then, under those bright lights, that Latham finally arrived at his own gathering.

He staged his entrance as though he'd just returned home from his years of traveling, poised to make his great impression, acting for all the world like some darkly dressed rajah from London. He handed his northern fur hat and gloves to the butler. He addressed his guests in fluent German and English, and made a toast in Spanish. The members of the Cambridge Auto-Racing Club announced that they wanted him to race for them in the faraway city of Chicago. The famous host was soon called over to a small, huddled group, among the horns and tanned hides of the Latham/Parmentier expedition. Here I recognized some of the visitors from earlier that day at the hall of nautical vessels, including Antoinette, who eyed Latham coolly. I was racked with regret that I had not spoken out to her in the stairwell.

"Hubert. Your cousin here claims that half of your treasure is still in the jungle somewhere." The one who spoke could only be Antoinette's mother. She had a compelling accent and the same slight duskiness around her eyes, which on her seemed regal.

Latham stepped forward. "Jean and his brother are excellent marksmen. They kept the expedition fed."

"He practically taught us how to shoot," said an easy gentleman, addressing the group. "And the poor porters—the translator couldn't explain why they had to keep lugging around an ever-growing bag of bones, day after day. So, when no one was looking, they lightened the load."

"Hubert," said the woman with the musical accent, "have you met M. Chaudberet, Antoinette's husband?"

But Chaudberet, a rangy, startled-looking fellow, immediately spoke up. "We've met several times."

"Yes . . ." Latham put his glass down on a shelf and reached out to shake hands, as if remembering something. He searched the group. "Yes. I remember you now," he said. "We met a few summers ago, in Switzerland."

"It is a remarkable collection," said Chaudberet, looking displeased to be brought to everyone's attention. "Especially if this is only a part of it." How tall he was, I thought, with high, wide hips and narrow shoulders, hunched so that he always seemed to be leaning forward to apologize. He had a small, tight head above those hunched shoulders, and despite his striking sideburns, his dark features seemed above all else mistrusting and private. Antoinette danced with no one else, and danced only once, looking odd in the embrace of those gangly elbows. The cumbersome Chaudberet brought Antoinette her glass of wine, and drank from one himself. But by the end of the night they both drank from the same glass.

Latham had a completely different aspect now—wan and thin, so thin in fact he seemed stooped and his pants were baggy. Everywhere he turned, some new face sought him out, yet he seemed detached, as if standing against a restless tide.

Already the guests were lining up to leave, each waiting to talk first with the host. The shimmering expectation I'd felt earlier had vanished, and rooms that had once seemed so endless were now stiflingly crowded. The babble of voices had turned harsh and hollow, echoing senselessly. Yet Latham's eyes remained amused. What an enchanting life this was, after all, they seemed to say, as each leave-taking guest sought him out with some unspoken need. His face was calm and good-natured in a way that made me think of a Hindu swami, though I'd never met a swami, or knew what a Hindu was, really. Still, he beamed with that special knowledge.

Then Latham saw me. He looked pointedly at me, then further. He took his watch from his vest pocket and flipped it open, and flipped it shut, and held it tightly in his grasp. The watch was like a solemn pact between us. He acted as though there was no one else he'd rather see.

"Potato," he said with an irresistible confidence, "have you been having a good time? I've been meaning to talk with you. There's someone I'd like you to meet."

And there he was again, on the mezzanine, Antoinette's father, M. Gastambide, a wicked old guzzler with side whiskers like the hairs at the end of an onion. He'd been eating some oily tidbit, and made Latham stand there as he withdrew his kerchief and ran it meticulously over his fingers and beard. Then, finally, he spoke.

"I was afraid you'd keep your promise. You know—" Jules Gastambide became everyone's favorite uncle again, with a paternal paw on Latham's shoulder and speaking above his face in mock secrecy, so that no one else could hear, no one except all those present. "You know, you could fill this party and one just like it with young men who were lost trying to fly."

"There's been only one fatality of machine-powered flight," said Latham. "Because of the Wrights. Their victim was a passenger—their secretary of war, or an officer of some sort."

L'oncle au monocle sighed. "Only because you insist. Only because I can't stop you." And he gave a rolling laugh to the gentleman across from him, who he introduced as León Levavasseur, the engineer of the Antoinette aeroplane and racing engines—a thick man with a vaguely nautical air and a stately bearing interrupted only by a beard that hung from his face like long, untended history.

"Remember you?" Levavasseur exulted when Gastambide presented Latham as the boat pilot of the great regatta. "Good god, one of the best days of my life. I was sad you did not stay on. Of course we need pilots. Or *the* pilot. The one who can fly. My machines are too expensive to keep putting back together. Is that you?"

"I was there when the American flew at Le Mans. I watched him from the air, from the advantage of a balloon. I saw how it was done."

"Perfect," said Levavasseur, who was currently working on a commission. But after that, he should have an aeroplane ready by February, and would let Latham have a look at it then.

✂❧

The appointment to fly the Antoinette aeroplane made Latham stride about like an athlete, entertaining his few remaining guests with genuine vitality and good cheer. By the last stirrings of the party, though, a quiet despair seemed to have fallen upon my aeronaut friend. Into the early morning hours I found him wandering the house, past the lotus-eaters asleep beside their flutes of *vin de coca* and extinguished cigars. In a room where two strong men were still bragging I caught him daydreaming over the trinkets from his own African safari.

"I remember now where I'd seen the color before," he said, as if he'd been thinking about it for quite some time—he always had a sense of his own dramatic purpose. I only looked at him, waiting for him to explain. "It is the color of melted glacial ice turned to water. It is the deep gray-green color of the bay where the glacier ends."

My evident bewilderment only seemed to agitate him, as if his reverie had been interrupted. "The gray-green color found in eyes," he said, finally, as if stating the obvious. "The certain profound color found in green eyes!"

And though I felt it all along, I had to piece it together, slowly—that in talking to *l'oncle au monocle*, Latham was reminded of the color of his daughter Antoinette's eyes. And this deep, milky sea-gray green was enhanced by her dark Eastern features and the alarming circles around them. Certainly, that was what he meant.

Book III

O Seasons, O Châteaux

O Seasons! O castles!
What soul is without faults?

O Seasons! O castles!

I have made the magic study
Of happiness, which eludes no one

—Arthur Rimbaud

21.

LATHAM'S MOTORCAR WAS PRACTICALLY A ROVING encampment. His sixteen-horsepower Grègoire had a sink, hot running water, and clever compartments of storage. There he kept his Scottish *canne à pêche*, a shotgun for birds, and a rifle for game. He even kept a mattress in the trunk, which served as a ready berth on overnight treks. His *coccinelle*—his "ladybug," as he liked to call it—had a futuristic custom body, rounded like the shell of a strange steel beetle. And to ride in this shaky mechanical insect was to hear only the demands of its raw, high pitch.

Gone were the common sounds of the country. No lonely winter bird. No lowing of the farmer's cow. We couldn't even hear the surge of the high winter stream as we crossed over it on an old medieval bridge. No, our motor ride was a loud, complaining river of sound, as when a riverboat chugs upstream. The noise seemed to push the woods around us to the periphery, heightening my sense of manly adventure. Neither of my two companions of the *Buontemponi* spoke, each squinting off into austerity, caught up in the purpose of the motor and its furious inner workings. The motor whined under its burden as it pushed the carriage uphill. In anger and pitch, the sound increased, but the car moved no faster, bumpily rolling over the ridge and into the valley.

The château came into view.

Its four lead-clad spires rose above the feudal woods.

The towers then receded as the motorcar wove along a garden wall of thorn bushes and espaliered vines as thick as a rain forest serpent, twisting back in on itself in the act of self-strangulation. This same root sent its leafless winter weave up the red brick of the castle manor and across the leaden sashes, finally lacing its frail, terrible fingers along the parapet above. The mealy ice on the moat was russet with autumn leaves.

On the drive before the house of Gastambide, the motorcar of the *Buontemponi* came to a halt. Latham hopped down from the motor. He paced along the driveway and then paused.

"We're here too early. Are you sure we have the correct day?" Without waiting for an answer, he followed a pathway through the snow.

"Auguste—," he said, and I believe this was the first and only time he ever used my name. "Potato, I'd like to show you something." As if gripped by some vexed superstition, he trod past the servants' dwellings and down to an idyllic stream that ran beside a pasture, to stand spellbound by the fast-gurgling currents that welled up here and there through the ice.

"This brook is usually not so fast-moving," he said.

Still, the babbling of this gray stream seemed to calm him as he began to tell me of how this same stream ran beside his own family home of Maillebois, not far downstream. After the exhibit at the Palace of Machines, he had been spending his winter here, inhabiting only one wing of the family estate, while the rest of the rooms were closed up with the furniture under sheets. In solitude he read and dined here, or fished away the short days along the banks. I pictured him casting his line here and there in the wintry water, and at the end of the day, venturing far enough to look into Antoinette's childhood home. Latham had told me that the stream was more treacherous than it appeared, with deep undertows that plunged into rapids. It even had a small waterfall, just around the bend. If you listened closely, you could hear it from here.

"Listen," said Latham, intently hearing something I could not.

Two days before, when César and I arrived at the Maillebois estate, Latham had taken us fishing along this stream. We immediately put our lines to the water, but Latham only stood back on the banks and watched, as though he possessed unusual powers. He never cast his line to the water, he told us, until he actually saw the fish. *Saw the fish?* It was the dead of winter. There were no insects to bring them to the top. I imagined them staying low in their deep, cold-water pockets. Still, Latham stared into the same gray, surging pools I did, which offered only shallow glimpses into the moving stream.

"You have to learn *how* to look," he'd said. "You have to learn what to look for."

And though I never did learn *to see* the fish, I never could look at a body of water—be it stream, river, or ocean—again the same.

≈≈

There was more to Latham's history with this stream than he could ever tell in an afternoon. It was into these same icy currents, on a stretch nearly impossible to reach, banked by a briary thicket and trees that reached down into the water, that Latham's father had waded one December morning to cut the throat of a beast wounded during the holiday hunt. Young Hubert was not yet three years old that Christmas Eve, when his father came home with the tremendous animal and hung it from a rope, only to climb into bed, catch pneumonia, and die himself three days later.

Over and over the young Latham had imagined how the wounded animal swam, chopping away at the ice. It had to dog-paddle in fierce circles just to keep its antlers from going under. Despite the danger of being kicked or gored, Lionel Latham had to wade in to perform the coup de grâce. His honor required it. In a mortal embrace, he cleaved to the drowning animal as they were both carried away. Pulling the heavy corpse back up onto the banks was the exhausting part. For a time he just sat in the freezing water, angry at the beast for being so tremendous even in death.

≈≈

The stream opened up to other memories farther down, beside the valley hospital, widening into a tranquil pond. There, the Gastambide girls once dove off an enormous rock as round as an egg into the middle.

In their gray bloomers, they shrieked and laughed in gray water as the sky darkened, and thunderclouds approached.

"You have to come swimming," said Antoinette, pulling the adolescent Latham from his lawn chair, and then in a lower voice, "I want you to stop looking at me like that. If you want to kiss me"—he even remembered her grammatical lapse, and her two buck teeth slightly parted, poised to breathe him in—"I will." She leaned so close he could see her hair clinging wet to her face and her eyelashes stuck together. There he sat, in the hospital lawn chair near the pond willows, where he'd been reading under a blanket. She seemed so impressed with his mysterious affliction, to the point of distraction, that she said, "I'm not afraid to die either." She'd claimed to be the keeper of secret attributes. When they were younger, she, with her sister and Latham, had once conducted a seance, involving the items in the Latham attic. She could read people's thoughts and inhabit their dreams.

Latham looked around at both families. "Come back here tonight," he said. "Meet me at this very spot." And Antoinette jumped again from the rock, knowing full well that the doctor had forbidden him to swim.

It was in its way a difficult memory for Latham, as it brought back to mind his sickly, skinny childhood frame and his ongoing bouts with albuminuria, a liver complaint of varying severities, which had him on a special diet of two liters of milk, ultraviolet rays, and much fruit and vegetables.

Later that same evening the two families took Latham out of the hospital and to the theatre. Some traveling players from the Folies-Bergère were in town. At one point in all the vaudeville and gymnastics, the dancers came out in high turbans and loose, golden togas that barely reached past their hips. Antoinette leaned forward as if involuntarily to peer around the others and look at Latham. In the row of dark seats, he imagined meeting her later in the cove beneath the low branches. It had been exciting to think that they might meet after dinner, but now, late into the night, after the performance, how much better? But after the show, their families' carriages traveled in opposite directions, of course, leaving young Latham stranded at the hospital. Still, he crept out of the ward that night, and stood in their meeting spot near the heavy willow branches and the black, undisturbed waters.

22.

Soon the keeper of the livery stable appeared. The hosts were worried over Latham, he announced. So would we please come follow, this way, sir, please, past the moat and sculpted fishpond, and back to the house.

My curiosity made me wish to stay, though, among the thatched-roof dwellings of the servants, and the stables for the animals, and the storing places of the familiar tools of my upbringing. I was awed. The heavy stone barn was filled with mighty Percherons, and the grey-hounds in their kennels projected the wisdom of kings. Everything was in stunning order and quality, despite its age. In the cart-shed I saw riding boots, hitches, saddles, and bridles of the deepest, reddest leather. I saw sabers, flints and arrows, and a tasseled bugle for the hunt. The yards of the servants' houses were lined with rhubarb and rhodo-dendron, and on the outskirts grew wild gooseberry. There, within the shrubbery, the wine press held its soggy, weathered promise, and I was seized with a sentimentality that was nearly savage, for here lay the domestic setting for a life with Simone, nestled neatly below those thin smoking chimneys, now heightened to the ideal.

At *la maison Gastambide*, we were guided up the three turns of the staircase and into a hall. Beyond, in the castle parlor, Antoinette and her family sat as if staged for a theatre play. But first we had to walk through the spacious vault where the treasures of the ages were kept. The walls gave off the sullen, chalky echo of an empty schoolroom. Likewise, the hall of paintings left us hushed. Surely all the stylized subjects from the *ancien régime*, even the children, had all perished by now, leaving behind their stark, painted likenesses to gaze back at us from across the peeling varnish and cobwebs of eternity. Seeing a painting that seemed to be the very Christ, I grew distracted and turned away, only to find a portrait of a baroness posed like a Madonna, clutching a single-stemmed rose and a pigeon to her breast. Each of the gilded frames had a name as long and unpronounceable as a far-off, forgotten province inscribed on its base.

I was brought to by the unexpected mention of my own valley home of Saint-Mars-la-Brière.

"You mean my mechanic?" said Latham.

Apparently I was being discussed.

"Yes, yes, of course." Gastambide left the parlor for the hall, where he paced back and forth past the open door, his barrel torso and short legs swinging. He had impressive wide shoulders, and his long arms extended from their frock coat and worked like bent bastards. "You've already established that, back when you humiliated me at the party. Just bring him. Whatever . . . whatever he does. Does he invent? Does he make machines up from the moisture in his brain? Does he? That's where we're headed. Right? Just. Don't say a word. Just drive. That's what you know how to do? Right? Drive?"

"Fly," said Latham.

"Ahhh—" Gastambide walked back into the parlor and balked. "The plane has never been flown before. Just wheel it across the field. And don't wreck it. If you wreck it, it's over. I'm an investor, you know, *the* investor. Do you understand?"

"They say the *Antoinette* is the most beautiful," said Antoinette's younger sister. Powdered face, like a music-hall mistress—it suited Sophia, who had a world-weariness about her that made her sharp and alive. "They're not at all practical machines. More like works of art. It takes an entire guild of artisans two whole months just to produce one. Then when the poor pilot climbs inside, no one knows what to do."

"Of course you can *mow the lawn* with it all day long," said *l'oncle* with sudden rancor, turning to pace the hall again. "But fly—like the Wrights? No. This machine has never been flown."

Latham shrugged and said in a near whisper, so our striding host could not hear, "I have your gift."

But whose gift that was I could not tell, for he seemed to be addressing the glass in his hands. For a long, awkward moment, no one spoke. There was no sign of her husband near, but Antoinette sat absolutely on edge.

I was still under the impression that the gift was for Antoinette. But it was Sophia who spoke up. "The rug, you mean?"

"Rug?" said Madame Gastambide.

"One of the trophies from his extensive travels," said Sophia.

"Really?" Madame's wide Persian eyes closed halfway in ironic curiosity. She turned to her husband, who was still occupied with his pacing. "Do you have space enough in your smoking parlor," she asked, "for yet another trophy from the intrepid sportsman?"

Oddly bent on the momentum of his thoughts, Gastambide could only mumble back into the drawing room, "What? What was that? What's the matter?"

And Sophia, so quick and pale, who could astonish with just a few words and a sudden lighting-up of her face, said, "Anna dear, did you see the fleeces Hubert brought us last year?"

Antoinette blanched before the sudden attention and hid behind her toddler son, who faced forward with a child's hypnotized stare. She brushed her lips along the top of his head and whispered deeply into his hair. The boy had the same dark, serious circles under his eyes as his mother, which made him appear disturbingly mature, or old, even. Constantly she admired the child with a full, private pleasure, and now she took refuge in it.

"My sweet." She caressed the toddler's shoulders and said so that everyone could hear, "Your uncle has journeyed far and away, and has brought us back the very Golden Fleece of the Argonauts."

Latham looked at her, alarmed. "How did you know it was golden?"

"Actually," said César, "it is believed that the Argonauts sailed eastward, past the Sea of Marmara and the Bosporus Strait. It is in Crimea, on the shores of the Black Sea, that the alleged Golden Fleece originates. Not Abyssinia."

"Were you active in its pursuit?" said Antoinette.

"No. But I find the speculations of history fascinating."

"Shall I wait till after dinner to retrieve it?" said Latham.

"Oh, no. Now," said Madame. "Better now, please. I fear I'll be too settled by then."

"Must we have an upheaval?" asked Antoinette.

"I think it's a splendid time for an upheaval," said Madame. "Besides, it's inevitable now anyway."

"Go on. Get it, will you?" said her sister. "It's my gift, after all."

There was a bustling at the door. "Sophie!" said Antoinette.

"What?"

A footman appeared, carrying a trunk of worn, water-damaged leather with rusted, capped corners and missing rivets.

Eyeing the suitcase with the rest of us, César said, "And did you know that the mountain ranges just north of Latham's safari were once considered the Atlas Mountains, the largest being Mount Atlas itself?"

Too busy to care, Latham sat with the suitcase across his lap and withdrew a key from his coat pocket. He opened the lid, revealing various articles, wrapped in linens and meticulously arranged.

"The pursuit of the perfect adventure," said Antoinette, "has desiccated his heart."

"And all other faculties as well," said Latham. "The remnants sit before you."

I recognized the telescope we'd used on the balloon ride, as well as the luggage that had held our unforgettable lunch. But now it carried a rolled-up sheaf of material, padded, listless, and obscene in the way it bunched in the middle, like a severed elephant's trunk. Latham shimmied the rawhide twines free. The tail had been used to keep the skin folded round itself, and Latham unwound it. The skin was a lush blond and gold and then spotted, each spot being of two colors, brown and an intense blonde in the middle.

"I watched this beast in the field every day for well over a month. Every third day, this splendid animal would pull down a beast twice its size."

"You see?" said Antoinette to the indifferent boy. "Your uncle has brought us the Golden Fleece."

The paws and then the legs unrolled onto the floor in a flat, ragged shape.

The poor toddler began to wail, and ran across the room away from the hide, only to return in horror and wail at the sight of it all over again.

"Good god, man," said Gastambide. "How many times did you kill it?"

The heap in the middle turned out to be the head—a golden, shriveled pumpkin of a head, with the evil reddish rind of its snarl peeled back, revealing yellowed incisors and the rest of its jagged mouth. The look was not so much of menace as of derangement, the derangement of a shrunken old man.

"Theo, come." Antoinette held out a hand to her son. "Help us to admire."

Everyone crowded round it.

All over, fur of that same fiery wheat color gleamed in the lamplight.

23.

IN THE OUTLYING TOWN OF PUTEAUX, we came to the aeroplane maker's shop.

It towered over the working-class neighborhood, a faded, industrial structure with the name Antoinette painted in black across its rusted sheet-metal roof. Beyond it lay a field of mown crabgrass, strewn with dirty puddles. And there, on the drive to the engine works, the three vehicles of our caravan came to a halt: two motorcars, and the landeau of *l'oncle* and *Madame*, drawn by two of those Herculean draft horses.

Jules Gastambide hopped down from his carriage and joined a small group of spectators there. As if the field did not allow entrance, he too stood on the outskirts, though he was none other than the director of the *Société Anonyme des Avions et Moteurs Antoinette*, its major investor, and chief member of the board. In the spreading gloom, only a few hung on with an awful sense of waiting, as if they should be somewhere else.

Leaning upon his cane, the president of the company turned a grumpy face to the scene below.

"They've been at it since noon," said one of the bystanders.

All of the Gastambides stood back, in keeping with the hauteur of the investor.

"If God had intended man to fly," said César, "he would have wings. And there! There they are, indisputably!"

L'oncle's scowl increased.

"You believe in a god?" asked Antoinette.

"I believe in that machine, Madame."

It's difficult to imagine that Antoinette saw anything uplifting in her name, written in such an obvious way across the sky. She cringed as she climbed down from her motor and walked under the roof's shadow. The name must have been a far more audacious statement when it was painted eight years ago, calling out with a brash optimism, *Here the sky will be conquered.*

And there, at the end of the field, stood the family investment.

The flying machine had only a single set of wings, tilted upward like arms, like true bird wings, outstretched into a V, as if in the act of reaching. The whole thing had a beautiful simplicity about it—the most birdlike flying machine I had ever witnessed. I'd seen this aeroplane before, on display back at the Palace of Machines. Everything about it supposed movement, and the will to fly, but until then the machine was so beautiful that it seemed apologetic and burdened by its own beauty.

The workers gathered round it like fervent disciples, though the demonstration was not going well.

Below, one of the workers readied himself before the propeller and swung it down. The prop did not take. The worker heaved himself down again and again, but each pull brought less success. The aeroplane was a slow, stubborn beast that would not be led across water. They showed the animal how shallow the stream was, they pampered it, they bullied it, they tempted it with soft voices. But always the beast stood perfectly still, perched above them with a mute, stubborn cunning. It was not a magneto that ignited the spark plugs, as I'd assumed, but a row of batteries inside the fuselage, which were now replaced with fresh ones. Then a cough of blue smoke came from the engine, and again, a third, and fourth time, until finally the prop caught with a roar and the mechanic stood smartly away from the disappearing blades. The aeroplane was a thrumming thing, throwing out wind. The aeroplane maker pulled his sailor's cap down over his ears. The chocks were pulled. They let go.

The contraption quivered like a great moth, stunned and excited, as it edged across the lawn. In the growing dark I could not fully make out its shape, though I remembered the American flying a contraption altogether square, with two sets of wings, one awkwardly set above the other. I remembered the elaborate catapult that had hurled the machine into the air. But here, the aeroplane trembled on its own front skid and two wheels.

I expected it to climb on its own power. I expected it to sail into the gray of the clouds. But instead the pilot kept leaning over the sides, as if to discover some troubling matter below. A wing dipped and a wooden runner dug into the grass, keeping the wing from dragging across the ground. Soon there was not field enough for a takeoff. The workers hurried as a group toward the machine. They grabbed it and spun it to face the other way. It taxied in the same jerky manner back across the field. The engine was cut.

Levavasseur came barreling up the knoll, stammering, out of breath, an excitable biblical patriarch wearing a small Greek sailor's cap.

Latham, who had been studying an earlier effort up on blocks in the barn—its missing wings giving it the overall appearance of a rowboat with a fluke—looked at him with vacuous curiosity.

This had merely been a taxi run, Levavasseur explained. They'd had no intention of sending the aeroplane into the air. Jules Gastambide turned a grouchy face to the rest of us and narrowed his expression.

"There's just not field enough here for a launch," said Levavasseur. "It was true with my last plane as well. But we thought it might be different this time around." He turned to Latham and then to the pilot Welfèringer climbing down from the wing. "Eugène will show you how to work the controls in the morning."

24.

THAT NIGHT I FOUND MYSELF UPSTAIRS in the aeroplane maker's office, in the company of investors and members of the Aéro-Club de France. They appeared to me like extravagant poets, dreamers, adventurers of the clouds, all of them eager to see what the motorboat racer could do once inside the plane. The talk centered on the upcoming flight season, of prize money and contests, the ultimate being, of course, the crossing of the English Channel, the purse now doubled after the craze caused by the American. Wilbur Wright, on an icy New Year's Eve, had made an unprecedented flight of two hours and twenty minutes—on his last day before departing Le Mans—resting any doubts as to who was master of the sky. He'd covered a distance that would have taken him across the sea to England, and brought him back, and sent him across again. Soon, as soon as the weather turned, someone would put an aeroplane together on the coast and notify the *Daily Mail* of their intent to cross.

"It takes great courage and skill to fly the ship," said Jules Gastambide, raising his cane like an ancient thespian, all the while eyeing the engineer Levavasseur and Latham as if to seal a pact. It surprised me to hear them calling the flying machine a ship, as the *Antoinette* looked more like a canoe with broad, bright wings.

César leaned forward and asked all those present to consider the ship and its sailor once the sky had been mastered and flying was no longer a question of *how*, but *where* to?

"What will the sailor find?" he asked. "Consider the treacherous unknowns. The wind will want to push him into the cliffs, or suck him into the clouds, or drive him against the rooftops, or throw him into the trees. And what about the cloud suddenly devoid of wind? Or the mountaintop engulfed in storm? Will the ship he rides become a dragon? Or will he be rushing out to find one?"

Levavasseur, who always gave the impression of wearing a cumbersome fur wrapping, enlivened also by a natural loftiness of spirit, shrank from the attention, unable to speak, at first. In his presence, I felt the heightened sense of agitation one always feels around famous people of penetrating insight. His deep, sad-bear, world-weary eyes avoided ours, but finally he spoke.

"I don't know what it takes," he said. "I rely on my pilot to tell me what additional control he needs, beyond what is already provided." He raised his glass to the pilot, Eugène Welféringer, who modestly smiled and tilted his own glass back. "This dialogue is crucial. I believe the first true Antoinette aeroplane is presently downstairs, being modified."

"To Number Four."

"Hear, hear."

"To health."

"To Four!"

Night wore on. Noises rose from the workshop below, then noticeable silences, then a grinding, whirring, clanging, swearing, laughter in coarse outbursts. Long into the night the lamps in the Antoinette barn burned, where a worker's shadow moved like a specter in the light that slanted from the window across the lawn.

I was compelled to go down and see the aeroplane again. The lank workers were just then finishing up, extinguishing the gas lamps, shutting down the electric works that drove a long overhead crankshaft that in turn ran the lathe or the band saw when engaged by a lever, or the router, the planer, all the workstations in a row, all moved by a wide canvas belt that came down from the shaft. The workers closed the doors of a red, glowing furnace. The barn went dark, and the wide-reaching aeroplane was lost in shadow.

The last few workers filed past—dark featureless forms—up to Levavasseur's office, a few, and the rest down the road. "Evening, sir," said one with salty irony as he strode away beneath the sluggish clouds.

I walked around the barn and peered in through a fence of wooden slats and into a graveyard of old flying machine parts. My mind seethed with industrial projects, with the forms and configurations of the half-built and half-taken-apart machines. Over the suburbs, the moving clouds burned with the pale, unreal light of too many thousands of electric light bulbs and gas lamps. Steam rose from the turbines of the day, obscuring the moon and stars. The humming engines of my brain were hard at work. Strange mechanical forms of birds took shape. In all of that surging mental turmoil, my attention was interrupted by two hushed characters approaching Latham's motor. They had the air of monks on their way to the refectory after a long morning mass. My heated ideas were stifled by their quickened strides, their bowed heads, their shadows like the end of Jesuit robes. One of them, who looked for all the world like Antoinette, climbed into the automobile, while Latham remained in front to crank the motor. It coughed and complained, and off they drove, the two of them, without bothering to turn on the headlamps.

How did they ever escape the shop without anyone's notice? Did they care? The motorcar came to a halt before it reached the road and idled there, and one of them—Antoinette, it turned out—came running back across the dark to the shop. Latham returned also, maybe a few minutes later, parking where he had before and cutting the engine.

In the disquiet of the streets, Latham lit a cigarette and paced before the windows of the engine works, looking in and making exclamations. Not like a madman, and not as if he were talking to himself, but more as if in congratulations. Yes, *yes,* he repeated to himself, over and over again, like a sportsman, a competitor sure of victory.

25.

THE NEXT MORNING THEY WHEELED THE *ANTOINETTE* onto the field again. Latham set a well-shod foot up on the pristine cloth of the wing and sat himself down in the pilot's wicker seat. He nodded in a slow, fixed way at his two instructors. The pilot and Levavasseur both spoke to him at once. He brooded on distant matters in calm, childlike absorption. If man and machine were thrust headlong through the roof of a barn, or plunged squarely into a field, it would only offer another matter for him to observe, as if it was happening to someone else.

The aeromachine was much brighter in the morning sun, gleaming all over in a sheet of white, and I saw how none other than shipwrights could have made it. The bow-shaped front, made of wooden panels and varnished to a sheen, was contoured like a racing scull. The nail heads sparkled like a row of jewels. The tail configuration was an empennage— like the fins of an arrow, triangular and weblike, in cuneiform, and here was where the ship looked its most Gothic.

Levavasseur and his pilot had a difficult time explaining the steering system to Latham. The cockpit had two large control wheels, one on either side of the pilot—the left one for the control of the ailerons, and the right to control the horizontal rudder of the ship. There were two more control wheels, a smaller one before the pilot, operating the ignition, and the fourth wheel, on the other side of the dashboard, for the inlet throttle. But four controls were not enough. The feet must also be busy. There were three foot pedals, two for the vertical rudder at the stern, and the third foot control as the ultimate brake, or as close as one could get to a brake midair, stopping the engine. Latham nodded, impatient, *Yes, yes*, his hands on the controls, ready to push on.

The motor started first try.

The field of weeds trembled, and the hectic machine taxied forward. But this time, nearing the end of the field, it had begun to climb the knoll toward the fence when Latham opened the throttle in full. It appeared as though Number IV would either hit the fence, or take off. But just as it reached the slope, picking up speed, Latham cut the engine. The aeroplane stopped just shy of the fence and rolled gently backward to a halt.

Levavasseur ran nervously over to his aeroplane, muttering under his breath. "Yes. Beautiful, my boy. Beautiful."

But upon reaching the aeroplane, he said, "What on this good earth are you trying to do to my machine? Let's turn this thing around and try it again, shall we? Without hooliganism."

26.

WORK IN THE ANTOINETTE BARN BEGAN EARLY, before sunrise, the same as any farm. Though the animal of the engine was an altogether alien beast. My first station was that of the stoker of flames, the keeper of coal, the shoveller. Through clenched teeth, I cursed and broke inside with mute affection for my father and the gift of the shovel that now defined me. Meanwhile, I heaped the blade-fulls into the maw of the forge. The glaring, metallic heat and grime-filled smoke burned away whatever watery feelings I might have, and my heart surrendered with all of my might to the work, employed now by the Antoinette engine company, maker of the pound-for-pound fastest, most prized engines in all of the world. I was given other duties. But if the fire was not of a roaring, metal-rendering intensity, I was roundly abused.

"Potato, I give you but one task, and you can't even do that. What if I gave you nothing to do—you think you could manage then?" With a crooked grin, the foreman walked off, as the works of electricity hummed all around him, the whirr of the fan belt, the grinding of the blade, and the ring of anvil and hammer.

Showing up in time for lunch, César remarked that I swung the shovel with such vigor, you'd think I was filling the boiler of a great, thrumming ship to China.

❧❧

Those days when Latham was learning to fly became a springtime picnic, yet better.

It was great fun to watch the people in the streets point to the aeroplane, as if it were a parade unto itself, roped to the back of the lorry. All of us workers accompanied the aeroplane to Issy-les-Moulineaux, the old military training grounds just south of Paris. Here, we were in the grandest of moods, César and I, seated on the sunny lawn, me idly pulling on blades of grass and César caught up in his usual mental vigor, his ongoing work of mouth.

"You know, don't you, that the first human to ever take leave of the earth vertically was most likely strapped to a kite."

The open expanse of the marching grounds was just the place to inspire such a thought. Long years had passed since the last war on French soil. And many believed that through such inventions as the wireless telegraph, the telephone, and the aeroplane, the world's borders would shrink; all nations would share the same collective interest, and there'd be no further need for war. Much of Issy had slowly changed over the years of peacetime—former grounds for military maneuvers had become a municipal park, where long crushed-gravel gardens led past low, rectangular ponds with small statues that served as fountains. The ponds were entirely satisfying, with their lily pads and underwater weeds, their large, white oriental fish as old as the ponds, cruising like ghost ships among the minnows. Beyond the public park was a field sanctioned for kites and the launching of balloons, but the majority of the grounds were reserved for the flying of aeroplanes.

Off in their quarter of the sky, kites hung stationary like military banners above a distant castle. None of them seemed large enough to lift a grown person into the air. Though most were the traditional diamond-shaped kites, some, because of the recent flying craze, took on strange, experimental forms—like the Australian box kite, miniature foils mimicking the aeroplane, and one like a pyramid that could be controlled by wires so that it dove wildly and swung in wide circles.

"You'd hope it was a stable kite," I said, "the one that took the first passenger up."

"Ancient Chinese writings describe such a trip."

Hardly a weekend went by when there wasn't some new flying machine rolled out onto the lawn. Here, all of the pioneers of French aviation flew, where they could compete and exchange ideas, side by side, out in the open before the crowds. And not hoard their innovations in secret as do the Wrights, until a military contract or a patent can be secured. César also instructed me on how technologies that naturally furthered the aeroplane had evolved from other inventions. "The screw, for instance—the propeller has been in maritime use for well over half a century, and now, in a modified shape, propels the aeroship through the air. The guy wires that support the lightweight frame, very similar to the principles employed in suspension bridges. Note the remarkable composition of the ribs in the *Antoinette's* fuselage and wings." Here César looked in earnest out to the distance beyond the roofs and chimneys. "The very same method of framing used in La Tour Eiffel. The rubberized fabric of the wings by Michelin, the lightweight, durable wheels from the bicycle, and so on, and on—the aeromachine is a continuation of all that came before it. Your boss, M. Levavasseur, was able to develop a motor that can produce one horsepower per one to two kilograms of engine. The Wrights' engine, in itself a marvel in this regard, takes all of six kilograms to produce this same unit of horsepower."

"Horsepower?" I said, considering the fifty-horsepower Latham rode behind.

"Yes, the power one horse can pull."

"You'd think one horse could pull that entire engine all over the field. Fifty horses could pull it to kingdom come."

"Only a potato like you would think such a thing." And César went on to describe the legend of the horse and a primitive steam locomotive from England engaged in the act of a tug of war—a team of horses, actually, nine tense plow animals. They kept adding beasts, and in this way, as the story goes, the standards for calibrating horsepower were set.

"Begging your pardon, sir," said one of the Welféringers, a brother to the pilot who instructed Latham, hunched forward with an offended manner. "But the inventor of horsepower got his idea from a mule in a mine shaft, hauling up a load of coal."

"I believe what you refer to is called 'pony power,'" said César, "established nearly one hundred years ago. Yes, the Englishman James Watt was trying to figure out a new scheme to sell his locomotive, his main source of competition being of course the old beast of burden. And so, after watching a mine pony haul, by means of rope and pulley, twenty-two thousand foot-pounds—or, in other words, two hundred and twenty pounds for a distance of a hundred feet—per minute, he then established the formula for 'pony power.' He figured a horse could pull twice what a pony could. How he figured that, who can say? And what sort of horse are we talking about? How old? Can the collective strength of a species be calibrated? So much for science. Using this same formula, he then established 'horsepower,' which we continue to use to this day. Still, it is far more romantic to imagine a legend, is it not? The story of a horse, or a group of horses, engaged in a single struggle against the machine. Remember now, this all occurred some hundred years ago, and what is the true purpose here? To bandy about and bicker over mere facts, or to try and come to terms with how we got here, by whatever means serve our imagination best?"

The Welfèringer brother could only tug on the long, worried bristles of his mustache, until they covered his frown. "I just wish that friend of yours would quit ruining our machine."

Yes, the aeroplane was often brought back to the barn for repairs.

Meanwhile, an ingenious flight simulator had been devised. It was essentially a half-barrel on a sheet of plywood, complete with the unique Antoinette steering system, and a series of pulleys and ropes. Within this half-barrel the pilot sat, while his instructors, consisting of mostly the brothers Welfèringer, jostled the flight deck vigorously. These weather reenactments by the Welfèringers were relentless, especially after the aristocrat cried "uncle."

Once Latham began riding the aeroplane into the air, it came back down to earth unexpectedly, and hard. The other pilot, Eugène Welfèringer, and Levavasseur were extremely gentle with their apprentice's many mishaps—mangled undercarriage, splintered wing, shattered propeller. Latham's two instructors seemed well aware of the difficulty of steering such a machine, and also patiently aware of the gifts of daring and natural mechanical fluency demonstrated by their pupil. During the time of short flights and tedious crashes, Latham complained once and only once to César about the odd steering arrangement, and in this roundabout way discovered why the aeroplane maker had put the two main steering controls in such odd juxtaposition—one to either side of the pilot's shoulders. César was not opposed to asking Levavasseur himself, who stated, resolutely, "So that the steering levers will not impale the pilot."

On this point Levavasseur was adamant. He knew that all the other aeroplane designers put the controls out front, as they were in the motorcar or any other logically steered vehicle. But the great bearded bear in his maritime clothes could not in good faith build a machine that might, even in concept, injure its occupant in such a brutal, obvious fashion. He would much rather suffer the consequences of developing a machine that was difficult to steer, and as such, difficult to sell, than position a steering column aimed directly at any volunteer pilot.

Soon our attention was drawn to the drone of the angry motor that after a while no longer gave offense. Latham gunned it until the wings no longer shook from the rough of the field. Soon he was lifting, sailing, just meters above the ground. Behind the blurring scythes of the prop he leaned forward, teeth clenched in a grin, as the wings circled slowly above the old marching grounds.

He flew in repetitive circles.

He flew before the temple of the horizon.

And before the smokestacks in a row.

The tower that was Paris.

The domes and spires.

And trees.

And river.

And hills.

And hills of chimneys and rooftops.

In calm weather, the ship practically steered itself. When the sheets of wind kicked up, Latham learned how to hold steady, making constant adjustments as the aeroship slewed sideways. He stayed above the marching grounds for as long as he could. It seemed as though he would never come down, so long as the temperamental engine kept firing, so long as no sudden gust or dip into the holes of "Swiss cheese air" upended him too low to recover. He found that the monoplane handled better at a fair distance above the lawn, so he kept flying higher and higher. Levavasseur protested, worried about a mechanical malfunction in the upper air. Until then, his pilots had come to the flight deck from the draftsman's table. Both Eugène Welfèringer and Demanest had been engineers long before they took the pilot's seat. But Latham was utterly arrogant to the internal workings of the machines he raced to their limits; he simply needed them to respond like extensions of his own musculature and nerves. Though he flew with little fear, he was careful, consistent, and deliberate, and quickly flew beyond that point where anyone could offer him sound advice.

The crowds soon grew used to the aeroplane overhead. Our faithful public no longer cheered and waved Latham on, though I thought I'd never tire of seeing the *Antoinette* and her wondrous birdlike bones sailing before the sun. The circling of the aeroplane was like the backdrop of a drowsy mechanical music.

Toward the end of day, on one very long flight, the sky darkened with clouds as a storm came in. The whirring propeller chopped the rain into a spray, pelting the pilot. The engine and radiator panels in the front of the ship hissed like a greasy teakettle, emitting the smells of sopped laundry, engine grease, and iron pots left in a fire.

Levavassseur's crew on the ground signaled Latham down. By the time he landed, the rain had become a downpour. The crew, distinguished members of the Aero Club, Levavasseur, César, Gastambide—all of them—were drenched and happy.

César adjusted a stopwatch.

"One hour, seven minutes, and thirty-seven seconds. That, I believe, constitutes a new world record."

"Yes, but for monoplanes," said Gastambide, a bit dour.

"Monoplanes!" said Levavasseur. "For monoplanes, my boy." He slapped Latham on the back. "*Monoplanes!*"

"Rain," said Latham, staring up at the conspiracy of clouds. "Rain."

His clothes, especially at the shoulders, were saturated in castor oil spat by the engine. He had the smell of a Vulcan demon about him, with his face rimmed in soot where his goggles had been. Only four months in the sky, and already Hubert Latham held the records for the longest flight in France, and in a monoplane. He'd won prize money for speed, for duration, for city-to-city flights. He flew from Paris to the family home at Maillebois on a lark and dined with his mother on a fine lunch of braised duck, liverwurst, and stuffed cabbages, of course joined by the Gastambides. To demonstrate the stability of his patron's machine, he took off into twenty-five-kilometer-an-hour gusts, at one point actually sailing backward. He landed the plane in a novel maneuver called the volplane, intentionally cutting the engine mid-flight and gliding the ship down to safety. The crowds were spellbound just to see a flying machine land in an open field and a man climb out—the birdman, flying bravely into a bright and optimistic future.

27.

LATHAM DID NOT EXPRESS HIMSELF WELL, unless you counted his well-worn phrases of inspiration and his obscure literary allusions, said sometimes, I believe, just to himself. He often made cryptic remarks that on the surface of it had nothing to do with anything around us. So when public opinion began to imbue him with celebrity and even otherworldly attributes, his behavior only furthered our adoration.

One morning, Latham took me from my duties in the barn. A handsaw in his hands, he bid me to come follow. I halted, looking back at my workstation. But the foreman waved me off. "Go on. See what he wants."

Latham led me beyond the engine works. As we approached the knoll at the end of the field, he said, "I can clear the fence just fine. With the right wind, certainly. But look beyond it."

He crossed his arms and leaned up against the fence, peering into the brick merchant's yard, where stood a row of crabapple trees in full blossom.

"I just need the top of one of those trees cut down. I just need a place to aim."

Latham held the handsaw out like a scepter and pointed at the middle tree. "That's the one."

"*Me?*" I said. "You want me to cut down the tree?"

Latham looked around as if maybe someone else had followed him and was listening. "Why, you can't expect me to do it, can you?"

"So I just hop over the fence?"

"Yes, Potato." He gave me the handsaw and assured me that what I was about to do was with the consent of all those involved.

I approached the middle tree with misgiving and began pruning it sparingly, as if to increase the yield of those branches thick enough to bear fruit—even though the fruit was mere shriveled crab apple. I would do the same with any orchard tree back home. Soon I would need a ladder, or have to climb the tree itself.

"But no, no, no. You have it all wrong." Latham made a slicing motion with his arms, at about eye level. "From here on up." He made a wide sweeping gesture. "Everything. Just hack it all away."

I blinked at him outrageously. There would be virtually no difference between sawing the tree off there and simply felling it with an ax, except the time involved. Latham's instructions simply made no sense. Still, I sawed away as he described. As the first branch fell in an enormous heap of twigs and leaves, strewn with flakes of white apple blossom, someone yelled. Turning, I saw a man in a long leather work apron, kicking away with the thick hams of his legs at the fallen branch. It was the brick merchant, M. Pellerin.

"What the devil's going on here?" Pellerin had a fat, red, flustered face. "My answer to Levavasseur is the same!" he said, marching in a blind rage through the twigs. "These trees are not coming down!"

I feared he'd call the authorities.

"M. Levavasseur?" I said. "Oh no, sir, you're mistaken. It's Latham who instructs me."

"Latham?"

"Yes. I've never spoken a word to Monsieur Levavasseur."

"Oh, well then."

The brick merchant mopped his brow. He looked out past his property and the nearby rooftops, out to the vagueness of the high morning clouds. Without a further word, he returned to his shop, and before long two of his brick workers appeared, one of them carrying pruning shears and the other a ladder and a handsaw. They then began helping me to prune the top of not just one of the trees, but all of them.

By noon, what remained of the tree trunks stood like poor blinded souls, their stubby arms raised in lame complaint.

❧❧

The next day, a favorable wind came in off the river. Latham ran the *Antoinette* from the work barn and took off from the knoll, the wheels barely, just barely, clearing the fence and stumpy trees. Without banking the plane back around, he kept flying in a steady ascent, sailing out beyond any field that might offer safe landing. Levavasseur glowered and turned his great beard to the sky. He had never agreed to the pilot sailing above strange brickyards and smokestacks and lumber mills, with nowhere to land safely should the engine fail, or the winds turn belligerent, especially during an anonymous test flight without one speck of publicity to further the reputation of his exquisite machine. He brooded, he paced. All of us workers stayed well clear. The drone of the aeroplane grew faint, sounding from above the river or thereabouts. For many moments now the flying machine had been lost from sight, and now, little by little, lost from hearing.

One of the Welfèringer brothers wondered aloud if the aeroplane was still in the air.

Levavasseur turned his face upward as if trying to recall some far-off troubling matter. The workers in the shop complained that the boss was by temperament a poor businessman. It seemed Levavasseur knew this and wished also to change but instead grew sour, year by year, thought by thought. His need for functional beauty had ruined him. "Everything must be perfect!" he was always saying. Though perfection never paid. Still, *make it perfect*. The attainment of which had turned him into a tyrant and a fiend. He could not abide a pilot who flew beyond the parameters of his vision. If his pilot died, it was the pilot's own fault, and the recklessness of this abundant talent would ruin the machine too, as well as Levavasseur's reputation. Long before his champion, Latham, had arrived on the scene, the aeroplane had been dubbed a man-killer. Though no one up until now had ever been seriously hurt.

The time it took to build just one of Levavasseur's flying machines was easily five times that of any other. Here, function and beauty were fiendishly intertwined. The copper tubing of the radiator was mounted at the front of the ship to catch the cooling effects of the air it passed through. Visible as they were, the pipes must not only cool the engine but also be visually appealing—no, perfect, the soft metal buffed to a golden radiance like a fresh-minted coin. Behind the radiator, the bowlike fuselage was sheathed in cedar panels, steamed in place, coated with various oils in the exact right order, and then given four coats of varnish, each of a different value. Each of the copper nails holding the panels in place was sanded with pumice until its flat head glistened. Here again, what was pleasing to behold must also slip aerodynamically through the sky. But his machines were hard to steer, and to keep aloft; they kept falling to earth. Word would spread: the *Antoinette* had finally earned its name as a killer, Levavasseur was an inventor, and a dreamer, and maniacal, consumed, like a dog, like an artist. And now his ship had just plunged into the abyss, beyond the steep-angled roofs and treetops of Paris, taking his pilot down with it.

28.

SUCH WAS THE SKY. No one knew if Latham was flying still—fallen, lost, or escaped—when a sooty, rain-streaked lorry pulled into the drive before the Antoinette barn. A thick, plain-looking man in dark clothes climbed from the cab. He did not step onto the field but stopped at the edge and looked down. This was Louis Blériot, Latham's rival aeroplane maker and pilot, and like Latham, he exuded the mythic aura of the birdman. The newspapers had made him out to be the figure of a Gallic chieftain: the "hawkish aviator's nose," the puffy countryman's mustache, the worried, brooding look.

On the flatbed of Blériot's truck lay two engines packed in crates— two very large engines, judging by the crates' size. And like dreams, the aeromachines they were intended to power were also huge. I'd seen the Blériot IX, X, and XI prototypes on display at the Salon de L'Aéronautique. One of these ships, intended to lift at least three, possibly four passengers into the air at once, had easily dwarfed all of the other flying machines at the Salon in magnitude and design. Altogether they comprised the largest, most varied offering of flying machines on hand, and by far the most ambitious.

∽◦◦≀

Not so long before, Léon Levavasseur and Louis Blériot had been in business together. But even before then, each of them had dreamt of inventing the aeroplane.

Before Alberto Santos-Dumont's historic hop of eight hundred yards at Bagatelle two years ago, and years before the Wright Brothers at Kitty Hawk, both Levavasseur and Blériot had built—independently of one another—unprecedented flying machines. In secret, so as not to rankle the investors of the Antoinette engine company, Levavasseur had built an enormous three-story-high flying ship with great curving wings. It had two propellers with blades the size of men, and an undercarriage that would run along rails until his sprawling superstructure lifted from the earth. By that time, in 1903, a year before Kitty Hawk, the rival Blériot had already built three ornithopters, propelled in theory by the flapping of wings. Whereas Levavasseur had turned his frustration inward, breaking apart his monstrous failure ply by ply with a hammer, Blériot turned his feverish energies to forming the first commercial aeroplane manufacturing company in the world. No one in their right mind would ever start up such a company until a flying machine had actually been constructed that could at once leave the earth, land safely, and prove stable enough to fly yet again. No one, that is, but Blériot. He had postcards made of all his early attempts, including his original flapping designs. He'd built a glider biplane that nearly drowned the pilot after being towed down the Seine; he'd built a plane with enormous circular foils on pontoons that never left the water; he'd made a plane that looked too much like the Brazilian's, another like the American Samuel Langley's "dragonfly." There were others, eight in all. All of them crashed. All of them were obvious, unsuccessful copies. None were wholly his own. Not one a Blériot. He drove his first company under, and then he immediately started up another. How could he afford it? He couldn't. He hadn't sold a single aeroship. His efforts put an increasing strain on the operations of the motorcar headlamp factory that was his only source of income, quite a hefty income indeed if it weren't being depleted by his ventures into flight.

From the Antoinette company's inception, Levavasseur had enlisted Blériot's trusted name and business acumen. Together they would establish the *Société Anonyme des Avions et Moteurs Antoinette* for the production of high-powered engines for racing cars, and eventually for aeroplanes. Their mutual friend Jules Gastambide was merely the president, and Blériot himself vice president. Soon nearly all of the wondrous and varied flying machines of France were driven by one of Antoinette's temperamental, lightweight power sources. The company's success brought far more in reputation than it did in profit, and was exclusively Levavasseur's brainchild.

But Blériot opted out the moment he learned that Levavasseur had been actively designing and building aeroplanes of his own, putting him in direct conflict with Blériot's primary interest. Blériot tried to sell his large portion of the Antoinette motorworks, but his shares went unpurchased. Their rivalry only increased as each of their subsequent aeroplane designs began to favor more and more the monoplane, of which both were soon the foremost builders.

Blériot still had an interest in Levavasseur's engine company, though it was in title alone. In a gesture as stubborn as it was generous, Levavasseur resolved after Blériot resigned never to appoint another deputy chairman. In answer, Blériot immediately appointed a replacement for himself to sit on the board, refusing to have anything more to do with the company. This only intensified their rivalry. They fought like brothers—no, more so. No other colleague had infused himself in Léon Levavasseur's dream to invent the aeroplane more than Blériot. You always compete most against those who are closest to you in temperament, interests, experience, proximity—the nearest, the handiest, the most like yourself.

⚜

Wandering the silent field, the bereft business partner Levavasseur paced in a coat much too thick for the springtime warmth. He turned his skeptical eyes to the clouds, to the rough of the meadow, to the gray ambiguity in the air, paying little attention to anything else, especially not to the visitor at the end of his drive, calling down to him with a ridiculous cheerfulness, "I heard you would be flying today!"

Levavasseur seemed haggard, as if unable to hear, as Blériot strode down the field. Of course Blériot would show up. He must have heard round about that Levavasseur had an aeroplane, and moreover a pilot, capable of flying from his truncated taxiing field, which would be quite a feat to see. Blériot had a nose for the wind.

As Blériot drew near, Levavasseur finally blinked him into his field of vision.

"Yes, we were set to fly. But I didn't know we'd fly"—Levavasseur made a gesture much like shooing off flies—"*away*."

"Away?"

"I believe I have just had my machine high-jinxed out from beneath my very nose."

"And your pilot?"

Levavasseur shrugged, his cumbersome stoic detachment his only answer.

"How long has he been gone?"

"Hmmm?" Levavasseur turned cloudy eyes to César.

César took out his watch. "Thirty-two minutes."

"That long?" said Blériot.

"It seems longer," said Levavasseur.

"The problem is usually the opposite," said Blériot. "To keep them in the air. The very reason I climb into the machine myself."

Yes, a few years back Blériot had turned his cruel impatience back down upon himself and began flying his own aeroplanes, despite having a wife and five children. He'd become notorious as the Prince of Bad Luck, having crashed well over two dozen times. He'd perfected a technique of diving out onto the wings at the last moment before a fall, sacrificing the plane but cushioning the impact.

Blériot stood as silent as every one of the astonished Antoinette workers. I considered them workers, but they were also engineers and brilliant artisans, specialists at the head of their trades.

"If you bring your truck around to the back of the barn, Sir," said the foreman to Blériot, "we can take these engines back."

29.

LATHAM'S FLIGHT THAT AFTERNOON was the most enjoyable he'd ever had.

Below his wings, he saw the pedestrians and how they pointed and waved. Horse carts came to a standstill. People leaned out of thrown-open windows to gape up at him. Sailing out over the green-water river, he looked down on bargemen and boaters along the quay as they held their faces aloft, shielding their eyes from the sun. In the feisty whirr, he followed the dull, peaceful curves of the river, all the more dull and peaceful from up here in the realm of the birds. And what was it they saw, the people of his town? A god. A hoax. A circus marvel descending. It amused him to think that if the machine should fail just then, he might crash down upon the inhabitants of the afternoon like some minor, escaped god, wreaking havoc on their sleepy normal life. Up here he was a conqueror, an explorer from some rare, special place, where his solitude seemed complete. The air whistled round his plane.

As he neared an industrial stretch of the river, a small flock of geese took off from the shallows near a factory, a dozen or so graylags hurling themselves in frantic instinct, one pacing the other, frightened and mercurial. In formation, the birds pumped away at the air as if of one mind, and Latham drew up alongside them, just far enough away that they would not disperse. From behind him in the fuselage, he withdrew a shotgun and stood. The shotgun was already loaded; he would have only one shot. In calm skies, like this, the machine flew on its own. This was one of the beauties of Levavasseur's design. The big broad wings and long tail of the ship made for great stability; the difficulty came in manipulating the controls. Latham raised the double barrels, steadied them, and waited for only open field below. He fired. The stricken bird tumbled through the air and fell just beyond the cattails at a bend of the river.

Latham circled several times over the site, taking a careful inventory of the surroundings. He noted the lush backwater ravine and the Spanish mosses that hung from the trees. He took stock of the nearby cottages, and the boathouse farther up. He had an even better sense of where his bird had landed by the honking and circling of another goose, most likely its mate, flying in lost circles until it could no longer endure the fatal sound of the approaching motor.

30.

BELOW THE GROWING DRONE OF THE AEROPLANE, people stepped out onto the streets for a better view, their voices rising, not quite cheering but more hollow, as if stunned. Never before had a machine flown over their streets and rooftops. For years they had seen the strange contraptions wheeled about, crated up, and hauled away, and now the marvel of *la vie moderne* had them leaning out of their windows and front porches to catch sight of the ghostly, gleaming ship, a white sail before the cloudbursts.

Levavasseur stormed up the stairs of his office, leaving Blériot to take the last of his two Antoinette engines, prototypes that never left the ground, down from the truck. Once inside, Levavasseur stewed before his window until his own competent Antoinette aeroplane came circling in above the truncated landing field. Then he removed himself from view, as if in protest. Outside, Blériot lost himself in the growing hubbub, as did we all, watching Latham's rough landing.

With great haste, Latham ushered César and me over to his motorcar. "Get in, get in!" he insisted, and started up the engine, utterly incapable of explaining why it was so important that we go along. He seemed stricken by some mad, superstitious ambition, yet as always had that unusual conviction about him, that absolute belief.

"What I'm searching for," he told us, "is a cottage."

We turned down quiet side streets, searching cottage after cottage. César eyed him suspiciously."Have you met someone new?"

What would bring Latham to the neighborhoods along the river if it weren't for some rendezvous? Though if that were the case, then why would he bring us along? The only thought that occurred to me was that Latham had found a place to land that afternoon, and must have had some remarkable encounter, which he was just then trying to relive.

"If you told us what we were looking for, then maybe we could help you," said César.

"If I tell you, I fear I'll never find it."

But it was as though Latham himself did not know what he was searching for. There was an impatience animating him, some crazed, elemental fabrication from the depths of his soul. He paid little attention to the cottages themselves. Street after street, he searched among the bulrushes, along the river, in the lumps of grass below the cattails. As darkness descended, we kept returning to the same riverside cove, until finally a meek old gentleman emerged from the shadowy privacy of his dark little cottage.

The elderly gentleman wore an ascot and a fine wrinkled coat, as if hurriedly put on for the occasion. How often did a motorcar stop along the roadside and three distinguished persons emerge from it, to admire his swampy riverside? He was the very picture of a lost and shabby gentility, hobbling over with his decrepit manners. Drawing near, he wished us a good afternoon.

"We are searching for a bird I shot here this afternoon," said Latham.

"Hunting?" asked César, seeming somehow offended. "You hunted?"

The old gentleman asked, "Did you shoot it from a boat? Where is your dog?"

"No," said Latham. "I shot it on my own. Did you hear anything unusual this afternoon?"

"Well, it isn't the season for hunting, if that's what you mean."

Latham seemed a bit deflated, as he often did when the world did not participate in his exploits. It truly puzzled him that anyone below his flight path that afternoon could not have seen his aeroplane. Still, he remained optimistic. "Do you mind if we search the riverbanks of your property?"

"No. Not at all, sirs. Do you care to join me in my parlor first, for some refreshments?"

"Only if we are successful," said Latham. "If we do not find it, we must keep moving."

But Latham might as well have been speaking Chinese to the ancient gentleman. Scouring the growth along the riverbanks with his gray, depthless eyes, he said only, "I'm surprised that they let you get away with the shooting. There are so many boaters out on a day like today."

César cleared his throat. "You see, our friend here, Mr. Latham, has just flown over your very household in an aeroplane this afternoon, and from it, in the sky, he shot a goose. A goose, was it?"

Latham nodded, but our ancient host gave no sign of comprehension.

"I believe we are looking for the first game bird ever shot from the vantage of an aeroplane," said César, speaking slowly and clearly. "Yes, one of the Voisons tried shooting at game while flying but—apparently—missed. Do you suppose that someone else may have witnessed the hunt, and picked up the bird before us?"

"That is why we should look now," said Latham, casting his gaze out beyond to the river.

"Let me know, even if you are unsuccessful." The old man began his small, even shuffle back toward his house. "I have something inside that should pick up your spirits. My niece has baked a sweet plum pie. I can't possibly eat it all. And she is presently putting on water for coffee." He disappeared back into his dark ramshackle cottage.

~❦~

The next morning, the goose was dressed in a basket. The knobby drumstick bones stuck up out of the folds of red linen, along with the beginnings of the dimpled, fatty skin. There was something obscene in the sheer nakedness of those two pale bird legs. A whiff of stale meaty breath came up from the weave of bulrushes. And jutting out alongside the bones was a corked bottle of sweet German wine, a garland of fresh river mint, and an envelope containing a letter addressed to Madame

Antoinette in the most painstaking hand, tied with a red ribbon. Latham gave me the basket, along with a set of succinct instructions.

I was to drive in his motor with Papagris the Sailor, the helmsman whom Latham had bested in the great Regatta. Our destination was *la maison Gastambide*, near the Place d'Italie. I was to drop off the basket at the Gastambide address. Wink at the foreign governess. Tell her of my rapture. But still remain aloof, for I was the one true Potato, the very apple of the earth, and not easily fooled—those were my instructions. "Go now, my friend. Hurry. Find her. For Madame Antoinette likes you and your trustworthy face. This is my thanks to her and the Gastambides, and my announcement that I will soon fly their family's investment across the sea. Hurry now. Off with you. We'll be leaving soon. Very soon."

So off I went, with Papagris the Sailor.

In his thick, heavy-lidded manner, the chauffeur drove. The surge of city life swarmed all around us, tooling motors, horse-drawn carts, double-decker tramcars, and factory girls out walking home at the end of the day.

And then I saw it—the picture Simone kept tucked in her apron to hand to me, the fine-looking people eating pastries at a sidewalk café. I could easily imagine Simone walking down the sidewalk just then, and, as she did on the farm, kicking her heavy skirts out with each step. I had an uneasiness of mind remembering a recent letter Simone had sent, informing me that the Professor of the Language of the Hands had begun paying visits again to the farm, trying to persuade her to resume her studies. I was torn. On the Normandy coast the next morning, I would write Simone a letter, filled with being near the sea. I'd soon be on a train with the flying machine, which was beyond comprehension, for I had never seen the ocean before. And there my friend the aeronaut, who had sailed in a balloon from England, would soon become the first to ever set sail across the sky above the sea. How could I conceive of such an event? The ocean and the coastal areas opened up inside of me as if they were prints in one of Simone's books, and I thought the air might be different out there, brighter, imbued with special qualities of light, as I imagined it to be in foreign countries, especially those close to the sea. I turned toward the heavy, unmovable features of the valet.

"M. Latham is flying to England," I said. "Will you attend?"

"Ah yes, England in the springtime." Papagris's thick, porous face peered round the hood of the motor. "A dapper and timely race, the English. Not as prompt as the Germans, mind you. And the women there, the English girls—such rosy complexions. Everyone should go there, at least once, for the fond memories."

Soon the motor came to a halt. "Well," said Papagris. "Here we are."

Hefting the rush basket, I walked in through a wrought-iron gate. Beyond the fence of white bricks and sculpted bushes, I found a small courtyard with raised beds of clematis and thyme. A row of small trees was sculpted into the shape of lemon drops, and in the middle of the courtyard stood a fountain, the statue of a woman rising up out of the pool, lifting a large amphora above her head. The door knockers here were not pitted with grime but of lustrous hammered brass. One of the wide double doors opened, and a thick German governess appeared, her hair in a net.

I held out the rush basket. *"Pour Madame."*

The governess held the basket with straight arms, so that it dropped heavily against her thighs. *"Mein Gott.* What is this? Stones?"

I stood, watching her heft the basket by its straining handle, suddenly burdened and twisted.

"Thank you," she said. "Madame thanks you very much."

Book IV
The Cliffs of Calais

*Among other provisions, it was specified that the flight would
have to be made between sunrise and sunset; that no part of
the machine should touch the sea during the crossing; that
the machine should be heavier than air, and without the
assistance of a gasbag or similar contrivance; that at least
forty-eight hours' advance notice of an attempt should be
given to the* Daily Mail; *that a contestant must furnish proof
of having successfully flown before; and that the contestant
must renounce any claims for damage to machine or person
in case of accident.*

—Henry Serrano Villard, *Contact!*

31.

THE *ANTOINETTE IV* WAS BOXED UP INTO CRATES and shipped by train to the cliffs facing England. There, five hand-picked workers placed the boxes beneath a large tarpaulin outside a rainy fishing village hotel. Beneath the eaves, the aeroplane hid in its crates, while the dismal, sea-drenched water pooled on the tarps. Inside the lobby, the day of arrival felt like a picnic, a seaboard holiday, a feast.

The dark, wet spring had left the seaside village unseasonably empty, so that now the dreary local establishments were quick to welcome the newcomers. By midafternoon many a newspaperman milled about the small lobby and café, filled with humid sea air, tobacco smoke, and a growing hullabaloo. The crossing of the channel was after all a stunt dreamed up by the newspaper magnate Lord Northcliffe himself, and so why shouldn't his kind create a peril out of nothing and wait for some sad sap to show himself up and hurl himself across the watery abyss for their sport?

He has arrived. *All hail! The birdman!*

Captive before the camera, cigarette holder clenched in his jaws, Latham stands, dangerous and polite, in photomythic fashion; beside him, his benefactor, the even prouder Levavasseur, happy to have found a way to contain his pilot by sending him into the clouds above the sea. Both of them filled with uncontainable childish glee. Levavasseur's inherent loftiness held at bay by his modesty, has given way to a trifling smile. One cannot help but admire the childishness of this inventor, dressed up in his father's sailor's suit, this active brain bent on the traverse of sea and sky.

It takes some time to set up the camera, with its hand-held flashes, black curtain, and tripod. In the stifling humidity, the photographer keeps having to wipe off the lens, then step back and hunch his shoulders beneath his black cape. Latham steps forward. Is it true, one of the newspapermen wishes to know, that in flying to England, Latham will also be returning to his ancestral home, only two generations removed? Isn't he then a citizen of both England and France? And isn't the flight across the sea a personal odyssey? Latham stands just as everyone wants him to, unnaturally for the photographer, sly artificer, request upon request, with that same devil-may-care, then—*vwoom.*

Flash of bulb.

❧

By late afternoon, the rain let up.

Now for a picnic of sorts.

All of us straggling along the cliffs above the beachhead to the tower, all of the party of Antoinette—her mechanics and inventor and pilot and investors loosely disguised as family members. We made our way along the clifftops, across the rolling meadows above the beach, the wet sedge grass soaking our trousers and dress hems. We strayed into the fields off the tractor road, and surrounding us, in the wet-salt air, always the same slow, cautious lull of sound, both far and near, at rest between storms, the mute dreaming of the giant, his drowsy snore, the surf's advance, the vast emptiness making itself known.

Latham had said he would always remember this day as if his life was somehow just beginning. He remembered the afternoon as he would a painting that he wished he himself had painted. He had the impression we were at once in a garden, a garden of such lush, magical beauty—with the orange-red poppies growing out beyond the fences and the cattle's reach—that it made him think of walks he'd taken through meadows when he was young, not of any one field in particular, but with a promising flush of light, as you feel when you are young. At his side was Antoinette's toddler and a slightly older girl, who had to pull the boy along, while he wished to stray and linger. Everyone seemed lulled into the enchantment of the cold, windy afternoon after the rains gave way. Languishing farther back, Antoinette walked, her blue muslin dress, worn for boating perhaps, now soaked nearly to the knees and sagging dismally. Latham wished to hang back as well, but the more he slowed his steps, the farther Antoinette herself fell back, until she was stubbornly lost to the party.

And now Latham's attention was claimed by the very mayor himself, at the head of the group—a round buoy-bag of a fellow, giving a tour of his domain. He led us in what seemed like a cherished routine of his, our benevolent, tweedy uncle, chockfull of local history, hearsay, and lore. Everything about him drooped. His eyebrows drooped at the corners, like catfishes' whiskers. His jowls drooped as he walked. A merry man who enjoyed his own wit, he called himself the Fish Mayor, for his work drawing up local trawling ordinances, which year after year secured his election.

The mayor turned with military aplomb. "Behold." He stopped before a large brick smokestack above a factory all by itself in the fields, and gestured grandly out beyond.

"Our neighbors! To the north!" he announced with the same grandeur to the wind. "It is here that we see the famous view of the cliffs of Dover and of Shakespeare, from the vantage of our humble village of Sangatte." He turned again and began walking with renewed vigor. "A view immortalized by so many generations of French poets and painters."

"But Monsieur Fish Mayor, sir," said César, "was it not here, in the nearby forests of Calais, that the Frenchman de Blanchard and his American passenger landed in the first crossing of the passenger balloon?"

"It is. The Channel was crossed not only by boat—and by balloon, of course, by the two fine aeronauts you see here today—but also by the sheer will of the human spirit. The Englishman Matthew Webb swam across it back in 1875—the longest recorded swim in all of history! The crossing of *la Manche*, and particularly at this very point, has since the very beginning held powerful sway over the human imagination."

Just then the German governess said, "Ouff, they fall, the two," in a quiet singsong in her native tongue, and soon afterward in French. Antoinette hurried over to help the two children up from the roadside swale, everyone laughing and *oohing* with exaggerated affection. The boy was fiercely displeased, finding himself soaked. The increased pace of the mayor must have tripped him.

It was then that the boy's father drew near.

That morning over breakfast, M. Chaudberet explained how he did so admire the traveling spirit, and that he'd already made arrangements for a charter boat to sail out beyond the jetty harbor. He'd found which beaches were best suited for the throwing of hand-nets for surf perches. Adrift without the busy, circular affairs of Paris to guide him, he cast himself headlong into the prescribed coastal activities. Before leaving, he explained, he'd had to copy in duplicate all of his outstanding ledgers, draft but not send his most pressing postal correspondences, and pay off all of his delinquent debts. Yet I sensed that anxiety still fed the rush he felt at finally taking leave of his complicated routines. He laughed with his son and threw him about—with a bit of violence, almost, though he was laughing—in a game of *gentille alouette*. He was a bit of a performer, with a fine tenor voice, and he sang softly, holding his son's hand as they walked with the rest, not solely to the boy, but to vent his fine feelings of being out once again on holiday in the open air of a seaboard town.

On we walked in a long, straggling line, broken up into small parties. Antoinette fell yet farther behind. Before us stood the tower—a defunct industrial smokestack—on one side darkened with the soot of time, and on the other battered clean by tempests. The mayor droned on, full of moldy dates, arcane facts, and illuminating anecdotes. He seemed particularly expert in the history of the century-old endeavor of attempting to dig a tunnel beneath the sea to England.

"It is rumored," he said, "that the old Channel Tunnel Company, whose brick smokestack you see before you, first took measures to tunnel a passage to England, beneath *la Manche*, over one hundred years ago, as far back as 1802 ..."

Approaching the descending path to the tunnel, we passed between two artificial earth mounds of equal size, worn smooth and grown over with stump grass, brush, and wizened cypress that seemed to stoop and twist coyly from our gaze, bent by the strong winds driving from the sea.

At the head of the fabled undersea thoroughfare, our little procession gawked, struck silent by a strange wonder. The boarded-up entrance looked more like an abandoned mine shaft than the grand subterranean highway uniting nations it was intended to be, and a small mineshaft at that.

"The British were to tunnel their way from their side," said the mayor. "And we from ours. They envisioned an undersea tunnel for the horse and buggy, lined with oil lamps, all the way to *Angleterre*. At the midway point, horses would have respite at a station providing fresh water and oats. Fresh air would be provided by a long, upward-reaching spout, extending all the way up to the sea's surface, midway. It would have been nothing short of the Eighth Marvel of the World. But then, fifty years later, in 1848, the attempt to join the nations was abandoned almost as quickly as it had begun, as the British feared that the tunnel might leave them vulnerable to attack."

"There will be another invasion, then," said César. "By air, by Monsieur Latham, when he lands."

"Hear, hear."

Our small party laughed and clapped, and the mayor recanted the sopped history, old by now, of futurists from the days of yore who wished to tunnel their way to the isle of the Brits. So grand, so epic, and yet so naive, as if from the brain of a child, or a fabulist in a fine frock coat, as if you could simply ride a bullet-shaped compartment to the moon. But there the artifact stood, right before our very eyes: the building of the old Tunnel Company with its brick smokestack and three large, brick-lined windows.

With a solemn air, Latham stood before the dull brick factory, as if it were an ancient shrine. Did he see a majestic flight from Delphi? Or some strange, antiquated failure? Or a chimney, just that, and nothing more, short and insignificant, not even nearing the proportions of a lighthouse?

Just then Antoinette separated herself from the tour completely. She'd wandered off to a lookout with a fence, somewhat hidden along the cliff, where she gazed out in an absorbed, disturbed way across the sea. Quickly lagging behind, Latham circled widely, as if to join her beyond everyone's notice. And I imagine this was the occasion she told him the following—for this, he would later say, was his golden season. She longed to walk out to sea, she told him. "Out into the blue." Not to swim—that held no interest—but only to step carefully downward out past the seaweed, on and on, until the waves carried her hat from her head, and still she would persist like a hypnotized patient instructed by her own submerged fantasies to inhale the cold, salty depths, her hair loosening into a swirl of ink and bubbles. "I've often thought it," she said. "To just—walk out to sea." She said it with an enthralled whisper, very close to abandon, knowing very well nothing would excite Latham more than a suicidal daydream.

He was beside himself with awe, beyond lust, smitten to the core. He marveled at the phenomenon of weather, of the miracle of clouds. Swallows turning in the air withheld their infinite mystery—just one instance of this precious day we call life—turning in the air after invisible treasure, after insects too small to see.

"Are you here on the coast long?" he asked.

"Are you?"

"No, I don't plan on it," he said, peering out to the floating chalk line of England on the horizon. "No. Not this coast."

"Nor I," she said. "We return to the city in three days."

Every once in a while a larger, more invasive wave struck the rocks of the cove below, so that a constant spray hung in the air, sent up by the wind at their faces. A look passed over Antoinette's face, and for a moment she could have imagined herself a Madame Bovary, believing in the endless future of reverie, of the feast unfolding without end, all in an afternoon—for Latham knew she had pulled this book down from her parent's shelf at thirteen, as do all good schoolgirls.

Then she turned abruptly and almost tripped over her rain-heavy dress. She stepped out to catch herself, though, and headed back to the group and the Fish Mayor's history.

32.

That evening we dined at the Fish Mayor's house.

Bottles stood, half filled or yet to be opened, of Spanish and Austrian wines, next to platters of opened shellfish, pickled herring, sardines served in a variety of Portuguese ways, crab appendages, and lobster tails, along with artichokes and pineapple. All of the food had this same pickled, sea-drenched translucency—soaked and salted cabbages, beets and onions awash in a pale vinegary brine, all manner of cod, smoked eel, and flounder served flat-down on a skillet, garnished with its own gory head smiling above its own stripped, steaming flesh, its bone pattern visible, and juices congealed into a cream around its fins. And here the mayor was more than just the mayor of fishes. A great, frothing capitalist dream had suddenly descended upon his little burg. Among his new celebrity guests, he regaled, he hugged, he surmised like a pope and smiled like a pasha. "Now don't you fly off tomorrow, you," said he, winking at Latham. "We have a fine celebration planned for you, during that great American invention known as *le weekend*."

In the rare, quiet moments off to himself, Latham kept an anxious eye on the view beyond the veranda. Sporadically the wind threw rain at the row of large windows as if tossing a handful of pebbles. Through the steam on those windows, in that great, ominous, windswept void of utter darkness, a lighthouse was flashing out from the storm. Then it would recede again, the dull casting of its own beam revolving into the engulfing chaos, only to flash out again a moment later.

Like an elder sea-trade captain or a retired admiral with a lookout over his own fleet—which was surely how he considered any ship that chugged its way slowly along *la Manche*—the Fish Mayor had a veranda with an excellent view of the harbor town of Calais, not far down the coast. He had two wooden telescopes, rolled-up charts, a logbook, a compass, a sextant, and many other fine nautical devices used to navigate and map the watery world. After dinner, Latham withdrew out onto the mayor's veranda, puffing away into the cold and the wind. He studied the lighthouse, and beyond it, the darkness, and the turbulence that moved unseen through the dark, where the lighthouse reappeared again—the only thing visible in all of that moving black, where the pounding of the breakers sounded from afar. Then, out of the chaos, a lighthouse asserted itself. It had seemed the clouds were engulfing the lighthouse, but it was just the sheets of rain engulfing the beam cast out over the storm-dark sea.

This time it was Antoinette who joined him, her hair darkly slicked across her brow by the rain. There was a stolen quality to their time outside. Latham knew she would not attempt it unless her husband was present, making her approach to him acceptable within her bounds. The two of them withstood a chilly discomfort that was entirely impractical in order to speak.

"This must be where the mayor keeps abreast of the comings and goings of the local inhabitants," said Latham.

Antoinette shivered. "It feels like a widow's walk."

"Perhaps it was, at one time."

"It seems unimaginable that someone can fly out into that."

"Somebody will be first. Surely by tomorrow, we'll be ready. Then I'd like to attempt it, on the day set for your return to Paris. If everything happens according to plan, there's no way you can escape. You'll be forced to stay here for the celebration. And besides—"

"Besides, there's already a pilot here, with a Wright Flyer."

"Maybe—maybe he will be first."

"But he hasn't left yet, for well over two months."

"The day will come," said Latham, "and not too far from now, when a flight like this will be commonplace."

"Do be careful, until then."

"Why?" he flared, contemptuously.

"Oh, please."

"Then why?" He leaned above her, as if to envelop her.

"No reason." She hugged herself against the cold. "I suppose there's no reason, if you put it that way."

They both turned and leaned against the railing, looking back, in at the party. Antoinette waved to someone, who turned out to be her husband, holding a glass and looking at himself through the beaded moisture on the window.

"He thinks of us as cousins, doesn't he?"

"How else should he see us?" she asked, her wet eyes full of reproach. "Perhaps as everyone else should too. You, of course, the dashing hero, ready to risk life and limb for the glory. And me, the pale, trembling waif—ready to fall, just eager for it. You love us most when we throw ourselves off bridges and underneath trains." She dabbed at her lips. "From where does this poison come?"

She was grinning now, full of mockery. He'd always thought she would make a wonderful actress, were it not for the self-defeating modesty that appeared in her like a reflex.

"Ah, there now," she said, "a whole party before us. Let's not spoil it, shall we?" She turned to go inside, but then caught sight of her sister, Sophie, talking with César. She stopped, and her expression bloomed full of affection. "Can it be that we have a romance brewing?"

Latham looked in at Sophie talking with César. Briefly, César put his hand over hers, and the lowering of her eyes gave the impression of pleasure and mirth.

"Oh yes," said Latham. "Just look at them. Do they know what traps await? Most likely they do, but they are unable to control themselves. Who is it I worry for most? He? Or she? See them, the dark pools of the eyes, they dilate, they open up, so wide just about anything can fall in." Latham no longer watched the scene of the party inside but was instead held by the eyes of Antoinette beside him, shimmering, bewitching him. "They say fluffy things, the eyes, the tilt of face."

Antoinette's head turned sharply, breaking the trance. Her husband was approaching a side window, adjusting his lapels in the reflection of the glass.

Latham ignored him. "The lovers, they say the most sweet apparent nothings. Rehearsed and refined. Since the days before the monkey could speak. And before, with all the chirps and croaks of the forest. Soon the corresponding male and female parts take to their throbbing. Overheated, the primal furnace roars! Uncontainable. And for what? They mate. They consummate, like barnyard animals, like fishes, like two frog lovers hopelessly intertwined. Is there any difference? Between us and the animals? Despite all the despair and poetry that brought us here? And why? For what?"

"Shouldn't we go inside?"

"So they can make another just like themselves, whom they can abuse with notions that make their own selves so miserable, so that their miniature selves will live life just as they do—so dull, common, and ultimately predictable."

"Are you hoping to offend me?" she asked. "Because if you are, you've only drawn attention to how stifled and ugly you've turned out. "

"Worse yet," he said, "is when the two lovers are nearly the same, each like the other in appearance, family background, social standing, as if of the same stock. Then it is as if they are merely in love with their own wretched selves. Now that is the stifled outcome."

"I couldn't agree more."

She turned abruptly toward the party but stopped just shy of the door, downcast, her face hidden beneath her hat. "I feel— a bit— so sorry for you." She turned again and made her way across the porch. "I hope you will excuse me." And she continued down the back steps of the Fish Mayor's veranda and onto a path that led along the cliffs to the fishing village.

Not knowing what else to do, Latham followed her, down the path where the clump grass and bushes trembled in the dim light cast from the house, and still farther down. Perhaps she had returned to the party, or to the village hotel. But he thought he saw her shimmering beige dress descending a path that made its way down the cliffs. But no, it was only wet glimmering leaves twisting along the wind-swept path, reflected back up to the house. Where had she gone?

Latham found the path that led down the cliffs. He wound round rocky ledges and cliff walls pounded smooth by battering tempests, down paths worn by human feet over the centuries, as if a widow's walk had been extended to the sea, a rocky veranda where she paces until her sailor comes home—either her sailor, or his ghost. If his own ghost were to emerge at sea, to where would the poor ghost paddle? To whom would he swim? Had he a home? Between the turbulent surf and the rocks of the cliff, he descended, the sea rising up in geysers in time with its sound. Who in her sleeping, dream-filled bed would his ghost meet, if he were lost at sea?

In the cove, a huge spuming wave rose up and crashed, spilling over and hissing as it returned, barely visible except for the foam. The dark sea tugged at the loose footing beneath him. He stumbled, stung cold, his legs lifting as if he might need to swim. His arm drenched to the elbow, he clung to the sharp weave of barnacles and spongy growth rooted to the cutting sea wall.

33.

With a grand sense of the history and poetry of the occasion, Levavasseur announced the next morning that his operations were to be housed at the abandoned old Tunnel Company building.

"Our new shop, headquarters, and base of propaganda," he said, to the few newspapermen gathered at his café table for breakfast.

Already a large striped circus *chapiteau* had been stretched into place above the wide barn doors of the factory, a makeshift canvas roof under which the workers could uncrate and assemble the aeroplane during the rains. Put together, the *Antoinette* was too wide, wing-to-wing, to fit inside the building. With fewer hands to take part, I was quickly ushered in to help.

Only once did Levavasseur speak to me directly. In passing, he put a senatorial hand upon my shoulder.

"Potato, is it?"

And without waiting for an answer, he sidestepped beyond the cramped work area, looking through me far into the lofty affairs of the inventor.

Meanwhile, the wings were reaffixed to the fuselage, the guy wires stretched to their optimum tautness. One of the Welféringers would pluck and listen until each wire made a dull, brief thrum, as if the guy wires were an enormous harp and the aeroplane a musical cavity.

Always the curious and skeptical alike stopped to take a look beneath the edges of the circus top—Parisians on holiday, farmers, fishermen, children. They stood with their umbrellas, sopped hats, and awkward faces, peering in through the beaded rain that fell from the tarp's edge. And there, beneath the dripping lean-to, I had an exalted sense of belonging, as the locals stared in as if gawking at some circus monstrosity—some strange wooden gift to be wheeled through their sleepy village.

Beneath the wind-rattled canvas, the longtime employees of Levavasseur had the *Antoinette* put together by noon. The rains subsided again after lunch, and three big wooden cameras were set up on their tripods just outside the old Tunnel Company, aimed at man and machine. Latham, in his jaunty pose, was soon joined by Levavasseur. The two of them talked and nodded, complete with hand gestures of grave, historical import, while another photographer turned the crank of a moving-picture camera, taking a soundless account of this crucial dialogue before the eve of the flight.

"And now," said one of the voices behind the capes, "If you please, a photograph of the namesake of this most beautiful of machines."

"Dear—" Levavasseur motioned to Antoinette, as if inviting her to waltz with him at a ball.

Antoinette hugged her arms and cringed in the ring of well wishers. "No—please."

But Levavasseur took her by the hand and pulled her unwillingly into the circle of attention.

"You can't be serious," she said.

"Yes. A must."

"There! A picture of the siren."

"Perfect—!"

Levavasseur stepped back and left a mortified Antoinette to strangle the knob of her parasol, facing Latham, who, with his hand on his hip, pulled back the flap of his sport coat and gazed upon her with a most ardent look of admiration. The cameras burst, one after the other, extinguishing their flash.

34.

AFTER A WEEK FULL OF GRUMPY SKIES, César said the obvious, that he'd never seen such bad luck, in the form of such bad weather, and that soon a break in this dreadful bluster would appear. The Norman coast, he added with gray philosophy, was famous for its dismal theater of clouds.

So we saw nothing of Latham's historic flight across the sea, unless you counted the enormous circus-striped canvases covering the aeroplane, drenched beneath the wind.

It wasn't just the rain or a still morning of fog that could ground Latham. A clear day of sunlight with just the slightest, most average ocean breeze would cause the pilot and Levavasseur to scowl out beyond the porch of the hotel, and agree to reevaluate the weather later that afternoon.

The days of forbidding weather, however, secretly excited me. Straightaway I took off for the harbor with its strong, salty smell of decrepit sea life and creosote, to watch the slow coming and going of boats and the many more tied up or at anchor. Beyond the jetty I could see distant smokestacks, sails, and tall ships fading slowly out to sea. On absolutely gray days, I sensed the beginning of some long, important journey at the blast of the foghorn, rising the discontent of some ancient baritone sea god to give us warning.

Not all are welcome. Not all shall pass.

⁓⁓

Our pilot of destiny had no real interest in seeing the camp of the alleged competition. But as the days of wind and rain wore on, César grew restless and suggested that somebody ought to scout out the only other legitimate contender for the *Daily Mail's* prize money. Like the other pilots, this competitor was a celebrity of vast potential—an elusive Russian of the aristocracy who flew not one but two custom Wright Flyers.

On a gray morning we set out, César and I, along the farm roads above the cliffs.

By all reputable accounts, according to César, the Russian was still learning to fly. As the Wright Brothers' first European student, and the first for that matter in the entire world, the Comte de Lambert merely practiced and increased his skills here, along the coast, but was nowhere near to venturing out beyond it. "And isn't it a wonder," said César, with a sweeping gaze out beyond the fields, "that the very wind that pushes our ships back and forth across the sea—in fact, they get nowhere without it—isn't it amazing that this same wind completely swamps the ship that sets out upon the sky?"

I listened but was more absorbed in the constant, far-off exhalations of the sea, the smoldering hues of the sky, the soaring gulls. A wide, unsettling rift opened inside of me as I thought of Simone, who was receiving increasingly regular visits from the Professor of the Hands, though this went unmentioned in her letters. I would never have known about these visits were it not for a brief note from her father, Odilon. When I wrote back to Simone about it, she responded that the nuns of the Suffering Silence could no longer understand the words she made with her hands. Signing exclusively with me had given her bad habits. And because she had not been born deaf, but had happened upon the state with a full ability to speak, she was the perfect assistant to help the professor from America develop his theories and further his studies—studies that seemed to me to have been going on far too long. The Professor of the Hands had himself studied with the

Canadian inventor of the telephone whose name meant bell. This 'bell' had also invented a phonetic alphabet that could sound out any word the human mouth was capable of. When Simone wrote to tell me that she was going back to school at the Suffering Silence, the pull of loss would have completely engulfed me if I gave myself over to it.

César claimed I was constantly under the strong sway of the first-time traveler. I had never spent any time on the coast before; I had only gazed over it in prints of books with Simone, and though she had never been here herself, she was everywhere now. She was the spirit of travel, and the longing to be back home.

❧❦

All of the houses on the coast were painted the same—a smudged white stucco with green trim. On the front porch of one of these farmhouses, three smallish children looked out from a half-open door, all of them with the same pale straight hair the color of straw.

"We are here to see the aviator," said César.

The children merely blinked back at him.

"Where is the birdman?" César spoke as if they were hard of hearing. "Are there any aeroplanes here?"

Without a word, the oldest child ran from the porch, his arms straight down at his sides. He made his way around the house to the barn, only to reappear. "This way, this way." He ducked and waved for us to follow.

❧❦

The formidable Comte de Lambert of the Russian region of Mondovia had commandeered the use of the entire farm for his operations. The farmer, the farmer's wife, his hay-colored children, wide-eyed and afraid—the Russian prince endured the doting, lingering curiosity of them all, which now included César and me. The farmer, a quiet elfin man who appeared on tiptoes, knocked timidly upon his own barn door. He was both the Comte's landlord and serf, and the Comte de Lambert, with his high, haughty peak and cape-like coat, was the mystic who haunted the farmer's horse stall. There, seated upon his ample bedding of blankets and hay, he seemed less like a nobleman than a religious zealot, or an angry hermit guarding his refuge, with two oil lamps on a nightstand strewn with many books. The farmer walked up to the Comte and set down in the hay, as if bringing him his routine provisions, a sack of apples, a half-eaten salami, a tin of tobacco, a flagon of spirits, a square of thick chocolate, and two loaves of bread. The Comte laughed low with scorn, as if this were half his allotment due.

Where were all the heaps of hay in the haymow, and, in the sow's stall, the sow and her suckling spring piglets? Or any pig, or cow?

There were none. All was machine—a barn of engine parts and aeroplane wings.

I kept looking beyond the stall, where the top wing of the Wright Flyer loomed vague in the shadows.

"If you're newspapermen, then go. Leave me." The Comte made a belittling gesture. "There's nothing here for you."

"My dear fellow—" César introduced me and himself.

The exquisite Comte gave a grunt.

"We are friends of the newly arrived pilot, Hubert Latham."

"Worse yet! You come to ply the enemy's camp for your advantage. Do you take me for a fool?"

"Oh no. Sir—We come simply as allies in the same cause. Yes, surely, there is a competition. A race to be first! But how does our being here hinder or help Latham's chances? Or yours, for the matter? You both have the same enemy: the raging tempest beyond the cliffs. We simply come here to wish you good luck and establish a friendship."

"A *friendship*? So you wish to see the Wright Flyer up close?"

His keen, accusing eye seized upon me. It was true I was still gazing above his head at the wing—the bright, broad wing in the shadows beyond the stall, the only part of the Flyer visible.

"No—," I said.

"Yes—come now. You want to stand before it, and sit in the pilot's seat. You want to work the controls. And start the engine"—the Comte made a gesture as if to gather the vapors to his face—"and take in its secrets intuitively, before you take the machine apart piece by piece and steal each secret as it unfolds."

César laughed. "Dear sir. Who do you think we are? I am neither a designer of the aeroplane, nor a flyer of such. I am merely an observer, but of a special kind. An aficionado, as they say. I humble myself before you, as an admirer. Bear in mind, though, that I too have attempted to cross the channel, by air, and have succeeded, via the balloon. I ask about your ship only because the Wright Flyer is the most respected in all of the world."

"*Hah!* It is true. You *did* come to see the machine."

Here the Comte puffed himself up and warmed considerably. He reached into the sack of apples and threw one to me and one to César, then took a raw bite into one himself, not bothering to wipe off the spittle of juice running down his beard. "Go ahead," he said. "Look all you want." He took out an enormous knife and began slicing the chocolate up into smaller squares, which he divvied out to the children, who retreated with them to the shadows and nibbled cautiously. He thrilled them further by making the mawkish sound of an ogre chewing on bones. Then he ripped off a heel of bread and sat down cross-legged in the stall, where he gazed with exaggerated rapture at a book he had opened across his lap.

Walking farther back into the gloom, I saw the famous Wright Flyer and was shocked. The plane was tragic. The back rudders leaned against the wall, along with the skids, one of them bent like mangled wire. The front elevator wings also leaned against the wall, lacerated beyond repair. It would be easier to construct new ones.

"And where is the other plane?" asked César, peering at the dirt floor. "Word has it there are two?"

"You see"—the Comte lowered his voice to the children—"spies, just as I said." Then, more loudly, "Outside, behind the barn. Intact, the aeroplane does not fit inside. Go on. Peruse at will. But remember, all of the mechanical innovations that make it the most advanced flying machine in all of the world are protected by both French and international law. If you violate them, the Minister of Inventions will come after you with his pitchfork. Or else he might send you his stern letter."

Outside, César lifted the tarp from the second Wright Flyer. It, too, was horribly disfigured. The violence of a miscalculated landing, perhaps, had demolished half of the ship. One set of wings had collapsed, and the propeller assembly hung loose from its mount.

Back inside, César cleared his throat, at a loss before the barn-ridden birdman and the tragedy of his two shipwrecks.

"Your pilot flies a monoplane, does he not?" the Comte said finally. "Don't worry. I've seen it. I've seen your camp. It's a beautiful ship. To the devil with the press corps, then. And the Marconi. Who needs to know what the weather is like in England? First, you must get there. First, you must leave the coast. How different can it be? From here to there? And who are you to trust? A group of newspapermen and the *cinema de photographie*? Can't you believe the weather at your face? They live by the wireless: 'Weather Leaves Pilot Grounded.' 'Latham Awaits His Chance.' Oh, then what did he have for breakfast? And so on. No. Unfold your own myth! Like a boxer, every pilot stands alone, and the truth—like the wind—hits you square in the face. Let us say that it is the ocean you wish to cross."

Here was the first student ever to be schooled by the Wrights, and the first European ever to fly their advanced, magnificent ship. And there they were, the first two Wright Flyers ever ordered and built, made to the Comte's own slight modifications, now grounded and lamed.

"You know of the Wrights?" I asked, hoping he would say more about these remarkable figures.

"In time . . ." The Comte de Lambert made a low face of disdain, as if to gawk over the American birdmen was an obvious fashion of the moment, a passing national craze.

The Russian called the commotion made by Latham here on the coast a vulgar corruption—base and sensational. Like a heated Bedouin who had forsaken his vows to Allah, the Comte had given himself over to lush dissipation. Madness lurked in him, now that he could no longer fly and was stranded in his barn, left only with the feverish turning of his own thoughts. "I wanted to learn about life, so I stood beside the river," he said. "I have crossed a great many waterways in my day—many raging currents, many turbulent seas, and also, an apparent calm that's just boiling beneath the surface. I have seen the sea rise up out of itself in walls of sheer apocalyptic grandeur.

"Consider the crossing of the sea in the age-old manner, across the waves upon its surface. You must first wade into its shallows, until you trust them. You learn to paddle and learn to swim. The first boats were most likely logs that you hung onto, allowing you to swim farther, or saving your life. Then, as a natural consequence, the logs were hollowed out. Boats came into play. Before you learned of the raging rivers, you learned of the stream, or of tranquil banks. Then, once the rivers were mastered, finally, you came to the sea. But the pilot of the aeroplane, he has only to take his first leap into the air, and immediately, he is out in the wide open. He is out at sea."

"Yes, yes." César spoke up enthusiastically. "Isn't it an absolute wonder that it takes only a single season for a bird's egg to grow into a nearly full-sized, capable bird? Once they leap from the tree, that's it, they are—as you say—in the sea. They must be fully established."

"I'm so sorry, sir. I forgot your name."

"César."

"César. It has been a great pleasure to meet you. Where did you study?"

"I am an active member of *LlAcadémie d'Histoire Synchronique*. We are always learning and contributing new findings, the pursuit of which is crucial to our membership."

"It is a fine institution, then."

"It is. Well," said César, "we'd best be going. It was a great pleasure to meet you as well, Monsieur le Comte de Lambert, sir. Thank you for the hospitality and the sharing of your machines."

"Comte de Lambert?" Here the Comte raised his face and laughed with a single burst, and the farmer, wife, and children all smiled one to another. "Oh no. I am just a man in the hay. The Comte de Lambert? He is *au travail* at the factory of the Wrights, in search of replacement parts for his machines and tradesmen skilled enough to apply them. Me? I am merely the hired guard. It was part of his contract with the Wrights that until the patent disputes are settled, of which they are many, the machine is to be guarded at all times. In fact, I understand that the latest model Antoinette employs the Wright system of wing-warping—is that true?"

"Yes, well, as I said before, I am not involved in the manufacturing."

"So you see, until all patent disputes are settled, the aeroplane must be guarded at all times. Of course, I take leave every now and again, when I ask the farmer to keep an eye on things. But mostly, I just sit here and watch over the planes."

"Then—your name please, sir."

"Félix Maximillien."

"Yes, I thought you were French."

35.

In a field outside the old Tunnel Company building stood a crude, high-reaching antenna.

The top portions of this citadel did not quite sway, but instead leaned and shifted throughout the course of the day, according to the prevailing winds. It towered precariously over the landscape, outreaching even the smokestack of the factory, and was visible from the tractor road long before we ever reached the site. Approaching the transmission antenna, César gestured in wonder.

"Our messages," he said. "They no longer need the wire. No. They travel through the very particles of the air themselves. They use the wind and even the rain as their conduit. Heedless of which way the wind blows, the messages—they spread out in all directions, at once! Like mercury! Like lightning!"

This new invention, the Marconi, had been installed here at the request of the great London newspaper magnate himself, Lord Northcliff of the *Daily Mail*. Just the week before, I watched the raising of this amazing instrument, by use of a steam-powered crane. Lord Northcliff had a similar Marconi set up at a Dover hotel just across the sea. In this way, his newspaper—and his alone—could keep abreast of the moment-by-moment developments of the camp Antoinette. More importantly, though, weather conditions on both coasts could be monitored, and the navy dispatched in a moment.

Close by, the wind stirred the drooping canvas top that protected our flying machine. Lashes of rainwater sprayed from its edges.

"Let's visit," said César. "Shall we?"

In one of the forgotten offices upstairs, which looked like the ruins of a schoolroom and smelled of leaf mold and rot, sat the Lieutenant Lord Martin of the British Naval Corps of Engineers, thick-browed, doughy-faced, and forever morose, one of the two operators stationed here for the Marconi. There always had to be one on duty, even though by 7:30 in the morning the fate of the day had generally been sealed. By then the velocity of wind had become constant, or would only increase, as the day's sun hurled the currents back and forth between the two shores at a force far beyond the aeroship's ability to sail.

"Good day, Lieutenant. And how is His Majesty's Royal Navy?"

The officer gave no answer. No change in the weather whatsoever could be expected, his demeanor suggested—you might believe, in fact, that the lieutenant and his outrageous tower held the winds captive rather than monitoring them. It was through him alone now that news of the world came. Behind his desk, wearing his headset, beneath an obelisk of equipment, he awaited urgent dispatches from the far shore, where the postponement due to weather now mocked the weighty messages this citadel was intended to relay: "Weather Delays Latham," "Frenchman from England Grows Anxious."

César thanked the British officer for keeping the French Navy at the ready.

The lieutenant's brow rose in curiosity and disdain. "Is there anything more I can do for you?"

"No, that's fine. Keep up the good work."

César strode out of the lone office and down the dilapidated halls, and soon he stood outside, under the dreariest of skies, in charge of both sea and air, hill and dale, all he surveyed. Yes, César was a monarch, but a happy one. Of all the members of the *Buontemponi*, of which there were few, only César truly upheld the principle of seeking out and having good times. This was his credo, and he practiced it when and wherever he could.

"Alas. Poor machine." César lifted a corner of the circus top and peeked in at the Antoinette aeroplane, dormant and unattended in the gloom. "I fear the pilot is faring far worse. Let's cheer him, shall we?"

Off we went to the Hôtel Neptune, where Levavasseur and the crew of the Antoinette had taken rooms, awaiting the great sea change. Though Latham had a room all to himself in nearby Calais, he also kept a room here, and often spent the afternoon at the public house of the Neptune. For weeks now the upstairs café had exuded an air of desperation. You could smell it in the rain-soaked tweeds, spent tobacco, and picked-at fish plates, now just a smattering of skin and bones. The smell of wet dog filled the room. César tried his hand at billiards, beating one of the Brothers Welfèringer convincingly, and then turned his attention to the piano. He knew many tunes—short melodies from rustic ballads, love songs, inspirational bars of patriotic vigor, and songs for marching.

"Just pick a song and stay with it," complained one of the brothers. "All this skipping around from tune to tune, it drives a fellow to suicide."

"Homicide, more like," said another, throwing his cards down on the table.

César let out a sigh. "This instrument," he said, "if you can call it that, so horribly out of tune." That seemed especially true when he played a ditty he must have been forced to learn by rote as a child. Everyone fell into a despondent stupor as the card playing wore on, and César stayed with his song, plodding his way dutifully from beginning to end.

Latham, on the other hand, seemed incapable of entertaining himself. I worried for the birdman who did not play at cards, nor even sit at rest at a café table. Instead he aimed his gaze out the window. He paced the roads until he found himself on a cliff above the sea, facing England. He puffed with great vigor. He chewed on the ends of his cigarette holder. Less than two weeks on the coast, and already he'd lost weight and taken on a ghostly pallor. He lived on seltzer water and radishes, which he garnished with salt. When he forced a smile, his lips seemed too raw, and his eyes were narrowed, predatory and alert.

Hands in his pockets, he stared at the sea. And all the while, the whole world, as it seemed, by means of the Marconi, followed his every move.

~~

One afternoon, Latham looked on as a motor came to a halt on the drive before the Hôtel Neptune, the motor of the Gastambides. Anyone watching him would surely have sensed a sudden air of anticipation uplifting his frame. Driving the motorcar was Antoinette, the great flounce of her hat cinched down by netting and a determined scarf. Also in the motorcar sat her governess and toddler son.

36.

THE SALON OF THE HÔTEL NEPTUNE HAD TWO main doors, each leading to a different floor that formed an altogether separate establishment. That evening Latham kept pacing between the two, spending most of his time in the café upstairs, but every once in a while showing himself in the basement tavern, only to turn back around and walk upstairs. When Latham appeared in the tavern again, he leaned over the table where César and I sat.

"Have you seen her?"

"I was under the impression," said César, "that her sister would accompany her when she returned to Calais."

Latham smiled a delirious grin—injured, crooked, and full of self-knowing. "Ah, the Gastambide girls, how would you say, ravishing or ravaging?"

"Both. My friend. Sit. Please. Enjoy. All women are such, are they not?"

"No. They're not."

He left.

Here below the veranda in a corner facing the sea was a sort of low public house that went by the name of the Hall of Neptune, frequented for the most part by sailors and a quiet mix of others from the professions of the sea. The waiter, a short, fair, sturdy fellow, seemed almost idle as he set down the half bottles of wine and jiggers of beer, and yet he performed these duties with a solemn expression, always the same open, serving confidence. Then there were the two, maybe more—yes, probably more—girls whose duty it was to attend to the clients of the hall. But in this hotel full of occupants devoted to the launching of one of their kind into the clouds aboard fantastical wings, there was such a special little buzz in the damp air that really the girls had little now to do, which they liked, at first, beside those men of important aeronautical pursuits. The new clientele seemed like scholars or monks from some foreign land full of strange, inexplicable customs. But also there was a bit of the traveling circus about them, and then overtones simultaneously of heresy and religion. Each morning these flying men woke in the small hours and stood on the porch to discuss the upcoming day's weather, curse, and then go back to bed. Then there were the restless newspapermen, as well as a motley mix of tourists and locals, the curious and, of course, the merely idle.

It was beyond César to only sit by as one of these intriguing locals stared about the drafty, sea-dank café one night as though she were a stranger in her own haunt. Moved by a natural neighborliness of spirit, César felt he must now comfort one so estranged. Soon he was whispering humorous nothings into the very blond and curly hair of a girl who introduced herself as Rosa. Rosa in turn had eyes only for César, so, hoping to deflect my awkward gaze, she introduced me to one of her friends, Raphaella. Here was a small woman of immense hauteur—dark, discontented, yet ebullient. She had eyes of polished coal, two dark points of feisty intent. Soon she and I were ignored by our counterparts, who laughed until they jiggled.

"Why does your friend call you Potato?" asked Raphaella.

I began to move my hands through the air to answer, but before I could show her what I meant, Rosa spoke up.

"The Potato is a colleague of *le monsieur*," she said, swinging her legs around; draped over César's lap, they did not reach the floor. "No doubt from one of his historical societies."

No, I told them; I was hoping for an appointment to work with the aeroplane maker, once the flight across the sea was complete.

"And what an impressive Potato he is," said Rosa. "Look at how long his eyelashes are! Like a child's."

Raphaella ignored her, only glancing down at her dress and then casting a look of magnificent boredom across the room. The low ceiling of heavy beams and posts added to the cloistered feeling of the basement establishment, and here in the evening, against the bustle of voices, the piano did not seem so out-of-tune. Bleached starfish, cork floats, and rotted strips of netting were nailed to the walls, along with the largest codfish ever in existence, a big horse trough of a fish, shellacked into a perpetual gloomy expression. The wallpaper against which it swam had faded to look much like the water-stained pages of a book, though in the deepest, darkest corners, it retained a greenish, smoke-stained hue, especially near the drafty kitchen. At times either the salty tang of the sea, or a beery stench wafted in, as the outside door opened and a harbor character or two stirred past. Along the back wall was a faded mural of a crude and most lovely sort, of a sea-creature that I supposed was a mermaid, but more human than that. She was fish only from the knees down, not from the hips, which is usually the case with her kind. Below the knees, her legs melded into a single scaly fluke that rested upon her floating oceanic lily pad. Poised there upon the waves near the shore, she clutched at one of her long garlands of sea-blown hair, tucking it between her legs in a gesture both prudish and provocative. Two winged zephyrs rose from the sea to float alongside her, blowing wind at her torso.

I swallowed hard and turned my eyes to the dark, brewing Mademoiselle Raphaella.

"You don't answer why your friend calls you Potato," she said.

She spoke like a foreigner, though from what country I could not tell, and this raised her greatly in my esteem.

"I don't think about it anymore."

"He says it as a joke."

"I like the joke."

"The joke mocks you."

"I suppose." I shrugged. "It used to. But not anymore. I like it when they call me Potato."

This answer surprised her. Her eyes, her deep, attentive eyes, had a dark spot on them that unnerved me, especially after I noticed that César and Rosa were no longer sitting at their table, and were no longer in the hall. Raphaella's expression of beautiful boredom intrigued me.

It made me wish to make shapes in the air before her face with my hands.

Before leaving, César had ordered a full glass of wine, and Raphaella sipped from it, edging in closer. She flattened my vest against me with a pull. In the swirling glamour of my fatigue, as she smiled at me with her small, sharp, discolored teeth, contrasting with the two square pearls up front, I began to see her as a dark ravishing gypsy princess.

Many things did I wish to say to her with my hands.

Instead of going upstairs with her, though, I said, "Look. Out there. There's something I want to show you." And I took her outside of the hotel—she protesting, smiling, shy, angry, shy, saying Why? Why? I was so strange.

Soon we were above the cliffs, above the cloud-dark sea. Her silken dress hung straight down her small, hipless figure, and her black lace-up boots were too big. Burlesque, tropical breezes, cypress and pine, I wished to draw pictures for her in the air. When I reached out to take her hand, she stepped back with an imperial distance. She kept me away with a great dignity, as if her hand were unavailable to me even while I held it, and all the rest of her was remote too, like a doomed, tragic figure, a foreigner in dark circumstances held against her will. There was a tension inside her, there, where the tragedy dwelt. But her heart was steadfast. Mute, ignorant, yearning, I pressed my face to find her, and like a deft Spanish bullfighter she dodged me.

"No, no," she said, twisting away. She screwed up her face in disbelief and then in sadness as she struggled. "My friend, what are you doing?"

I found myself in the swirling grass, waving my hands around in gestures of loss and regret. I felt the urge to explain the deep mysterious languages of the sea and the vast emptiness of the clouds in a world beyond words to her with a large sweep of my arms, but she was not there. No one was there, not a soul, as I waved my hands through the air, wishing to bury my head in Simone's lap while she hummed as she sometimes did, a warm, tuneless warbling from somewhere deep within her thoughts, that turned like the music of the spheres, like the wind and the stars, in an ether only she could hear.

37.

I FOUND LATHAM IN THE VERY EBB OF THE NIGHT at the upstairs café of the Hôtel Neptune, in a state of utter composure. The lone waiter stood back in the shadows, idly wiping down a glass. Otherwise, Latham was alone, staring at nothing in particular. He had the air of someone who did not wish to be disturbed, so I excused myself.

"No, no. Sit, Potato, please."

We sat, both held captive in our separate, apologetic states. Latham finally broke the awkward silence, telling me of an observation that was troubling him. I cannot be trusted to relay his exact words here; he seemed haunted by his upcoming journey, and I was just an observer, unperturbed by the dangers that surely awaited him. He told me of the difficulty he had of seeing England. "You simply cannot trust the sea air," he said. "Have you ever studied the coast of England in the daytime? Have you?"

He sat back with his arms crossed, having made this enlightening statement of undeniable truth. "Sometimes the ocean air seems to magnify the coast. Everything becomes so large and close, you can almost make out the cottages on a hillside. You can see whole villages, as if looking through a telescope. Yet we all know what a trick of light that is. Ask any number of the villagers here how far away England is. Go ahead. Ask them. How far away is England?

"Twenty-two and a half miles," he answered himself, guessing at my ignorance from my expression. "And no wonder no one knows. On even the clearest of days, the mirage rises. It comes up out of the sea and floats there on the haze. The white cliffs of Dover stretch out in startling contrast to the sky—and to the rest of the low, gray horizon. Some of it is land, and some of it is water. But which is which? And if you stare long enough, I mean really study one spot, that feature of land disappears altogether. It drifts off, or sinks to insubstantial depths. Then, on these apparently clear days, the sea mist holds the land hostage in its mysteries, as in a dream, with sharp clarities and stretches of vagueness set side by side. But on most days you cannot even make out this uncertainty. What you can be sure of is clouds following upon clouds across the sky, until soon a deep, brooding sky blankets all of England. A long stretch of menacing vapors mimics a rocky coastline, like an England floating up into the sky, and there's no way of knowing whether you see an illusion or the real thing. But on most days the clouds come in so low they smother just about everything altogether, and you cannot make out the terrain of even the French coast. All is lost in a gray, abysmal rain. Every day you look out, it's a different England out there, it's altogether a different sea."

Without provocation, Latham also explained why he felt at ease telling me of possibilities he would otherwise never express. For instance, he wondered why one of the investors of the aeroplane had taken the time to show up on the coast today. He always wondered if someday Antoinette would want to fly the aeroplane herself, and why she had not been given the chance. No, it wasn't that. Perhaps she had no desire to fly. Or perhaps she did. Still, there was a quality about her that had him perplexed.

Why had she shown up on the coast at all that day without sending notice?

There was always some vague, as-of-yet unnamed project ahead of her, something close to a vocation or a passion that would engage her untapped sensibilities, a masterpiece of energy, as if she were a painter, or a photographer of the soul. This purpose had not yet been realized, but it was always lurking within, always drawing near, and always, without knowing it, she lived close to life's sacred fires. He actually said this phrase—life's sacred fires—as if he'd read it once somewhere and knew no one else to whom it applied, and I believed him, as strange as that was. I too believed that she perceived me cleanly, and I always felt a subtle grace when she was near.

It wasn't long before the waiter asked Latham if he wanted anything else.

"No, no." Latham shook his head, a kind of monastic simplicity moving across his features. "No. But thank you."

He then stood with astounding awkwardness. It was the awkwardness you feel when you have told someone perhaps too much, and now stand in a position to be judged and exposed long afterward.

"Good night," he said, and I sensed he felt a little unburdened by what he'd said. Then he turned and left.

38.

To HEIGHTEN THE SEABOARD EXPERIENCE of the bourgeois inlander, the hotel room held a thick volume of yellowed nautical charts, scaled down to fit within a book, large and finely bound though it was. Also provided was a tide table, three years out of date. Latham would often spend the last few moments before sleep here, at the desk, musing over the depictions of the coastline, the shallows and shoals, the sea currents and coastal hills. There was a walk he liked to take along the cliffs each night, but he did not want to miss the desperate entrance of Antoinette, shivering up in her room. She stayed at this very hotel, and still they had not had their scene yet, he and she. If not now, tonight, tomorrow, when? When would she risk the wicked vigilance of the German governess, who knew better anyway, so what did it matter? Instead Latham rode the writing desk of his hotel room far into the nighttime sky, studying the charts, wondering how he would appear when Antoinette did. Finally he climbed into bed. Night after night, the same. Who would awake him, though he couldn't sleep? One of the brothers Welféringer, or Levavasseur himself to tell him of the favorable conditions and that the flight was on?

Up from the harbor sounded the knocking of ropes and tackle of boats, auguring the impossibility of flight tomorrow, a foregone conclusion. Still, before his eager hopes rose the cliffs of Shakespeare, a throng of admirers, sheets of wind, billowing sails, windmills and castles, the green fields of Dover and their sad little sheep cowering below the dreary sky. What were the jagged seawalls called before the time of the Bard? There, floating above the nameless sea, between the two lands, Latham had a vivid sense of sailing the Olympic heights in the balloon. How the sea sparkled, where the sun hit, furrowed like the rind of a lime. His first balloon crossing had been in a June much like this one, though sun-drenched and clear. César had instructed his cousin, the prodigy, on how to find the winds, though he wasn't doing a very good job of it himself. Some Junes you want the winds, and some you do not. Yet despite their failure to find them, let alone control them, still they saw what the gods see: an illusion. Instead of a sea-blue globe stretching out below, they saw the horizon rising at an incline all around, a product of what César called refraction, a striking phenomenon that left the two aeronauts feeling cupped within a bowl of gently rising seawall.

Where below:

The tiny boats plied.

Tall masts reached up as they passed.

And ocean steamers followed their own plumes.

Sailing, yet not seeming to sail.

Motionless in the deep gray sea.

And farther out, near oblivion, the Isle of Wight, where not even gravity applied, only sunlight. Sunlight off the water, much brighter than sunlight from the sky. Much brighter now, all just a memory, all that remained, all the want excited by memory, by the hope for its repetition, for the inevitable ache of it all over again. The profound low note of a foghorn boomed out again, and with it the suggestion of a distant land heaped in violence and myth. In his sleepless, cloud-filled turning, Latham felt sick inside with a disturbance as vague as the weather. The room around him tilted and rolled, as if he were in a boat. He saw a woman wading from a lake, jumping from a bridge, leading him into an attic; his mind could not fix her. Constantly the wind blew through the caverns of his head. Rain pinged against the windows. Voices urged him. A restless circus tent fell all around him, capturing him as if in a net.

He heard a knocking, and it was not the wind nor his exhausted brain.

"Léon? César? Is it time? Shall we go?"

The only answer was the same gentle knocking.

"Come in."

With a sharp snap, she shook the water from her umbrella. Antoinette wore her hat cinched tightly, with white netting over her face. In the predawn gloaming she looked surreal, as if she'd come to him from beyond the world, already a shadow. He took her in, nobly, like a condemned man, wrongly accused. She looked at him with unnerving calm behind her shroud.

"I'm driving back to Paris today," she said. "I just came here to say goodbye."

"Goodbye? I didn't even know you were in town."

"Come now." She sat down on the edge of his bed, and he heard the familiar smile in her voice. "I arrived just yesterday. I heard you were looking for me."

Briefly she took one of his hands in both of hers, leaning over him. All the various layers of her dress pressed up against his side, and he wondered if she could feel his heat.

"Listen," she said. "I had a terrible dream. I dreamed of you in the water. You were bloodied and hurt. I dreamed you did not make it."

"Why do you tell me this? And why now?"

"It's why I drove here. Only to tell you."

He held on to her white glove and felt its folds where it yielded. "You know this only serves to remind me that I have no other choice than to go, and even more so now. How can I not? With all that has been put in place."

"I know, I know. But I had to tell you. So that you can—I'm not sure—take precautions."

"And how do you suggest I prepare for my fall from the sky?"

"Can't you do *something*?"

"Yes. Land in a nice, green English field."

"You know I hope to God I'm wrong."

"So do I. But either way I have to go."

"And so do I," she said. The rustling of her heavy dress sent out the scents of a hearthside fire and the secrets of her cooped-up, married sex.

The impulse to reach out and pull her into an embrace overwhelmed him, but she was already standing beyond his grasp. "There, I've told you. Now I can go with a clear conscience."

"You know," he said with a mocking air, "that when a sailor drowns at sea, his soul swims home to his lover, or his wife. To whom will my soggy, sea-drenched soul swim? I mean . . . since I'm already swimming to you in your dreams."

"Ah, Hubert." She paced, looking out the gray-weather window at the dull morning beginning to dawn. "Even if you did believe in the soul, which I'm sure you do not, do you believe that you have one?" She walked up and stood above his bed again and took his face in both her hands. "Then where is it?" She turned his face this way and that. "Where?"

She lifted the netting from her own face, and he felt that she was a nurse and he her patient—her features gaunt, her eyes impoverished by lost sleep, grown large and full of emotion.

"Are you really leaving today?" he asked. "Going back? To what?"

"Oh." She walked the small room, finally settling upon a dark window, and faced out. "Those who do not learn from history are doomed to repeat it."

"We should only be so lucky," said Latham.

"Listen, dear friend. I've already done all this. I've sung my recitals, and lifted my skirts, lightly, like so, and waltzed before a room full of men. Believe me, my comedy's over."

"Over? How sad. And what is my role in your little comedy?"

"Ha. You see, you think too much about yourself. Don't be such a tragic fellow. Or is yours not a comedy?"

"Look," he said. "If you're going back to Paris today, do you think you could go a bit farther? I have a favor to ask of you."

"I suppose . . . I could. Why?"

Latham held out a sealed letter.

Antoinette took it. "What? What is this?"

"My mechanic has asked me to post this next time I'm in town."

"You mean—" Antoinette blushed furiously through the netting bunched into her hat. "You did not write this?"

"No." Latham reached over her to his nightstand, over the elaborate flowing of her dress, and produced a good handful of others. "I think he's written more," he said. "But he's had no reply."

"Your young friend from the country?"

"Yes."

Antoinette shuffled through the letters, one by one, looking over the addresses. "There's two different addresses here," she said. "One to a monastery."

"I believe all the letters should go to the monastery by now. Expressions of young love," he said. "Perhaps you know something of that."

She sat herself down at his desk in a slump that seemed all the more impressive in her traveling dress. "Will you be flying today?"

"That's why I'm asking you to post them."

She turned in her chair and leaned toward him, as if swayed by a complete change of heart. "Life is never so easy around you. How do you do that? You didn't answer my first question. Are you flying today?"

"Listen—"

The rain beat down steadily, battering the eaves with every gust of wind. Then, from the hallway, they heard a door, and the sound of voices and footsteps.

"What am I to do with these?" she whispered, cradling the bundle of letters in her hand.

"Hurry," said Latham.

Antoinette let the netting fall again over her face, grabbed her umbrella, and stood to leave. Opening the door, she peeked out beyond it, and only then did she walk into the hallway, the rasp of her boot heels moving away as the door swung shut.

39.

A GREAT GRAY LULL HUNG OVER THE SEA.

Latham drove his *coccinelle* down the puddled farm roads, below a volatile sky for the moment at rest. The rains from England had subsided, apart from the occasional drizzle. But the visibility was poor, very poor. The dark skies obscured whatever fate awaited him on the far shore. Still, he drove, fighting his own impatience, trying to extricate himself from the doom of Antoinette's dream. He didn't believe in dreams, not as prophecies, at least; they were only manifestations, as the nervous activity of a worried brain. Yet still he feared them. No, it wasn't fear, but the need to know, or to prepare in the face of unknowing, or to go, to simply go, but do *something*—just go.

At the Hôtel Neptune, the fraternity of Levavasseur and Gastambide took their breakfast, which was over but for the coffee and frustration. They perked up, though, when they heard of Latham's case, all of hope, skepticism, and weariness, but mostly of agitated hope to get the aeroplane over the sea. He impressed them all with his impatience.

"Tomorrow," said Levavasseur. "We'll get you into the air then."

"Besides, we've long since sent our dispatch to the hotel in Worcester," said César. "The *Harpon* will be at anchor all day."

Levavasseur went on to explain that before they attempted the Channel, they must first make a complete and successful flight up and down the coast, until they'd burned through an entire tank's worth of fuel and seen how the engine handled the damp sea air.

Latham had heard all this before, but he no longer believed it. "But we haven't even had a day calm enough for a test," he said.

"And this sky's so thick," said Levavasseur, "you won't be able to see the ends of your arm, let alone the beach."

"That's it," said Latham. "*That's it*. Just up and down the beach."

"In this sky?"

"It's calm enough." Latham grinned. "Let's save the first beautiful day—for England."

Levavasseur stood. "Yes, beautiful, my boy. You heard him. Put her to the field."

So they hitched Gastambide's ceremonial draft horse by means of a rope to the skid at the front of the aeroplane. The horse hauled the clumsy contraption as if it were the lightest of cabriolets, and the stableman led the beast by the snout, constantly having to calm it against the turmoil of the growing wall of spectators—well-wishers, newspapermen, tourists; boys on bikes were the most nimble. Constantly the horse was inclined to snort and yank the plane off-kilter. The brothers Welfèringer walked beneath the aeroplane to steady the wings, and Gastambide and Levavasseur rode behind in a motor. All the while Latham rode in the aeroplane. Boys paced abeam of the aviator as they do at train stations, just after the conductor climbs into his compartment and swings the door shut and the train lurches into motion. Except most here were not boys. Intense speculation lit the faces of grown men as Latham rode atop a teetering bug-like contraption that sprawled out over the edges of two adjoining fields. He sat above the wings of one of Jules Verne's fantastical machines. With the great rim of England to the north, Latham felt sure there'd been far too much caution up till then. He should have made the test flight weeks ago. A light mist fell, leaving a slick of dew across the wings' white-doped cloth.

There was a tic, a submerged flinch of dark feeling, that he could not quite shake, nor quite remember, though it was always there. Here in the daylight, even this milky daylight, Antoinette's dream of him in the water, struck him as nothing more than her own private anxiety, and the sadness of the dreams that she was too afraid to follow. All around him a more public, courageous will buoyed him up and whisked him along, growing in force, urging him into the clouds, across the sea. All of us—inventor and pilot and crew and well-wishers and the curious as well as the aeroplane—we all approached the farm, the empty field that Levavasseur had rented out, a field that lay flat and fallow, grazed by sheep right down to the nub.

Perfect for takeoff.

⤜⤛

Latham's plane rose into a ghostly, sea-gray gloom, not as thick as a fog, just a dull wash that covered up all distances. Still, the visibility was better than expected. Beneath the clouds, he saw wide stretches of field. Chimneys rose into view. He flew well wide of the slender church spire, and then the brick stack from the old Tunnel Company building—once again an oracle, but foretelling what? Then past the leaning Marconi tower. He took the *Antoinette* a little higher, in case another augury should suddenly appear.

The plan was this:

To simply go up and come immediately back down, when they would top off the fuel tank. Then he'd take off again, to begin in earnest the test of duration. Through the treetops, fog moved like wool through a comb, and then all gave way to the sea. Against the rocks, the great waves lifted and crashed, as if the element were sucked out from below him, only to rise up again. The wind above the sea was more turbulent, too, and sudden pockets and bursts of air racked him. The wings dropped from beneath him, like the sudden stopping of his heart, while he actually rose up from his seat, and then he was caught up again, just above where the surf broke into geysers and sea spouts. The gray-green water surged up against the beachhead, and the wet, barnacled rocks shimmered with kelp. He flew out farther, where the sea cloud thickened. All else was ocean, traversed by crested waves that turned to foam. What if he just . . . kept . . . sailing to England?

For a while that was his course.

But without proper notification, there'd be no prize money. And what if he sank in the sea, with no navy to rescue him? Or missed the island of England altogether? He never thought he'd need a compass, and now he had to calculate his turn back to land. For a while he was completely lost. He made a wide sweeping turn, which would become wider and wider, if need be. But soon he saw the beach, and the small fishing boats beyond the harbor. He saw the jetty, and the great ocean steamers, and the military juggernaut, the *Harpon*, at anchor, waiting to properly accompany him across the sea.

As he approached the takeoff meadow, he was gripped by dismay. Where would he land? The pasture was completely overrun with spectators, as were all the nearby fields and the roads that led to the farm. They seemed to sprout from the ground itself, their cheering so enthusiastic, it was as if he'd already reached England and was making his return. Like a circus hero shot from a cannon, he arched over them. Their adulations increased. He passed over them again, trying to wave them away, to clear a place to land. But the more he waved them off, the more they cheered. They milled leisurely about like a crowd at a country fair, his aeroplane's approach to the field only consolidating their mass. Finally even Levavasseur waved him away. He and Latham yelled to each other. There was no getting the crowd to move.

Levavasseur began emphatically to point. *The next field over.*

But even from up here, Latham could see that landing in a field of wheat would be difficult at best. No telling how deep the crop was, or what lay beneath it. He could see no better place to land, though. Perhaps he would not even make it out over the sea before Antoinette's dream proved true.

He circled in.

The wheels rattled the wheat like the shuffling of a deck of cards as he cut the engine. He braced himself as, just as he'd anticipated, the runners dug into the field, and the machine upended, coming to rest at an incline, as if it meant to bore into the ground. Latham jumped down from his wicker seat and into the midsummer crop, and only then, standing waist high in wheat, did he realize he was unhurt. Spectators were climbing over the fence and running toward him, parting the tall stalks. And he was glad—euphoric, even, though the aeroship would be under repairs for at least a week. He'd outlived Antoinette's prophecy and survived the landing, and now the sea lay before him, untouched.

But then, as he stood beside the broken sails of his wallowing ship, the wheat rose in swells all around him. The field was a purgatory where Antoinette's dream kept him captive.

40.

"Up, Potato. Up."

One of the Welféringer brothers barged into the hotel room and shook me awake. Two weeks had passed since Latham's crash landing in the wheat, and we'd come to the conclusion that the windows for flying were all too brief and could be blown away within the instant. So one of us was appointed to keep a constant watch of the weather through the night.

"If the weather clears, wake up your boss. It's your watch."

The big beef of a brother still ridiculed me for my friendship with the celebrity birdman from the valley of châteaux. Worse yet, he begrudged my very presence on the coast when too many of Levavasseur's long-standing workers, far more deserving, were not asked to attend. I could sense, though, a deep lethargy overwhelming my spiteful colleague. He would soon give himself over to sleep.

"These rains should keep you company," he said.

I heard the door slam shut, and the brother's footsteps falling off.

∽≋∾

"Potato. You awake?"

César barged into my room.

He approached the nightstand, huffing and yawning, snapping like a duck. He stood and began splashing the water in the basin and making distinguished faces into the mirror as he preened his beard and mustaches. Soon we both stood on the porch of the hotel, inspecting the dark skies for both tranquility and clearness, as well as for signs that the sudden calm might remain until daybreak.

An intense moon, brighter than a coin, shone through the clouds.

"Stars," I said.

"Yes. I think your esteemed associate observed incorrectly," said César. "The lummox."

"And above England, a sky full of them."

"Oh yes. As if some kindly soul had suddenly thrown a few more to the firmament."

On we walked, to the cliffs above the sea.

While on weather watch, César left nothing to chance. Shortly after midnight, he took out an instrument for divining weather that looked very much like a timepiece on a chain. His "barometer" gave a very solid reading, he explained, remaining constant. Still, César worked to curb a hasty assessment. He breathed in deeply and told me he smelled a very wet and oceany air, the same as always, but wasn't there also a hush? As if we stood in the wind's ebb? And the ocean breakers too seemed slower and farther away, as if the surf had diminished. César strode energetically despite the early hour, so that I was forced to hop-step to keep up.

His vigil carried him out to the very point of Cap Blanc-Nez, where he looked out. "Why—if this truly were the day to wake Latham—did that brother fellow not save the glory for himself?"

And I began to wake to a giddy pride. I might get the honors.

"Well, if you must know, very well then, I will tell you." Beginning to pace, César explained that my friend, the Brother Lummox, suffered from what the ministers of health called "a softening of the brain," especially the cerebellum and cerebral cortex. It was not just the palpable living tissue of the organ itself. He lacked discipline and constitution, and begrudged those, like César and myself, who demonstrated such qualities in abundance.

I was especially enlivened now, moved by the spirit of César's boundless knowledge, which seemed to encompass all things.

"Still, our friend the lummox will live long," said César, his thoughts fuming round his head as if they rose from a boiler. "So it goes. Dullness endures. Some lost souls—"

"However," I said, "he's an expert joiner, who reminds me of many tasks I've overlooked."

César stopped me abruptly. He took a long, contemplative look at the nighttime sea.

"Some lost souls," he went on, "when confronted with the task of watching the weather, become frustrated, waiting on what they cannot comprehend. They wish the task of staring out into the dark empty void were finished. Done. Or better yet, done by someone else. The varieties of reaction of the soul to the sea are many. Some natures, when confronted with the sea, they see the tractless waters, the wide, stretching horizon; they become painters, or poets. They hear a depth and musicality. Soon they aspire to recreate the ocean's wonder. But they can only ape this splendor, like a monkey banging with a stick."

César's inspiration produced a strange effect on him. He rushed along the cliffside path, yet I was not sure where he was headed.

"Other souls," he explained, "when confronted with the sea, are drawn irresistibly to travel. To adventure. Other places. Strange new lands. New foods, new customs, new clothes! They feel the excitement of immersion into a world of complete otherness. They want to seek out the unknown, to indenture themselves on a merchant ship, to purchase tickets aboard a steamer to exotic ports.

"We not only have great ocean liners, we have machinery that can bring us down into the very undersea world itself. Hence the invention of the submarine, the observation compartment lowered by crane, the deep-sea diver. We can greet the fishes. Commune with whales. We can look up as if the ocean were the sky, and the fish like birds flying through it. What do the birds see of the heavens above? Such is the limitation of all understanding. Yet we go on, as busy as bees—or as sardines, if we're to keep with our metaphors.

"I know many who stand at the edge of the sea and see only the continuation of railways, undersea thoroughfares, ocean-going freighters. They see hulls packed with livestock, textiles, dry goods. For them, the sea excites the desire for profit. The monkey must have more and more sticks. Always more. To what end?"

Here César picked up a flower or a leaf—I could not tell which, in the seaside dark—and twirled it between his fingertips with a flourish, then took in its aroma, held up close to his face.

"Yet we know some who see the sea as a conquest, and merely that, the conquest of a woman, or a title, a destiny. Agh." He sighed and tossed the flower to the waves, to the dark, rushing sound below. "Is it folly? Or the threshold of a magnificent day? A magnificent *era*? Regardless, I believe this is it. We must wish our dear friend good luck in his upcoming journey."

I was at a loss to add anything that could assist our good friend in his flight across the sea. The watery unknowns of the dark would be beneath him the entire way.

"Truly, if his flight is successful, is it ultimately a good thing? Do the advancements of science enhance us, or enslave? Observe."

César stepped forward onto the very precipice of the cliff, a little dangerously close, it seemed to me. He leaned into the wind, as if it were a buttress that would keep him from falling to the rocks.

"On rare nights"—he spoke loudly now, as if trying to project over the cliffs—"the foam of the sea is eerily lit. Everywhere the sea breaks, it is illuminated by a green phosphorescence. The sea has elements within it that self-illuminate. Like the brightest, most clever of minds. If you were to go undersea, they say, the submarine terrain is covered with this luminescence—underwater shoals covered with mollusks, jellyfish floating, glowing phosphorescent from the deeps; tiny fish with small lanterns on horn-like appendages that they wag to and fro, to attract prey or light their way through the interminable dark. Yet down in the sea, it is not dark—not at all. The ocean floor gives off its own brilliance. At this very time, scientists are hard at work, close to unlocking the secret of this glowing process, when they will create a paint that contains this very quality." He waved his arms, carried away. "Imagine our town squares and roadsides painted with this illuminating substance. Our cities will glow naturally, brought out of the ever-lasting night. Can we say the same about all machinery and applications of science? Do they foul or enlighten our sky? If we fly to England tomorrow, what of it? Will it further our experience? Our scope and our span? Will the work of scientists and adventurers light our way? Or will we just be finding another way to go back and forth, or gather more sticks, or throw them down upon England? Because we can."

César pulled his watch from his vest pocket and began to rewind it. Occasionally the beam of the lighthouse shot out over the night sea. Out there, a boat's light blinked, ducking below the horizon and rising again, going on, and off again, a tiny, lone light, somewhere between here and there, steaming between the Baltic and Atlantic, away to ports unknown.

"I taught him how to fly the balloon, you know," said César. "But who put the heart in him? Who taught him how to steer the machine with such effortless daring? We are so lucky, you and I, to know him, and be next to him as he follows his arc, wherever it may lead. Look at where he has brought us so far."

César moved back away from the cliff and handed me his watch. "Here. You'll need this to wake Levavasseur. Soon. Very soon."

He turned to walk away from the cliffs. "Tomorrow, we lunch in England, you and I. I'll leave you the honor of waking *Le Père* for yourself."

With a calm, ragged dignity, César moved off toward the hotel. "I'm used to setting my watch by the chiming of the bells of Charbonneau. But we've been gone from its tolling for so long."

41.

I WAITED UNTIL FOUR IN THE MORNING BEFORE I knocked on the first door of the hallway. The door to the hotel room opened slightly, and a woman peered around it, making me feel as though I were an intruder. In the private, slumberous light of her room, *Le Père's* wife stood, somewhat suspicious—small, aged, and ropy, with a prominent rib cage beneath her robe.

Then from beyond the door came a booming voice:

"Wake the others. Then—*go!* Go to the aeroplane."

I had not even uttered a word yet, and my achievement of weather watch would go unnoticed by the great elfish industrialist and inventor of aeroplanes. Still, I knocked on the doors up and down the hallway to rouse the others.

But first in the hall was *Le Père*, with his swollen, sleep-encrusted face. "Why aren't you at the aeroplane?" he said. His well-to-do bulk seemed comic and enchanted as he ran around in his sleeping robe. Then, "YOU!" he said to me again. "*You?* Why aren't you at the Marconi?"

When I left the hotel, he was leaning over the lobby counter, staring at the concierge, who had the phone up to his ear and the mouthpiece to his face, calling Latham's hotel.

❧❦

I ran to the old Channel Tunnel Building and up the stairs to the moldy headquarters of the British Naval Corps of Engineers. There Lieutenant Lord Martin stopped me from ever uttering a word. Not only had the glum operator already corresponded with the press corps at the Dover Hotel, he'd sent his dispatch to the French navy and then on to the *Calaisien*—the British tugboat set to guard Latham in the waters off the other shore. In addition, the great White Star liner the *Oceanic* had been ordered to halt, at the passengers' request. Their departure to America would have to wait; the liner sailed in perfect waters to view the aviator. So there the three-stacked steamer lay adrift, its passengers strung along the rails, waiting for the magical birdman to come sailing across the sky in his rattling circus contraption.

At last, the dull, uneventful weather everyone had been waiting for. The Lieutenant turned his attention to the window and the scene below.

Already, as the crew began to uncloak the *Antoinette* from its tarps, a small crowd had gathered. Gastambide's fine Percheron was harnessed to the aeroplane's front skid, and there everyone awaited Latham.

❧❦

Before any flight of record, it was customary for a certain woman of dark skin and large, dark eyes to pin a rose to Latham's lapel. I remembered her as the stage singer from the Folies-Gobelins who had performed at the party. She had been more prominent as his muse back when he raced motorcars and boats, but still she was there at the launch of every one of his flights, with her full, falling hair of the south, her tragic mouth, her illustrious beauty, always running after him with a harried look of love in her eyes.

Latham lifted up his lapel and savored the rose, drawing it to his face. Then, quickly, he swung himself over the wing and was aboard. Like the austere Wilbur Wright, he had become the unwilling performer, ignoring the hubbub of the crowds yet buoyed up by it.

Levavasseur and Gastambide stood just outside the tent overhang, looking up at the pilot. What do you say to your champion before you send him alone across the abyss, either to oblivion or world renown? I never found out. As I worked through the crowd, both investor and inventor, along with their small, distinguished party, made their way to the motor coach, bundled up in dark coats for the short sea voyage. There was a grave ceremony about them, as if they were leaving or entering a cathedral. The motorcar set off for the harbor, where they would board the boat that waited at anchor to ferry them across.

Latham took his exalted place above the wings.

The draft horse pulled.

A growing band of spectators followed the sprawling machine as it began to roll in a slow, jerky manner down the road. I helped the brothers Welféringer steady the ship, as bicycles wheeled past the aeroplane along the path. The long-reaching blades of the wings shook above the fields on either side, and I thought something I'd often thought as I helped maneuver the ship, or sometimes when I saw it fly overhead, that it was a cross made of wood, and the man riding it an unknowing savior. On this morning, though, the thought overwhelmed me with superstitious dread. I looked down the tractor road to the takeoff field, where already the well-wishers were gathered.

≈◦≈

Once past the mouth of the harbor, the *Harpon* fired its cannons once as a sign of readiness, the dull charge echoing in the damp sea air.

Full of impatience, Latham had the brothers unhitch the horse, and he taxied under the aeroplane's own hectic power along the road, scattering the crowd along his way. At lookouts along the cliff, cameramen stood at the ready beside their tripods and cameras. The crowd parted just as the *Antoinette* entered the field, and Latham turned off the engine so the mechanics could take one last look over the ship. César put a hand on one of the reporter's shoulders, and, striking the pose of a venerable orator, began, full of importance:

"The time?"

The bystanders silenced.

"Six forty-two," said a reporter, his notepad wedged between his elbow and hip, checking his own watch.

Several spectators also took out their pocket watches. I noted that César's was twenty minutes slow.

Like a scrappy street fighter, Latham leaned forward. The paddles of the prop disappeared in their own whirr, and I received a blast of air that smelled of seawater and fuel. The spars of the tail wings trembled. We let go. The aeroplane rolled forward, a flurry of field clippings hanging in the air behind it, as if we were in the wake of a mechanical thresher. The aeroplane circled once around the lone industrial brick stack.

The *Antoinette* flew up and down the beach, then swung back again over the crowd at the farm. Then it banked seaward like a fan-winged cormorant, as if that were the most natural and uneventful of acts. Every face turned upward—the investors, Parisians from the Aero Club, friends and family of the Gastambides, Félix Maximillien and the farmer and the Fish Mayor, remarking that soon everything would return back to normal in their sleepy little village. The mayor congratulated César as the aeroplane continued to grow smaller, its contained fury diminishing to a sad, solitary whine that sounded more like the sea than itself, and finally, slowly, gave way to no sound at all. Everyone stood at the edge, leaning toward it, at a loss in the after-din of a miracle.

Cheers rose here and there along the cliff. Latham grew smaller and smaller, while boys on their bikes rode round in aimless circles.

42.

IN THE SKY, HE FELT HE'D BEEN LIED TO. Not by his observers, nor by the fates, but by his own eyes. The visibility had been ten miles when he took off from Calais. Now a dull, oppressive mist hid all of England. Usually the winds blew away this infernal fog. But it was these same winds that had made the flying impossible up till now.

On a chain in his pocket Latham had a compass, but he believed only in the thrum of the engine. He climbed, shaking and tilting, until he leveled off at around two hundred feet. Looking down at the automobiles parked behind the line of spectators, he thought he recognized a few of them—but not the one driven by Antoinette. She wouldn't be there—he knew that, and berated himself for looking.

And now, coming into view through the sea-mist like a world of miniatures, the jetty, the estuary, the small fleet of pleasure boats gathered to send him off. Once again he was a minor dispossessed god, looking down on a world that he could sway for his own amusement. He overtook the *Harpon*, which was steaming the wrong way—back to France. Perhaps he had been too long in taking off, and the navy ship's captain had turned back around. No matter. Latham kept soaring out over the sea. Fair waves, small to none. The oceanic calm as still as a tub's water, dull as the sky. Good signs all. Behind him now the *Harpon* was turning around again to follow him to England.

But what?

The pitch of the engine dropped. The propeller slowed.

Seven minutes beyond the coast, he began to lose altitude. The two paddles of the propeller came to a halt, and Latham gave the fuel line a jolt, smacking it with his open palm. He climbed out over the wings as best as he could to give the propeller a turn, careful not to grab the iron-hot engine. Holding onto the blade, he could not find leverage enough to turn it with any force. Not even slowly, as if moving the hands of a clock. He hung onto the aeroplane and heard the damp cool atmosphere whistle by, and that barely perceptible hiss of the sea, its vast steaming fields tilting as they drew near. Latham took his seat again. Once again he would have to perform his now famous volplane, but this time on the open sea, with no one there to witness it. The ocean below took on a peculiar vividness. He couldn't believe this was happening, yet he'd always known it would. Instead of a crowd pressing in all around him and his aeroplane in a field beside a British castle, he saw the cold blue-gray of the sea, the patterns of foam on the waves, the different hues, the hidden depths. He braced himself for the swim with calm detachment. Long before nearing water, he felt its chill. He inhaled its sharp briny scent, the scent of both the unknown and the inevitable. And then the aeroplane belly-flopped, bouncing across the troughs, jarring him violently, but for only a second. He perceived no injury. On the contrary, what a gentle, beautiful landing! Seawater hissed and steamed off the scalding engine as the *Antoinette* came to rest perfectly, like a handkerchief draped upon the sea, becoming more and more heavy, until it no longer moved from the momentum of its fall. The aeroplane's tail rose slightly as its front dipped, pulled down by the weight of the engine. He hoped it would not fill completely with seawater and pull him under.

Until then, though, he bobbed.

Like a cork.

Upon the great gray sea.

Norman born, in Anglo garb.

And the clothes still dry.

Except for a sock.

And even that not wet, really.
Adrift in the middle of no-man's-land.
Or no-man's-water.
Gentle trough of a wave.
Welcome and kind.
He rose.
And fell.
On the calmest of ocean swells.

∽∾

Usually in the middle of the sea like this, you are protected by the rails of a boat, at least a story or two up. But now the placid ocean was nearly at eye level. Beyond the horizon, as far as he could see, projected the stolid stacks and sails of ships, as they'd be on any given day, as if he'd plunged into the middle of a watery world that had no notion of his fall. He heard only the calm against his hat and hair, and the carbonated hissing of the sea, the waves nowhere near to breaking, only softly lapping against the wooden panels and fabric of his doomed aeroship.

The reflection of a low-riding gull passed over the waters, and a single gray seabird feather floated on the surface, the down of its quill stirred by the breeze. He searched his pockets. Excellent. His matches and tobacco were still dry. Far off, the gray outline and black smoke of the navy ship could be seen, now turned and steaming his way.

43.

To celebrate the historic flight across the sea, César had made arrangements to cross the English Channel with none other than the Fish Mayor himself. I was of course welcome to ride along in the mayor's ancient double paddle-wheeler of Le Havre, a tidy relic of the shipyard from 1862—and, given the calm weather and the festive occasion, the perfect vessel to ferry us across. Until then, though, we made our way back through the scattered crowds to the old Tunnel Company building to catch news from the Marconi. The onlookers were also in the grandest of moods, in the loaf and ease of a summer vacation, and now enthralled at having witnessed the making of history.

By the time we made our way along the hallway to the Marconi station, though, doubt had begun to arise. Even if Latham were bucking a headwind of seven knots or more, which he was not, the aeroplane's average speed of forty miles an hour should have put him in England a good twenty minutes before. The Marconi office itself was unreachable, the hall just beyond it filled shoulder to shoulder with members of the press corps of Britain and France. By the gravity of his connection to the birdman, however, César insinuated himself into the office. After an unbearable wait, he emerged with a slip of paper in his hands, the correspondence from the Marconi operator at the Dover Hotel.

In a grave orator's style, he read:

SEVEN TWENTY-THREE. NO SIGN OF AVIATOR.

"He's in the sea!"

The hallway burst into a chorus of groans as César ducked back into the crowded doorway of the Marconi operator's office. If the *Antoinette* had flown into the ocean in the same way it had flown into the wheat, then Latham had plunged into the sea and sunk under the waves. What if there was no trace of him at all? Or maybe he was swimming, impossible to see, out in the middle. I found the hallway oppressive, but could do nothing but wait for more news. After a great long while, César pushed his way again between the shoulders at the office door:

SEVEN FORTY-SIX. NOTHING IN SIGHT. REQUESTING ASSISTANCE. FISHERY CRUISER TO SEARCH.

In the hallway, I paced. Dejected reporters lowered themselves against the wall. Feeling seasick and bereft, I could not imagine Latham falling halfway across the sea. An even longer time lapsed before César appeared again with the next correspondence:

EIGHT-O-SIX. VERY ANXIOUS HERE. CANNOT SEE TORPEDO BOAT OR LATHAM.

44.

LIKE THE SEA ITSELF, LATHAM SAT ABSOLUTELY STILL while his strange, elaborate raft filled slowly with seawater. The black bulk of the navy boat grew larger and larger, its dark stack belching up an enormous cloud. Its horn blew three times in greeting, and sailors lined the rails. But the lowering of the launches did not go well. The bow of the first lifeboat was lowered too quickly, so that when it reached the waves, it scooped up water like a ladle. Once three launches were lowered and free, the sailors rowed like so many water bugs, two by two. One lifeboat had a camera up front, set like a gun mount at the bow. Black-caped avenger, the photographer could actually stand unhindered in the calm, and so could his tripod, poised to humiliate Latham as the oarsmen plied behind as ordered. Latham cursed at the preparations made for his failure. Yet the birdman breathed air and not seawater, did he not?

The first lifeboat drew up alongside, and an oarsman threw him a line.

"The Captain wishes to know if the aeronaut is in good health, and if he is thirsty?" The officer of the rowboat, a thick, hairy man with a calm dog-like face, held a flask out to a mate, who scurried over the legs of the others to hold it out in turn to Latham.

"Yes. To both." Latham raised his throat to the sky.

The sailors had dressed up for the occasion in their formal in-port uniforms, with a smart blue ribbon hanging from their caps. They stared at Latham as he was accustomed to being stared at, their open faces agape, as if he were a half-god, or an experimental man that the half-gods preyed upon for their own dark amusement. Latham took hold of an oar and climbed onto the boat, happy to be alive enough to drink strong drink, to have it burn his sternum and gut.

❧❧

Upon seeing Latham climb from the launch onto the deck of the *Harpon*, the inventor Levavasseur put both of his hands up to the pilot's face and shook him, full of woe and worry. "You—," said the woeful patriarch. "I could not be more grateful."

But immediately he leaned over the rails with the rest of the crew to catch a glimpse of his beautiful floating machine. Léon Levavasseur, who'd traipsed off to the *Académie des Beaux-Arts* as a youth, who'd turned his desire to paint and draw into engineering machines, now gazed at his airy skiff, half above the water and half below, only its rudder and tail fin above the seas. Like a wreath it floated, and the enchanted sailors could not look away. Never before had there been a machine so animate, so beautiful, so tragic.

The curious fog that had descended upon the water only added to Latham's calm and alienation. He sat on the bridge like an aquatic Orpheus, wearing a navy-issue jacket but no socks, mesmerized by the ship's flags that hung heavily in the mist. A growing number of boats—pleasure boats, rentals, yachts—had appeared out of the haze and plowed in aimless circles, trying to gain a last view of the flying machine as it sank slowly into the sea. Beyond them, a three-masted sailing ship approached slowly. It towered over the water and the other craft like a ghost ship, fading in and out of the apocalyptic mist.

Special provisions had been stored to commemorate the Frenchman's successful flight across the sea. But in view of what seemed closer to the heroic, or at least closer to complete demise, the captain ordered to have the cases brought from the hold anyway and the bottles opened. There were five officers altogether up on the flying bridge with Latham, while the entire navy had gathered on the deck below, leaning over the rail, staring helplessly at the aeroship.

"To the aeronaut!"

The captain raised his glass to the pilot and then to his crew, now gathered around the ship's cannonry.

"To the aviator!"

"To France."

"Vive la France!"

Along with his blue sailor's jacket, he now wore a mate's cap, as if he'd become a mascot. His countrymen could make a celebration out of anything. But the sight of the soaked, half-submerged wings injured him, finally. He'd failed.

Below, on the deck, a fiddler began to play, and a sailor waved a tricolor back and forth, a glorious victory in semaphore. A group of sailors began to sing. One saluted. The ship motored forward until the *Antoinette* lay in its lee, protected from the wind until the tug *Calaisien* could arrive. To keep the aeroplane from sinking, the captain ordered it lashed to the ship's rails.

∽∘∾

We watched the plane that had been so competently and historically landed in the ocean now dragged up along the hull of the *Calaisien* by the tug's crane. The boom proved too short; once it was hoisted into position, the wings of the *Antoinette* struck the hull with each swell. A mate climbed from his rowboat onto the plane's wing to better rig the aeroplane up, but he fell—not bending the spars or slipping off the side, but plunging straight through the wing's canvas. For a moment it appeared as though an additional rescue might be needed. Fished quickly from the sea, the wrung-wet sailor jumped right on to the aeroplane from his new station aboard the life raft.

Again the crane began its work.

The *Antoinette* rose, drifting and knocking up against the tug's hull, bending under the weight of the seawater that filled it and spilled from its sides. One wing warped heavily, and then snapped in half. One catastrophic break followed another, until soon the damage done by the sailor falling through the wing seemed small and incidental. Even the fuselage gave way. As soon as the horrible mess had been hauled above deck, Levavasseur asked that the *Harpon* be brought alongside, if only to take inventory of all the reasons he must now order a completely new machine if he ever wished to fly the Channel. It was a hopeless task. Mangled and shattered, just ruined, better if both wings had been shorn off. Everywhere the fabric hung in soaked, jagged sheaves, the wooden spars in splinters.

A small armada of pleasure boats and fishing vessels followed the *Harpon*, which in turn followed the *Calaisien*, where the *Antoinette* hung like a poorly gutted fish strung from the tug's crane. As the navy ship steamed into port, the inventor stood stoic on its deck, his dark, somber collar lifting in the July wind.

45.

AS IF PART OF A GREAT VICTORY PARADE, a steady swarm of well-wishers made their way along the tractor roads to the harbor town of Calais. Motors of the well-to-do chugged behind, impatient to pass. Meanwhile César and I watched on from the empty tent of the Antoinette motorworks, strangely empty now without an aeroplane inside it, and no one knowing if the ship would ever return.

"Good God all-bloody mighty, Potato. Just a few minutes ago we thought our friend was lost to the deep."

The birdman had fallen into the sea and been fished from the waves—like a watery Phoenix.

He survived!

In its way, the disastrous outcome of the day was more mythic, more amazing than success would have been. News spread quickly, though reports varied. Some had it that the aeroship had actually sunk below the waves, that Latham had to swim for his life. I pictured a sailor firing a projectile life ring into the waves. César and I figured that seeing our friend in his hero's hour would be virtually impossible in the small, overrun town of Calais. We remained behind in the striped canvas lean-to at the old Tunnel Company building, content for now that Latham was safe.

From down in the harbor came a triumph of boat horns and bells.

≈≋

Around noon an unexpected motor came bounding in.
The car was filmed with layers of dust and mud on the underside, as if just come from a long journey. Stranger still, the car was burgeoning with womanhood—scarves, hats, riding nets—and a child. The motorcar seemed strangely familiar to me at first. I thought I saw Simone riding in it along with women with netting hung from their hats to shield their faces, like beekeepers. The bonnets of the beekeepers stopped their toppling as the vehicle came to a halt.

Simone was of course not wearing any such heavy equipment, and the more I looked, the more I was sure I was seeing things. It seemed both perfectly natural yet utterly impossible that she should appear all of a sudden in a motorcar. In writing all those letters to her from the coast, I'd thought it mattered little if I actually sent them or not. We haunted each other; we circled, she and I, like ghosts. When she stepped down from the motor car, I was brought back to that spring day when she emerged from the carriage of the professor and the nuns. And just as on that day, she had a completely different aspect about her, as if she'd grown to where I no longer knew her. In just a few months, her face had sharpened with age, and now contained ways of looking at things and concerns I knew nothing about. She untied her blue printed kerchief from her head, and her hair fell stiff and wild about her face, wind-tousled by the long journey.

Then something just as unlikely occurred. Once she removed her beekeeper's hat, I realized that the chauffeur of the motorcar was none other than Antoinette herself, in tight hair netting and goggles. She looked defiant like a wrestler, but with that elusive beauty, grim beneath her fierce mask. Rushing down from the motorcar, she demanded to see that the aeronaut was safe, despite César's assurance that all was well, or, more to the point, that there'd be a public rally held that evening to celebrate the pilot's successful "ditch" into the sea. César even offered to take Antoinette up to the Marconi office himself, to view the accounts of the heroic rescue. But no. Antoinette insisted on seeing firsthand how their company's employee had fared. She feared for the pilot's spirit as much as anything.

Immediately she drove off, taking César with her.

～～

The striped awning I sat under sagged in the lazy seaside afternoon. There was no aeroplane here anymore—no crew, no newspapermen, nobody else at all. All was lost at sea.

When I saw Simone approach, I did even not stop to think of how she had come here, or why. She asked if I wanted to be with the others, to catch sight of the birdman and witness all the great to-do.

No, no, I told her, it would be hard to see him right now. But if she wanted, we could go on a favorite walk of mine.

We left the old brick building and walked along a path to the cliffs. I pointed out how all the houses were painted the same—the same dirty white stucco with green trim.

"So you wrote me," she said, "in a letter."

I watched how Simone squinted over the fields, so different from the fields back home, how they swept out and out and kept going. It seemed that the way she perceived things had changed. She stared more intently at my mouth when I spoke. She stared at everyone's mouth more intently. She'd been so attentive to Antoinette and her sister when they spoke of the arrangements made with the hotel. Her speech had vastly improved over the summer, which must have been a result of her studies with the professor. When she studied the way I spoke, it was as if her balance was about to give way, as if she might fall into the point of her overly focused attention. I kept losing track of what I was about to say, and let my arms drop. She wasn't watching my gestures at all. Her time with the professor had changed everything.

I asked her what drove her to come here. "A woman came to me," she said, "an angel dressed like a lady. In her hands was a stack of letters, written by you. She said she could take me to you."

The path wound around the cliffs down to the beach, where we found a stretch of empty chairs in a row. It was noon, and the morning's fog had burned off to reveal a hazy, windy sea. Patches of seaweed lay on the sand like abandoned beards, surrounded by a hovering of flies.

And the wind brought the sharp scents of salt air and rotting sea vegetation.

Simone's impaired sense of balance made the going hard for her in the sand, so she took off her shoes and carried them as we walked on that strip of solid beach that shimmered where the waves fell back. Closer to the jetty, the chairs were actually occupied by tourists, Parisians who sat in dark clothes beneath black umbrellas and watched the sailboats cut back and forth across the waves, one sloop so close I could hear the violent whipping of its sails as it tacked.

Simone, of course, could hear none of it. She stood still for long periods in order to feel the breaking of the ocean over the sand beneath her. That last advance of swift, foaming seawater—moving in a gray sheet at first coming in, and later going out—made us feel as though we were moving, dizzy with sunlight.

"I've been having the same dream," I said, which was not quite true. I'd had the dream only once, but it had fused itself into my waking. "Ever since I've been here," I said, "I dreamed of you and I—we go on a boat."

With one hand, Simone held onto her shoes, and with the other, she picked up a half shell from the beach and held it up to me and squeezed my arm. She had never been to the sea before either. She spoke aloud just as I could feel her urge to gesture, even as she hung onto the shoes. But now she pointed out over the horizon and said aloud, "Bateau," pointing to another sail, farther out. A thin cushion of mist hid the waters out in the middle, and above it England seemed to float. The more we stared, the more vague the island appeared, until it too shrank from sight, enveloped by thin clouds.

"Where do we go?" Simone said now, waving her shoes about, and my attention fell into her gestures. "In your dream?"

"Just"—my hands moved in answer—"on a boat."

"Yes, but where to?"

"Nowhere." I shrugged. "Or anywhere. We just—keep going."

❧❧

Evening fell over the harbor town of Calais as Simone and I approached it. On either side of the main road into town, the crushed stones had been freshly raked beneath beech trees in a row. In the cooling air, Simone hooked my arm for warmth. And instead of striding in silence, she could now speak out into the dark, while I had to wait until we were beneath the light of a gas lamp to reply, sometimes having to stop altogether so that she could follow the movements of my face. And when that didn't work, I had to let go of her altogether and gesture. Then we resumed our walking. The boulevard had the air of a carnival—street vendors, country folk, musicians, nuns, dogs, children, gentlemen and ladies out strolling like great courtesans to the hotels and restaurants. As Simone and I neared the commotion of the town square, we were immediately approached by César, who was more than eager to give us an account of the day.

Why was it that kindly people often called Simone an "old soul"? Surely it was her apparent humorlessness, her reluctant expressions, and her ever-attentive eyes. César behaved as if it were his duty to speak very carefully to her, giving a deliberate account of what happened to Latham that day.

On dry land, he'd been besieged—by the press, by the crowd, by dignitaries of influence who felt they should stand the downed aeronaut a drink. All that day Latham strode around in his new navy-issue jacket; he joked, he promenaded. The crowd was the most curious mix of tourists and locals. Those who followed him most closely either had some business with him or wanted to be a part of the public photography. Tourists and children followed him around, as did farmers, everyone, everywhere, always a crowd, sea-salt characters, adoring teenage girls walking hitched at the elbow, throwing flower petals into the air. Under a sky of gathering clouds, fireworks were set off in the aviator's honor, paper lanterns hung from the trees, and an impromptu celebration began in the form of a gathering of newspapermen. As the clouds darkened, the evening turned warmer. Smells of low tide and tarred dock pylons came up from the harbor.

The first to take the podium was an ancient dignitary, the president of the now defunct Tunnel Company, rumored to be ninety-nine years of age. His face was wrinkled as a shriveled peach. Two stout women led him up to the podium. Then *Le Grand Visionnaire de l'Âge Industriel* spoke:

"You are my rival," he began, his voice wavering in and out, and he paused, as if slurping soup. "You wish to go over, while our aim was to pass under *La Manche*. But you have done magnificently, *mon cher.*" Unsure what to do next, he simply stood there tentatively within his frock coat until his handlers led him from the stage.

After that—the entirety of his trembling, venerable speech—the crowd broke into outrageous celebration, just as the sky rumbled from far out over the sea with a slow, sullen thunder.

Then the Fish Mayor stood at the podium and quieted the crowd. His whiskers shook enthusiastically with each word.

"Like Icarus, here is a man who has flown close to the sun. But also, he is the first to fly close to the sea, and close to our hearts. Half bird, half man, and half—, half—, *fish*. Yet! Unlike Icarus, he comes back to us."

The crowd reacted with laughter as jolly as the mayor's, who, surprised at his own wit, left the podium with a smile absolutely bubbling over, shaking hands and carrying on.

Then, from above the sea, a sudden clap of thunder broke alarmingly close.

It pounded the rooftops, and shook the trees and windowpanes, and then rumbled off into the distance.

A few of the crowd ran for cover, but most moved in closer to the stage as Levavasseur was introduced to the podium. He took a small slip of paper ponderously from his coat pocket and unfolded it with great dignity. It looked as if he might have written his speech on an envelope or back of the dailies, and the paper was highly wrinkled, as if visited and revisited all over again. Then he read, a bit self-consciously, in a voice so low that the crowd had to move in closer to hear. He was greatly disappointed, he began, that they were not just then celebrating in Dover, *Angleterre*. But the day's journey into the sea had given him an even greater faith in the tough little flier that was the *Antoinette*. She'd kept his pilot safe. That was the main thing, and also above water, and dry, too, most of which must be attributed to the skill of the craftsmen who had built her. What was important was that they had developed a machine that could go on land, in the air, and in the water. It ran, it flew, it swam. *C'est un triomphe!* It gave him a great sense of pride also to know that our pilot, the courageous Hubert Latham, the most skilled aeroman in all of France and the world, was ready to try and fly again, crossing the sea to England. Already a new *Antoinette* was being shipped from Paris, to arrive the very next day!

At the height of the cheers and applause for the brave birdman of England and France, who was to speak next, Latham was offered a kiss from the town's young Fish Princess, crowned with a tiara and draped with a sash, a little plump, and very flushed. So he kissed her quickly, to wild applause and shouts of public optimism, just as the clouds released their heavy summer downpour, and the crowd ran for cover.

46.

LATHAM AND HIS PARAMOUR FROM PARISIAN circles had finally escaped the crowds and the rain to sit at one of the shadowy tables in the basement Hall of Neptune for a *champagne demi-sec* and absinthe.

"Ah, there you are," said César.

We took chairs at the next table over.

"Hardly," said Latham. "Surviving this day has been more trying than a rescue at sea."

"Is that so?" said the diva, who unpinned the wet hat from her head and shook loose a few strands of her luxurious hair.

"Until my glorious rescue." Latham lowered a hand over hers and patted it. Being with her seemed to somehow help separate him from the crowd. "My savior." He addressed both our table and the next over, consisting of dignitaries and personages and the like.

Apparently Simone and I were not the only ones spellbound by the Parisian actress. Of course Daphné de Cassandra wished to witness more of Latham's flights. But she felt she must always be in Paris with her daughter, who really lived under the roof of the grandmother, allowing the illustrious diva of the Mimes and Les Folies-Gobelins to follow her gift: that of speaking and gesturing before the bright electric chandeliers for a hall filled with so many eager, awaiting eyes. It was a duty of passion for her to live under the sway of the moment like this, always in the public's eye, even when no one was around. It was she, Cassandra de Dauphinois, who would pin a blood-red rose to the lapel of Latham's coat just before any major flight of record, or even before a quick publicity stunt to further the reputation of either Levavasseur's engine or flying machine. Latham, of course, would receive all of the adoration and acclaim; her part was that of a shy, naive beauty with lowered eyes, who would pin the rose to his coat and look up at him once with a brief, salacious grin. Then she'd turn away again with reverent shoulders, increasing, through her display, Latham's fame as a devil-may-care *homme du monde*.

Meanwhile, the man of the hour hunched forward with a bone-thin intensity beneath the borrowed navy-issue jacket, staring at nothing below the heavy beams of the basement barroom. Here in the Hall of Neptune, crowded with seaside folk, the aeronaut could feel anonymous. The regular customers merely tolerated him, despite all the gawkers in the town of Calais, searching everywhere for a glimpse of the birdman. Soon they would all be gone, and the quiet seaside life of the villagers would return. Still there was a mild, grumbling curiosity surrounding the pilot, but that too would vanish.

At the top of the stairs, the two Gastambide sisters, Sophie and Antoinette, appeared, and suddenly the smoky hall seemed to brighten. Not so much by an increase of light—for it still had the perennial comfort of a dark public house, lit by dim yellow flames—but by a rise in voices and an attention in the air

The two Gastambides stood before the low table with the silent understanding of siblings, who, over the years, have established a constant friendship, while Cassandra stared back at them from kohl-rimmed cat's eyes. Glancing down at the taffeta trim of her sleeves, she pulled up her stiffened baleen collar.

"*Ma chère*," said César, stepping back to make a place for both of the sisters to sit and immediately cozying up to Sophie, as though this was an expected rendezvous.

"I am so glad you're safe," said Antoinette.

"Whatever do you mean?" asked Latham.

Antoinette said nothing, and once again the dark waters of her prophecy moved as a dream between them. For a while it seemed as though Latham felt guilty. No, not quite guilty, but constrained, yes, as if he'd broken a pact with her.

"Yes. Yes, I am. Thank you. Thank you for the cautionary tale." And Latham went on with the introductions, beginning with Cassandra de Dauphinois.

"You mean de Dauphinois of the theater?" asked Antoinette.

The olive-skinned actress, with her thick mass of curls piled up on top of her head, nodded ever so slightly, acting out a modesty that was like an unspoken pact between them all.

"These are my two dear cousins," said Latham to Cassandra.

Here Antoinette bowed her head in reverence to the great renown of the actress. "I loved you in Molière's *L'École des femmes*."

"My dear—" Cassandra fell into deeper tones of confidence, fingering the wings of her collar bones just below the neck and then running her fingers over her necklace and across her clavicle. "That performance was so long ago, if I'm thinking of the same. I'm so overjoyed that you not only saw it but remembered. I don't think I can ever again deliver anything like it, though I am so grateful to you for remembering."

Then an obviously soused gentleman, wearing a navy-blue blazer with a coat of arms stitched to his breast pocket, stopped gravely before Latham's table. With the solemn dignity of the intoxicated, he raised his glass to the low ceiling and beheld it as though it were a torch. He held this pose of triumph for so long, we wondered about his wits.

"*Vive Latham!*" he announced proudly and stoically, and, staring at his glass, which he still held aloft, began to sing "La Marseillaise." Quickly the piano player joined in, and soon the entire room was singing the national anthem on the aviator's behalf. Afterward the piano player started in with a folk song. By the time the pianist had played beyond the first verse and chorus, Cassandra was the only one singing:

> How I regret
> My dimpled arms,
> My well-made legs,
> And my vanished charms!

When the song ended, Antoinette said, "What a wonderful pleasure it must be, to be able to sing with such beauty!"

"It is not always such a blessing," said Cassandra, "to live under the sway of your emotions as passionately as the theater requires."

"Still," said Antoinette, "it seems so much like a dream. Like a wish that will never come true: to travel somewhere that opens you to dreaming. Or to be kidnapped; that sounds inviting, does it not? To the imagination. To be onstage. To be an inventor, like a man. Or to own a great possession." She looked at Latham and Cassandra with a hint of reproach. "But I don't think such things are ever possible. Only to persons such as yourself." She stood and gave Latham her hand. "I am so truly relieved you are safe," she said, and then excused herself and said good night to her sister.

Cassandra turned to Sophie and spoke of the wonderful presence of her sister Antoinette. "I hope we are joined by you two often."

"Oh yes. *Nous aussi!*" Sophie shot an amused look at the actress, then at Latham, then at the actress again, her eyes dancing.

"Yes," he said. "Let's all go on a picnic together, shall we?"

"Here? Or in Paris?"

Sophie was even more delighted that Hubert's chanteuse had entertained the invitation further. "Here, here. Still, Paris is better, I think." And again she glanced between Latham and actress.

Latham stood and excused himself. Tomorrow he should be awake early enough to receive the new aeroplane, arriving in parts from Paris, he said, and headed back to the hotel along the cliff path, alone.

47.

Unable to sleep, I went down to the hotel lobby well before dawn. Simone and I had not set a time to meet in the morning, so I had prepared myself for a long wait, but she was already seated on a chair beside the window, looking out. We took a long walk along the blue fields before sunrise, talking about our valley home and her studies at the Suffering Silence. I sensed acutely how there were vast portions of me that could be animated only when I was with Simone. And like the swallows that dove down over the fields, our thoughts flew up over the houses and cliffs and out to sea. Long before the train was set to arrive we found ourselves at the train station, where many from the Antoinette motorworks were already gathered, among them César.

He greeted us on the station platform and gazed up into the tranquil sky, full of promise. He saw bright, fair, rounded clouds, sailing their way from England. He was a great fan of the weather. He was a great fan of the clouds. He missed them, he said disparagingly to me and especially Simone, almost as much as he missed the silver aeroship of the *Buontemponi*. And my heart swelled at the thought of riding again in the balloon, but this time with Simone, who was scanning the clouds as if she were already deep within them, full of her calm, placid wonder.

César was surprised to find an old balloonist friend of his, Alfred Leblanc of the *Aéro-Club de France*, standing on the station platform and waiting for the train along with the rest of us. A stickler for manners, meticulous in all respects, Leblanc inspired César to recall the simple, carefree days of ballooning, before all of this clamor of attention fell upon the aeroplanes. Once again César became the Explorer, the Antiquarian of Synchronic Histories, who had sailed the English Channel by air as often as any explorer he knew—he had sailed from *Angleterre* to France, true, not only in June but also in the winter, when the damp winds blow fiercely toward the continent. Leblanc listened without as much as a smile—thin-lipped, matter-of-fact, and eagerly awaiting the train as much as anyone, the only one present with an umbrella.

The last to arrive was the inventor Levavasseur, who walked from his motorcar and joined the Gastambide family already on the platform. To accompany his sailor's cap, he now wore the woolen sweater favored by the local fishermen. Relaxed and cheerful, he told us he was awaiting the first component of his new *Antoinette VII*: the engine, again a fifty-horsepower V8. The rest of the aeroplane would arrive piecemeal by train over the next few days.

Even for spare parts, yesterday's sea-wreck of an aeroplane would be useless. It had been left overnight at the docks, and the lingering crowd had worked it over like a pack of grave robbers. By the morning, it was like the picked-over carcass of a mythic bird, drying out in the morning sun. She would be a comely ship, the new *Antoinette*, with more or less the same lines as her wrecked predecessor, but this model would be steered by wing-warping, the system of the Wrights, which was thought to be even more effective on monoplanes.

Latham was at the station, too, leaning toward the investors talking with *Le Père*. One of these was Antoinette, who stood as concerned as any financier.

Very quietly, though, she said to Latham, "I had no idea you attended the theater."

"What? I am to live forever in the past?"

"I've enjoyed her performances very much," she said. "And you?" She arranged her hat to cover her face.

"Look at them," said César, who turned an amused face up to the sky, just as Latham and Antoinette separated. "How easily the clouds sail across the sea."

"Yes," said Levavasseur in mock grumpiness. "But *from* England."

"To or fro, back and forth." Latham shrugged. "We've waited a month and a day for weather like this."

"Two months," said Levavasseur. "And still these winds are stronger than some days we let pass."

"Friends," said César. "Behold the shifting shapes of the sky, so regular and friendly, as they make their way across the sea. These are the clouds of fair weather, are they not? Ones that bring to mind things pleasant and hopeful to behold. Like fishes. Or romping horses."

Yes, they were the clouds of voyages aboard ships that sail the sea, clouds of hope and clouds of glory.

"Or!" said Gastambide, "the profile of your favorite politician emblazoned upon your money."

"Yes," Levavasseur grunted. "Let's hope these clouds bring us some of that."

∽∘≈

The train arrived, announced by vast quantities of coal-black smoke rising above the treetops along the line. Passengers stared blankly through the cars' grimy windows as it rolled in, oblivious to the fact that the engine that drew them was also delivering its new promise—of more machinery, from a greater, grander era yet to come, where overwhelming white ships sailed the sky and brought back their denizens, from one city portal to the next, in a world made pure by thickened clouds of spent fuel and steam. These new galleys would not need the sea. Instead they'd set sail to all cities at once, unbound by roads and held aloft by combinations of wings, balloonish reservoirs, propellers, paddles, keels, and sails. They would send and receive their messages, one to the other, floating like an entire city unto itself, reaching ever outward. And each city below would have its own busy aerodrome, ready to gather these floating islands and their traveling populations.

Smoke and steam were the sweat and will of the engine. Sparks flew, brakes howled, and the great grinding burden came to a halt.

Of the seven train cars, three were for freight, and one flatcar had a green-striped circus top tied across it, protecting a large, familiar contraption. I beamed with anticipation and pride. The new *Antoinette* had arrived early, its dismantled wings beside it, I thought, and gestured to Simone. What providence!

But right away there was something altogether odd about the shape beneath the soiled canvas top. It was too small, for one thing. A lorry pulled up beside the train, and a group of workmen I'd never seen before emerged from one of the train's passenger cars. Efficiently they began taking boxes and provisions down from the flatcar. Then, pulling off the canvas cover, they lifted the entire ship. For such a large machine it took only a few men to lift it, and without a word of instruction, as if in a well-worn routine, they set the aeroplane down upon the lorry's flatbed and tied it up. The plane was all business—squat, dirty, and well flown, the fabric of the right-side wing already degenerated from the castor oil thrown by the engine.

Then from the train, Blériot, the famous aviator, appeared, with his rounded shoulders and tired mustache. He made a miserable hop down from the passenger car, and then his wife stepped down too, carrying a set of crutches, which she handed over to him along with a kiss. Then with a much-practiced hobble step, he fit himself over the crutches and began a begrudging, invalid sort of walk. One of his feet, which he would not let touch ground, was thickly bandaged. Despite a stubborn impatience, it was very slowly that he lumped along the length of the train platform, past Levavasseur and Latham and all the investors and workmen of the *Société Anonyme des Avions et Moteurs Antoinette*, of which Blériot was still vice president, though no longer a member.

From beneath his troubled brow, the *Aviateur Militant*, as he was known, looked up at last. "Léon," he said.

"Louis," said Levavasseur.

And Blériot continued at his slow, brooding pace until he was joined by his workmen at the far end of the train, where Leblanc also waited, the esteemed member of the *Aéro-Club de France* to greet the newcomer and offer his advice.

Like an angry sea captain, Levavasseur turned to the crew. "Where's our engine?" he barked. "It's on the train here somewhere, isn't it?"

The brothers Welféringer looked at each other, tentative, uneasy, dumbstruck. We approached the train, unsure of which boxcar to search.

❧❧

We worked until well past midnight. Normally we would have waited for the rest of the machine to arrive. But now, like a heart removed from the body, the new engine needed the ship's viscera around it to make it pump. This we scabbed from the wasted sea-wreck of a plane down in the harbor. It still had a fuel tank, which we dismantled and screwed down to a wooden crate. Because the engine needed a crank to start, we equipped it with the backup propeller and mounted the whole heavy ordeal up on a block to allow the blade to spin.

César strolled in just then with his balloonist colleague, Alfred Leblanc. Although they were in effect auxiliaries in different camps, they were also monks from the same order, who for the moment saw the competition as mere rhetoric, subsumed by a higher cause. Leblanc informed them that Blériot had chosen as his camp a small farm nearby at Les Baraques. And the Comte de Lambert had also announced to the office of the *Daily Mail* of his intention to cross *la Manche*.

"What if we all three fly at once?" Latham asked.

"There are not enough navy escorts," said Levavasseur.

"There's a meeting tomorrow morning, here, at the Marconi operator's office," said Leblanc. "Blériot asked me to tell you, so that you can also attend."

"Then Blériot will not be flying tomorrow." Levavasseur made a wide, superstitious face out the canvas opening and to the weather beyond. "At least not early, he won't. Thank god for this weather."

"We depend on our old enemy, Aeolus," said Latham, "to ground our new one."

"So the race is on," said César.

"Not yet," said Levavasseur. "We need a machine first."

48.

THE TRAINS DELIVERING THE NEW *ANTOINETTE* were late. All morning and on into the afternoon, one or another of us was squinting up into the clouds above the station, listening for the whine of Blériot's twenty-five-horsepower engine. I had a supernatural respect for the prowess of this new rival and ex-business partner. We'd all seen Blériot fly at the maneuver grounds back in Paris. We knew he was an expert at the crash landing. It was from him that Latham had learned the art of throwing himself onto a wing just before impact, sacrificing the machine but softening the blow so that he could walk away from the incident. But Latham had used the technique only once, almost twice, whereas Blériot, the Prince of Bad Luck, had crashed various aeroplanes well over two dozen times.

The crutches Blériot presently wore were due to severe burns he'd suffered on his left foot recently, when the asbestos lining of the engine exhaust of his number XII had blown out—two different times. For this attempt to cross the Channel, Blériot planned on taking his crutches with him, tied to the fuselage on one side. On the other, he'd have an inflatable airbag, intended to keep his aeroplane afloat should he fall into the sea. The jacket he would wear was made of cork. Perhaps the *Aviateur Militant* would take off without first consulting the wireless and

keep sailing his way out to England. Or perhaps, during the meeting at
the Marconi station, he'd simply announce that he'd begin his flight.
How would Latham ever have a chance? All we had was a twisted,
busted-up machine down at the harbor and a wholly untried engine.

⸲❧⸱❧

That night, under the clearest weather, Levavasseur's new aeroplane
took shape. César wondered aloud whether the absence of all but a
few newspaper reporters meant they were following the activity of the
Blériot camp instead. By midnight, the *Antoinette VII* was well enough
put together that Latham climbed into the cockpit and in his usual impatience, extreme with fatigue, bid us to start it up.

The engine roared into life. The blast from the prop stirred the
tarps. They billowed and flapped, and beyond them, Antoinette Gastambide held on to her parasol handle, braced against the wind.

The engine died down, and the canvas walls of the work area
relaxed and floated down too.

"When will it be ready?" asked Antoinette, loudly, in a public way.

Latham shrugged. "When I'm over England."

"How long until then?" she asked.

"Tomorrow," said one of the brothers.

"Yes, a day," another grumbled from somewhere beneath the tarps.

"In the best of all possible worlds, three," said Levavasseur. "Three
days."

"As an investor," said Antoinette, "I'm wondering if it's wise to take
an entirely new machine across the ocean on its maiden flight."

"No. No, it is not wise," said Latham, climbing down from the wing.
"Not wise at all. Gentlemen . . . Madame . . . To the new *Antoinette*. May
she be christened in England."

"Hear, hear."

The brothers, thus inspired, resumed their work in the dim light
under the rustling tarps.

⸲❧⸱❧

Late that night, Latham walked up the stairwell of the Calais hotel. Alone, exhausted, he had finally felt the full impact of his rival's aeroplane on the coast, and it numbed him.

Everything around him seemed dismal and surreal in this stupor, another day begun in the dead of night without his notice or under-standing. So why shouldn't the beauty of his dreams also appear for no reason other than simply that she should? Like a self-conscious Cleopatra, she stood poised at the head of the stairs. Who was it that moved aside to let the other pass? Still, they kept moving in each other's way. Two steps above, her dress spread out and blocked what little light penetrated the gloom of the stairwell, so that he still could not make out her expression as she lifted the veil from her face. He cleaved to her dress. He nuzzled his face into the linen flounces at her hips and felt the tense back of her legs above the knee, beneath the straps and girders of her undergarments.

He asked, "Are you here to forecast another of my gloomy events?"

"Who was that woman you were with?"

"I introduced you."

"Yes. But do you even like her?"

"Well, she's not married, for one thing."

"Must you mock me?" she said, her fingers as nervous and unplanned as a change of thought.

He wrapped his arms farther around her and picked her up as if to carry her in a standing position up the steps.

"*What,*" she said, "are you trying to do? You can't just pick me up and arrange me as if I were another one of your things."

Latham released her, stepped back, and looked austerely up the stairwell past her. "Will you allow me to pass, then, so I may get to my room?"

"You just picked me up off the floor."

"I did?"

"You see, all along I've been worried about your health, and now your back too, when you so desperately need rest. Just look at you!"

"You exaggerate," he said, and tried to walk past her. "Out of kindness."

"Wait, please. I found a letter I've been meaning to give to you."

"You *found* it?"

"Well. Yes. I mean ... yes."

She retreated past him down the steps, her dress rustling like a shuffling deck of cards, and he followed. She continued through the lobby and out to a neutral spot on the porch below, and it reminded Latham of the night on the Fish Mayor's veranda. Now, though, at the height of summer, the thin clouds vanished into long streamers in one of the clearest, darkest skies Latham had ever seen. The wind was electric, and from beyond the cliffs sounded the regular advances of the sea, always the same, throwing out their questions and answers, distant and near, always in flux, like life, enlarged, so rarely, Antoinette. He sensed the mysterious floating of her skin around her bones. Sudden changes of mood passed over her, animating her, and over her eyes, darkened and inflamed from a lack of sleep, fell long curling lashes of disappointment.

"What do you mean to say, you found it?"

"What do you want me to say? What I have to say will be in your hands, if I give it to you. If you come with me, I will show you."

She led him back through the darkened lobby and into the street. The unsteady wind had extinguished all but a few of the gas lamps in the town square, where just two nights before, the great public rally for his crash landing into the sea had taken place. Now the last flames in their glass cases flickered, nearly out. And the leaves of the beech trees shook and rustled, their branches yielding to the gusts. On the boardwalk, with its abandoned disquiet, he had the urge to reach out and grab her and turn her around to face what had become a madness. But walking beside her also calmed him, as composed as she was, with her arms folded, drawing her shawl in. They walked past a marble-tiled stairway that led to a terrace of Doric columns. It was the public entryway to a civic hall, where beyond the ancient threshold, the laws and sacred values were stored. Beside him Antoinette seemed inaccessible, her head bent down, leaning forward into her pace. All he could do was walk beside her, feeling mute. The constant disturbance of the sea surged like blood through his temples. Walking beside her, he felt constricted and bruised, as if slapped by an open palm across the ribs.

They took the road back to the Hôtel Neptune, past moonlit fields of grain stretching out, moving like turbulent waves on the sea, desolate and alive. Looking down, she was too lost within her purpose to see a thing. Latham wished only that their walk would be over, so that he could talk to her again.

Inside, the hotel lobby was even more desolate and somnolent. In the hallway upstairs she reached for a door handle before she turned to him, as if to quiet them both.

"Here. The letter is inside."

He followed her into her quarters. A child's crib had been set in the parlor, and one of the adjoining doors was left ajar. Antoinette shut it, and let her voice drop.

"Here." She reached into a small valise on a nightstand and handed him the letter without looking at him. Instead she stared down at the crib where her toddler son slept, wrapped in soft wool blankets. Then she put her ear to the closed bedroom door and listened.

"The governess," she whispered. "Wait here."

She opened the door and disappeared behind it. While waiting for her, Latham peered down into the crib, moved by a curiosity and then a godliness he felt even in this pale little creature. The child slept with the perfect serenity that only the small and helpless can achieve, and Latham envied this tranquil innocence, undisturbed by fate, or failure, or days and nights of wanting and regret, and he worried for the sleeping child that these things would show soon enough.

When Antoinette returned, she held out a thick bundle of letters before her. Her hat was off, her hair was down, her beauty overflowed.

"There," she said, walking nearer to the door, as if he should too. "First, I trouble over your health. And then your heart too, or what's left of it. You say the most awful things. I wish you the best of luck and happiness after you make it to England. Good luck. Now please, good night."

She opened the door to let him out, but he stopped outside in the unlit hall, baffled by the bulk of the letters in his hands. She also was still standing at the half-closed door, leaning into it while holding it ajar. Evidently, there was more to discuss.

∽≈

She walked out in the windy street, rubbing her hands up and down her bare elbows and arms; she'd forgotten her hat and shawl. Latham took off his jacket to put over her, but in her distraction she walked out from underneath it just as he reached out, and it fell to the ground. Stooping to retrieve it, he hurried after her. She kept her gaze down, apparently absorbed in the air somewhere before her, or her feet or the rustling seas of wheat. One shoulder of her dress had slipped when the coat fell, so that her shoulders seemed half naked.

"I can't get that dream out of my head," she said. "Why did I have that dream of you in the sea? When . . . look. Here you are. Just look at you. You come back to me."

And Latham fell back into the strange haunted feelings of his youth, when he had only one more year to live. Except now he had only a week. Or a day. Just a day. When he'd much prefer to die in the comfort of his bed than drown at sea. How did she ever instill those feelings in him, again, so desperate and so near the end?

"Such nervous superstitions." He laughed, with a sneer. "People have them all the time. Do you really believe in them? That you have access—into the future?" He grabbed her and peered into her face. "That you sleep below some sort of—Delphic oracle?"

"No," she said, wide-eyed and sober, suddenly spooked. "No. I don't believe in such things, either."

"Good," he said, and let go of her, and turned down the road. "Good."

"But if you should ever crash into the sea again—my father's patience in this enterprise is not unlimited. These are not your toys to keep ruining as you please."

"*Toys?* Everyone expects me to go—León, your father, everyone. What choice do I have? If I don't go now, it's as if I do nothing. Or worse. If ever I had a purpose—"

"What if the other pilot leaves before you?"

"I can't think of him. Just where I have to go."

"So you believe you were put here for a purpose?"

And just as she said it, Latham could tell she'd wished she had not, as he finished the thought for her—that one could dream or have an intuition about such a purpose. And once again the dream hung before them, like a mistake, like a bottle of india ink spilled out across the sky, a dark flood that made the stars flicker. It stirred the wind that drove the clouds against the moon, which seemed to struggle just to hold its place in the sky. The winds parted round the stars too, lighting them up at their fuses, and they had never seemed so bright, though still they flickered, some of them, as did the distant lights atop the cliffs of England, or maybe they were the lights of boats below. Here and there a glowing dome signified an English town beyond the sea, and these were fixed.

Without Latham noticing it, they had been following a route that simply went round and round the hotel. When her toddler began to cry, Antoinette could hear it from the opened second-story window. "Oh, please my sweet, stop," she said. "Please." And Latham watched her hitch her dress up so that she could run the short distance to the hotel and up the flight of stairs to the veranda. The doors opened, and she disappeared.

～～

Latham stood outside the dark hotel long enough to see Antoinette's window dimly light up, and a lone figure, pace into view. The old familiar pull had him now, like a turning, tortured music. No, not quite tortured, more like a broken music he longed to hear all over again, to relive its magic heartache.

There was nothing left for Latham to do except walk around her hotel a few last times, her lit room filling him with its unseen dramas of yearning and dreaming under the waves of interrupted sleep. He felt all over again those trips of his youth when the two families—his and the Gastambides'—made their seasonal rounds. There was a restless traveling quality to his memories. Antoinette's face hovered over a constantly shifting scene—winters in Paris, summers up north, off to Cannes, Jouy-en-Josas, St. Moritz, Schaden, Innsbruck, in some vast plaza hotel, a shared summer home, an Alpine resort. All night came the furtive sounds: a door opening, the creaking of a floorboard, the pop of someone's knee. Then stocking feet tripping lightly over the hardwood.

The hotel window went dark, the figure disappeared, and Latham walked the tractor paths back to his own hotel room in town.

49.

THE FOLLOWING DAY DAWNED ON A QUANDARY. We desperately needed more time, a window in which we could send Latham up on a test flight of the new *Antoinette*. But in the same window of tranquil weather, Blériot would be on his way to England, sure to win the *Daily Mail*'s prize if Latham weren't also out over the sea. Luckily for us, perhaps, the winds off the coast had regained their force, stranding us under the familiar unsettling sky.

The rigors of the race kept Latham at the old Tunnel Company building well past noon. Overnight it seemed that he had been plunged into aviation's golden age. With the great race came important committees from Paris and London and tedious reviews of the rules. The meeting at the Marconi operator's office began when the navy arrived, and as many reporters as would fit. The air grew tense and officious. Blériot was there with his wife, his crutches, and a colleague, an eccentric Italian engineer with waxed mustaches and the mouth of a trooper, who designed the very engine that had replaced the original *Antoinette* motor in Blériots' machine.

When it was established which naval escort would follow whom across the sea in case all three aviators were in the air at once—for the

Comte de Lambert had officially thrown his hat into the ring—the first mate of the *Harpon* wished good luck to Latham personally.

"Monsieur," he said, just a shy lad, braving himself to speak before our champion. "*Bonne chance.*" He had no need to hide his partiality; he was one of the sailors who had fished Latham from the sea.

⁓⁓

With little to do beneath the circus tent of the Antoinette station, Latham took one of his regular walks along the cliffs, followed by the usual group of newspapermen. The procession came to a stop at a prominent lookout, where he presumed to inspect the shores of England. He'd even brought his telescope, which he aimed over the sea. But the great expanse glared back at him, like a dull mirror, overwhelming any of his instrument's focus. His spyglass was more adjusted to the flat beach below that stretched out and out in the ebb of a low tide. There, Latham saw someone. He further sharpened the glass. Yes, it was Antoinette, on the beach below. She sat on a chair next to her sister, her governess, and the mute girl from the farm, all watching Antoinette's child play in the sand close to the waves. Latham tried to make sense of it all, while trying to disguise the fact that he was spying on the tourists below. Perhaps it would tarnish the birdman's growing legend if it were known he spent the evenings meant for rest and important preparations pursuing a married woman instead.

Latham hastily turned the telescope away, and instead searched for the train that did not come along the tracks. A rough line of rubble and driftwood high up on the beach showed where the tides rose and fell back. He followed gulls and other large seabirds wheeling slowly through the air, and everywhere his intensified view, framed by the glass, seemed to contain the dense passage of time. Children were throwing rocks into the waves, having escaped their grown-ups, and nearby dogs' attention wandered. Latham fell into a curious, calm elation, as if this might be the last time he ever saw such a scene, a scene from a life that included Antoinette. Tomorrow he could be either dead or immortalized, but either way, completely altered, in a way that made it impossible that she could ever see him as he was.

He allowed himself one final look at her, this time with more courage, not caring what the newsmen thought. But the more he looked, the less he recognized her or her companions. Their figures and their clothes were not right. There was a little girl there he'd never seen before, and the child playing in the sand had nothing to do with the women sitting on the chairs. Antoinette was not one of them. She was nowhere to be seen.

It hardly mattered. The world he'd seen through his telescope for a moment was not one he could have entered, even if it were real. And tomorrow was a long way off.

⚓

That night, while the seaside fishing village slept like the dead, again came the furtive knocking on Latham's door. Opening it, he found Antoinette clutching the same thick bundle of letters.

"You forgot these," she said, hotly offended, and with a shove that was more like a collapse or a fall, she entered his room, smelling of linen and hearthside smoke, with the salty taste of tears around her mouth.

50.

SHE EMERGED FROM THE TANGLE OF BED LINENS and clothes like some enchanted sea bride, sprung up out of the vast mythology of his desire. In the darkness he could see her as his memory of her, a younger, freer Antoinette. In calm resignation, she said, "I'm always just fine, feeling just fine about everything, until you show up again. Every time you return, it's the same, I'm in ruin."

"Do you want me to leave?"

"What?"

In the bed beneath them, he sensed the illimitable, dark and endless. And in the vastness he felt adrift beside her. Latham looked past the curtains to the clear sky and the stars that shone there. He saw the sad, reflective, loneliness in the spheres of her eyes.

"Do you think," he asked trying to coax her, "that man will ever fly to the planets?"

"Whatever happened to your ambition to discover the North Pole?"

He really couldn't say what had happened. The idea had never quite come to him after all, but it had never gone away either, it had always been. The histories of voyages taken in the spirit of discovery made up a great deal of his father's library, he reminded her.

"You know I waited for you to return," she replied.

"But I never set out." He'd once believed that the North Pole was a land of eternal light and splendor, where the sun never set, and that beyond the continent of snow and ice was an oasis of lush tropical diversity. It would be a veritable Garden of Eden—preserved since the beginning of time by uncrossable seas of snow and ice. And he'd imagined himself hunting the strange, prehistoric beasts that roamed there: the mastodon, the saber-toothed tiger, elk with antlers more vast and magnificent than any that had ever been seen.

"Haven't the poles already been discovered?" she asked.

"According to some. More than a few explorers have claimed to have taken their sled teams to the very poles. But in those endless lands of snow and ice, none could prove that the prize was ever reached. Not definitively." And Latham fought to drive the impossibility of this frozen landscape from his mind. "Still, the planets," he said, "the stars. Do you think someday we will ever fly there?"

"It seems yet more a miracle that you and I are even here."

"Think of it, though. Do you believe that someday we shall ever fly to the moon, as they do in the cinema?"

"What else?" She smiled absurdly. "The moon, the stars, what else?" In his elation he asked her if she remembered that one particular afternoon, or summer of afternoons really, when their families spent Sundays at the small pond by the stream in their valley.

He wasn't sure why he was courting memories of his sickly youth, but yes, she remembered it, and there she was again, shining, a girl with spindly legs who climbed up out of the lake like a dark water nymph, spraying him with droplets as she breathed, hardly suppressing her laughter. And there was also the giddy excitement that he and Antoinette could now share: *Look how far we have come.* And they could share past experiences of loneliness that had been endlessly relived in solitude.

"Do you remember," he asked, "that night at the theater?"

"Remember it? I can hardly attend a show without—"

And Latham considered her unread letters lying on the nightstand, and also the letter he'd once written to her that he'd never sent, about the mountains above the Galla-lands; and how he followed their elusive terrain up into the clouds; and how he had come upon a lake of such astonishing natural beauty, it reminded him of the lakes up high in the Italian Alps; and how he'd tried to impose upon them a shared sentimentality that perhaps did not exist. For both his family and Antoinette's had vacationed at those very Alpine lakes. And somehow that summer he was able to separate her from the complicated web of mundane commitments that had him always fascinated. She did not act startled when she caught him in the unlit hallway late at night. Instead, "Are you cold? Yes? Me too. I absolutely cannot sleep." Her hands were cold, and they crept back to their respective rooms for sweaters and shoes and left the villa hotel and walked along the bridge at night, above a black mill pool that opened up to a lake. Bronze carp rose from the darkness at the sound of their footsteps. Antoinette remembered then too the appointment they could not keep back at the infirmary, and they laughed at the memory of it. It was, after all, the shortest night of the year, and the next-to-the-last night of their excursion to Italy. The sun was beginning to show, spreading its silvery gloom, and Antoinette began to shiver. So they turned back to the hotel, when Latham tried to pull her into the covered boathouse, and she followed. What happened next became more real to him than any memory or dream, though he felt he'd made it up, how they chose a wooden rowboat they had to climb up to, and how their clothes formed around them and made a pillow in the bow, where the boat smelled of dried lake life and summer, and they slept.

When she awoke to nearly full morning, Antoinette cried out in astonishment. "Hubert, we must get back." Hurriedly she kissed him, dressing herself, and said, "But you must wait for me," and ran out, pulling her sweater over her shoulders, her heels clacking over the wooden planks.

The next morning she seemed utterly unchanged by the events of the night before, except for a giddy sleepiness that gave her voice a husky, exhausted-sounding quality. Otherwise it was as if that night had never been. The usual arrangements of her day took her away again, and then everyone left for the train back to Paris. But after that day, their shared family vacations ceased. His suspicion that their affinity—his and Antoinette's—was being meddled with only increased his belief, both the impossibility and inevitability of it; that she would always be there, always more in the future than she was now, awaiting him in the next villa or mountain resort like a secret, an innuendo, one of the last to adjourn for bed. Above all else he believed, come what may, that the perfect future moment would arrive in the form of her.

51.

SLOWLY, VERY SLOWLY, the sound of a fly buzzing, and then of a far-off motor, grew louder and louder. All that night he'd slept poorly, he and Antoinette clinging to one another as only fresh lovers can. In the shadows he'd lain awake, musing over the tranquility of her sleeping brow. How unbothered she was by the upcoming day, serene in the valley of embroidered pillows. Was she dreaming? Of something pleasant, no doubt. Endlessly he wanted to be beside her. Or was there a cringe of worry—a slight, electric tension—tightening her face? Everywhere in Latham's drowsy thoughts, he heard the drone of rain.

He blinked.

His eyes opened.

Was there a motor?

Blériot's angry Anzani, directly above the hotel!

"God, no! No!"

Latham leaped from the bed, struggling with his trousers, leaving Antoinette deep within the depression of the tangled sheets. Already, before he was even awake, he realized, he'd heard reporters in the hallways and lobby and café below, awaiting his reaction.

52.

Because Levavasseur had taken Latham's alarm clock the night before, and because he said he would wake Latham himself, I kept expecting a knock at my own door at any minute. Yet well past sunrise I heard nothing, except for a distant, echoing report of what sounded like gunfire in the gray morning, and the far-off barking of a dog.

But then an engine started, and I immediately jumped out of bed. The noise was foreign, distant, and with a disturbing mechanical intensity. My chest froze at the realization that Blériot had taken off first—a natural consequence of sleeping at the same farm as your operations. Yet my greater fear was that the *Antoinette* was being towed by horse to the takeoff field and I'd overslept. At our greatest hour, I'd missed it.

As I neared the Antoinette circus tent, I felt trapped within one of those sluggish dreams where everything you attempt never begins and nothing makes any sense. I saw the *Antoinette VII* beneath the overhang, the canvas of its wings a pristine linen hue, like a well-ironed tablecloth, unsmudged by use. I felt a sudden rush of relief that I had not slept through the flight, but then utter alarm that it had not yet begun. Nothing had begun. Yet surely the milky haze of the overcast signaled daytime. Something was off—horribly, horribly off.

As I drew closer, again I heard the unmistakable sound of Blériot's aeroplane start up. I asked a stranger on the road what time it was—6:51 exactly. What came next was stranger still. As my agitation grew, I spotted Levavasseur at the workbench under the tent overhang. Hearing the aeroplane overhead, he did nothing but look up in calm detachment. In his heavy state, he slowly walked out from under the eaves and surveyed the sky as if to confirm the perfect weather and the fact that his rival's aeroplane was just then flying overhead. His only further reaction was to go back under the tent top, wipe off the glass face of a pocketwatch, and then meditatively put the instrument back into his pocket and turn to his own flying machine with a sense of private admiration. Through the tent overhang, for a brief moment, I thought that Levavasseur had seen me. But then immediately he changed his expression as if to say no, no, he had not, and that was that, and I had better not enter.

⁂

By midmorning the wind had picked up as usual. In a futile drill, we pushed the new aeroplane around to a ready position in the farmer's field. A greater crowd than before gathered during the two-mile trip to the takeoff field, where Latham sat up high in his aeroship, inscrutable, his absorption so fierce that he was unable to acknowledge what had occurred, as if constant forward motion would dispel whatever news might come from the far shore.

Levavasseur, who had not bothered to drive his motor to the harbor boat, looked ponderously up to the sky. "This wind," he said, "it's impossible. Can we risk it?"

"I've taken off in worse."

"Don't forget the landing. Was there such a thing? A landing? Could you call it that?"

The aeronaut looked down, hiding his welling-up eyes, as Levavasseur spoke as if to himself.

"England, yes, England will still be there on the morrow. Can we risk it? Can we?" Levavasseur looked out beyond the fields, to the clouds above the sea and the birds that turned there. "We can only hope that Blériot gets there before this wind."

Then Levavasseur walked through the idling crowd, as if through a great, despondent fog, leaving Latham still seated above his wing.

53.

Beginning at the Marconi operator's station, cheers rose, news spread, church bells pealed out over the coastal towns.

In the days and weeks that followed, it was impossible to avoid the bombardment of accounts of Blériot's landing on the cliffs of England.

All that morning, César and I huddled in the hallway along with the members of the press corps outside of Lieutenant Lord Martin's office as the reports came in: long messages about the conditions Blériot had to overcome, the low fog that had obscured the aviator's view. The gunshot I'd heard that morning was fired from none other than the pistol of the mad Italian engineer Anzani, to wake his crew. Upon the starting of the engine, a dog ran into the propeller and instantly died. A more inauspicious opening to Blériot's flight could not be imagined.

Blériot too had a flair for publicity, and had made himself out to be somewhat of a sullen, unwilling hero. He would have been happy, he told the newspapermen, to be told that the wind was blowing and no attempt was possible. After a quick trial flight, Alfred Leblanc of the *Aéro-Club de France* trained a telescope down on the Antoinette camp but saw no activity. Then Blériot was 250 feet in the air, beyond the telegraph wires of a small cliff, and overtaking his navy escort, the *Escopette*. The depthless cloudbank hid any sign of either shore.

The torpedo boat trailed behind until it lost view of the aeroplane. "The moment is supreme," Blériot recalled after his flight. "Yet I surprise myself by feeling no exultation. Below me is the sea, the surface disturbed by the wind, which is now freshening. The motion of the waves beneath me is not pleasant. I drive on."

All the patriotic renderings and photographs showed the same, images not only of the aviator's historic feat but also of the publicity stunt pulled off by the French newspaperman who guided Blériot down.

In Blériot's pocket was a postcard. It depicted quaint North Foreland Meadow, a picturesque little English green space complete with sheep and castle, overlooking the sea. It was here that Blériot intended to land. This colorful navigational device had been given to him by the meticulous Leblanc, who received it from Henri Fountain of the Paris daily *Le Matin*, who'd dispatched it from Dover via channel boat two days earlier. Since Blériot saw nothing but cloudbank ahead and uneasy ocean below, the postcard remained in his pocket. In any case, the image of the field and castle was seared into his brain.

"For ten minutes I am lost. It is a strange position, to be alone, unguided, without compass, in the air over the middle of the Channel. I touch nothing. My hands and feet rest lightly on the levers. I let the aeroplane take its own course. I care not where it goes."

Soon Blériot found that he had flown too far down the coast; three fishing boats had appeared beneath him, all pointed in the same direction.

He yelled down *Which way to Dover!* and the fishermen called back in English, waving and pointing. After following six miles of shoreline, Blériot found his friend Fountain, waving the tricolor enthusiastically through an opening in the cliffs and then running up a hill, to guide Blériot to a green meadow and safe landing. *Bravo! Bravo!* Blériot was almost blown into a group of red buildings as the wind caught him and whirled him around two or three times, so that he had to stop his motor and land in a free fall of sixty feet.

Still, Blériot did not land upon the lush fields of *Angleterre*.

He crashed there.

As with the thirty-two other aeroplanes he had crashed, he was able to crawl away from this one—only the front and undercarriage badly damaged. He was greeted in the sloping fields outside the Dover castle by a policeman and a few soldiers. Two constables of the British Bureau of Immigration and Foreign Affairs walked up. They asked Blériot for his passport, and if he had any items he wished to declare.

～◦～

Beneath the tarps at the old Tunnel Company building, Latham listened distantly to the news from across the sea, knowing it all beforehand, it seemed, his forehead pressed against a wing that he had never really flown, aware of all eyes upon him, and lost now to an England that had once been his—and robbed also of that part of history that was his destiny. Gone, all of it, gone.

"Still, I will go," he said. "I will." He cast a worried, toothy grin to the sky as César reminded him of how the weather was working against them, as usual, the morning fog having blown away and the winds ripping along the coast, as turbulent as ever—much too much sky over that cold thrashing element of the sea. Impossible Neptune, always in a rage, even while he dreamt. Then Latham took a folded slip of paper from his coat pocket and handed it to César.

"Will you give my congratulations to Blériot at the Marconi?"

"How can I not?" said César, taking the note. Still, he explained that Blériot would magnanimously share the prize money should Latham reach the shore by nightfall.

But it would take a week or so to see the full extent of the collaboration between the French media and the Blériot camp. Not only had *Le Matin's* Fountain arranged to be first on hand to collect Blériot's account, he had actually participated in the famous event. César had tried to hide the papers before Latham could find them, but there they were, everywhere: full-blown artist reproductions of Fountain running through the meadow, trailed by the tricolor; Fountain astride a rooftop, waving the flag in victory. In a posed photograph, British officials watched on as Fountain guided the injured Blériot from the wreckage, and behind them all, the tricolor with its heavy braids, draped in patriotic splendor, captured by the French photographer Pompetou, also under assignment from *Le Matin*.

But before César could even deliver Latham's note to the old Tunnel Company building, more bad news came: Blériot congratulated by kings and queens, ministers, heads of state. Banquets, parades, and holidays announced, on both sides of the sea. Meanwhile Latham stood under the wings of the aeroplane in the smoky wreck of disillusionment. And Levavasseur, his disappointment too great too, perhaps greater than Latham's—Levavasseur also seemed unable to act.

"This day," he said, "you've done your best, as always. Don't be too harsh on yourself. But note, this day, it is already won. Are you sure you want to risk it? Are you? This day? Or any just like it?" He spread his elfish fingers out in an open-palmed way, presenting the trees on the hill and the clouds in the sky. Or was the inventor just tormented by that stubborn, maniacal pursuit of perfection?

Levavasseur turned again to his pilot. Then he cast his grave, forgiving eyes on Antoinette, hidden among the shoulders of those gathered.

"My dear, shall we have lunch?" He held out his arm, and slowly, as if brought back out of herself, she accepted. "Come with us," he said, now suddenly the quaint old uncle he was. "At least our pilot is safe."

"Though I'm sure he'll make it otherwise," she said. And again, that hidden look of rebuke in her eyes.

"I just can't stay here in this curse," said Latham, so quietly that only she would hear.

"*Cursed?*" Her face was suddenly open, stung. She would have gone off defiantly into the sea of well-wishers, were her arm not linked with Levavasseur's.

In the gray morning Latham wished only to exchange further words, but always there was someone near. His mother, for instance, or his cousins, the Parmentier brothers. There were also rumors, laughed away by many, that a woman was responsible for the demise of the *Antoinette*. "The luck of the woman," cried one of the Welféringers. Still Latham managed to catch up with her.

"Forgive *me*," she said. "And how am I a curse?"

"No, I meant, that . . . only that . . . you warned me."

"Of what? You think I cursed you. You just said it."

"Remember, my boy," said Levavasseur. "It was I who didn't wake up in time. Not you." He had said the same thing earlier, but stressed the point this time, putting a hand on Latham's shoulder.

Latham stared at him without comprehension, incapacitated by the magic stupor of defeat. He saw only the beauty of an old man walking away with a woman as familiar to him as a sister, or more so, or less—such distinctions had been obliterated by the swiftness with which life's bright fire could be snuffed out. The aeronaut stood by his machine, not lost in thought so much as lost from it. César too took this time to walk away, murmuring that he would now dispatch Latham's congratulations to the operator of the Marconi.

Latham did not hear that either. So César bid Simone and me to walk with him. Even César—who claimed to be so objective in his understanding of events and human interactions—even he could not help but be moved by the forbearance of his fellow aeronaut of the *Buontemponi*.

The three of us set out along the cliffs, toward the harbor, where César suggested that a brief jaunt on the sea might do us all good. Had either Simone or I been out on a boat yet on the water? No? Well, he knew just the thing.

54.

To while away the long days of boredom and restlessness, César had at his disposal a small open boat that he rented regularly from a whiskery old dock worker who worked in some mysterious capacity around the wharf. For well over a month now César had been using the *Little Turtle* to set his wooden lobster traps close to shore, hauling up mostly scraggy crabs too scrawny to boil. Still, he found the rowing relaxing, especially while the rest of the *Antoinette* crew were stewing in weather-enforced idleness.

On this, the historic morning of Blériot's crossing, César desperately needed some escape from the crew's low spirits, but he didn't think he would enjoy rowing out alone. He seemed grateful to Simone and me for accompanying him to the docks.

At the harbor, I was at first disturbed, and then a little saddened that all of the world was not disappointed that Latham had lost the great race. Instead the waterfront was bustling with a distracting vitality. Porters and passengers clanged up the narrow gangplank to a Scandinavian steamer; stevedores gesticulated as they saw to the loading of crates; a hoist raised a horse into the air and lowered it into the ship's hold. Shouts of the longshoremen drifted to us in the easy wind, the sound redolent of far-off tropical ports of call.

At the end of a rotting-out dock, César had me steady the weathered little dinghy as he took Simone's hand and helped her onto the tiny bench at the bow.

He asked if I wanted to row, and we set out. I'd never worked the oars of a boat before. A bit wobbly at first, we maneuvered out from underneath the rows of masts and beyond the bobbing hulls pulling on their lines. The air was heavy with engine grease and creosote from dock pylons. The water grew choppy, the sleepy green sun leapt off the waves. Farther out, beyond the harbor entrance, the rough sea would swamp our little boat, but here behind the jetty rocks, we were only tossed about a bit by a heavy chop. A white sloop approached under sail, and César waved. Leaning on his tiller, the sea-calmed boater waved back, a ritual that captivated Simone and me. We too waved as the sloop sailed past, tilting at a brisk angle, around the jetty and out to sea.

These simple gestures put César in a fine mood. "Whoa," he said, "you don't want to capsize us now," as I turned around to see how far we had to go.

Again the clouds were those marvelous swabs, like islands in the sky, with inviting shapes within, if you were in a daydreaming mood, as César was. I turned back and rowed again; César sat at the stern, looking forward; Simone, behind me in the bow, faced him in her kerchief and apron, her hands clasped, as if saying grace.

"Just the starboard oar, pull on that side . . . easy now . . . easy. . .," César said, looking over my shoulder to see if Simone could admire his captainly directives, or at least the changing expressions of his sagely manner.

In the lee of the jetty, the humming of the wind and the toss of the waves calmed considerably. Then Simone tapped me on the shoulders, and took my place at the oars. She rowed with such surprising strength that César did not bother to offer his instructions, even as she began to pull the boat out into rough waters. She stopped just short of the open sea, the boat dipping precariously into the watery violence.

In the wind we could see everything.

A three-stacked steamer loomed against the vague horizon; sails, too, rode in and out of view. We three in the *Little Turtle* looked out beyond the mouth of the harbor where white-capped rollers surged and broke and fell again all the way to England, which you could not see, but felt, a mythic land beyond the mist, with its jagged cliff tops and green hills. The huge stretch of the sea overwhelmed us, and beyond it a name, a personal essence, like a voice, that urged us with its own call. Soon we drifted back into the lee of the wind, and I felt saturated, yet clear, in the vivid, drowsy colors, the infinite greens of the sea.

Here, on the verge of the open waters, César began a set of elaborations concerning the Aristotelian theories of what is beautiful. "What is beautiful? We ask." He took on a scholarly air, looking out over the sea. "What is beauty? For instance, combinations of mathematically arranged notes form music—" He looked at Simone imploringly. "Not all music, mind you, is beautiful. But it can be of the highest sort of beauty." And César took in Simone's sea-bleached smile as she held the oars at rest. "Properly aligned relations, they are extremely beautiful—in symmetry, to the eye of the beholder. A waterfall is beautiful. Or when the wind topples an enormous tree. When a proud wild animal is hunted and killed, there is a beauty in the tragic. A hero transcends beauty, and is morally obliged to satisfy our expectations, and so, before the tale is done, he triumphs. He becomes sublime only when he struggles, and fails."

César squinted out at the dirty-gray gulls whose whitish underbellies gleamed like dull ghosts in the sky. Our eyes followed one gull that flew singularly close overhead.

I drew pictures of what César had said in the air, and later gazed at the reflection of one of the oars on the shimmering water. We continued our discussion on beauty in silence, each of us lost to our own thoughts. We bobbed for quite some time. Finally Simone tapped me out of my reverie and made a set of elaborate gestures of her own.

Out loud I asked, "Why is it, then, that when I struggle, I am not in a beautiful mood, I am just dismal?"

And here César took hold of Simone's hand, then one of mine, and held us both. There was a sort of despair like a low rumbling in his soul—all of that contemplation of the ideal and the sublime—and also a gentle, distant optimism that seemed to come from sadness. "And here I was, thinking I was the only one of the *Buontemponi* who knew how to have a good time. Please, let me row for a while. No, no. You two sit together, up front. Together. There you go."

And César took the oars and pulled, the three of us riding our small, solitary thing on the sea-green immobility, tossed about without moving, caught on the shifting surface of an expanse that turned dangerous to our tiny craft, out beyond the harbor entrance, just twenty-five feet before us, with an angry indifference, at that point beyond which we could not go.

55.

Two days later Latham took to the skies again for England.

Back on French shores he was told that the wind blew from three to seven knots, but in the sky it blew stronger. There was no telling how fast he flew. He passed the boats in the channel as if they were sailing backward, their hulls crashing down and their dissolving plumes traveling north with him to England. The slightest turn of the rudder increased his skid along the wind. Occasionally the dense flow of air was interrupted by a brutal slant or empty pocket, voiding the harmony. Losing its drag, the prop caught on nothing, and the engine's thrum changed. He'd never flown so fast, he thought. No one had. England grew brighter, always brighter, the ramparts of the Shakespearean cliffs rising up ahead.

At the harbor entrance a flotilla of boats gathered, a welcoming fleet. He heard their horns and bells. He saw the flags of both nations. Those aboard waved to him with straight arms.

All hail! The underdog!

Sentimental favorite!

Second to fly across *la Manche*—but the first to fly beyond it. He had a surprise planned for them all; he'd turn eastward and keep flying all the way to London, where he'd land by the Thames.

But less than a mile short of Dover, or maybe two miles, the drone of the engine changed, losing its angry triumph, ailing him yet again.

The aeroplane pitched seaward. He reached out to the engine and opened the throttle with his hands but burnt them. Through the slowing whirr of the propeller came the cold saltwater smell and the gray-green light off the sea and the even greater gloom of defeat, as he crouched low to brace against the fall. A wing caught on a trough and turned the plane violently. His head struck against the throttle control, or a spar. He couldn't tell which, but he could taste the coppery red of blood mixed with seawater. The side of his face turned cold as windy dreams flew in and out of the hole in his head—out of the skull's cave and back to the sea, the all-imbibing sea. A fellow was not made to bob around like a cork so far out. Funny, though, hardly feel a thing, like pain, anyway. Nervous system protects and shuts down for a pleasant enough watery grave. Any death probably pleasant enough once you approach it that way. Just float away. As if on a bed across the sea. A berth with the hatch slung open and the hull burst apart. How unfortunate, to let the sunlight and waves interrupt your sleep, where blood, breath, and bone pour forth, all out the wound. So much debris. Awash in the rips. Pocket, wallet, watch, tobacco, valise, handwritten notes, all of her letters, all of it sunk, descending into the varied hues, different depths, colder temperatures. Down there for the fishes. Though some of him floated. Cabbage of a head, mostly. Awash in the fabrics of his clothes and his swelling raft. Pages drenched and floating, one from the other, words washed away, memories soaked and dissolved, flowing out the hole in his head like water down a stream.

Until he realized he'd been knocked unconscious, and lifted himself, heavy with saltwater, and shook the strength back into his being.

Seawater sloshed deep within the canoe of his boat and broke over the canvas walls. Latham took off his cap and began to bail out the ship, but the soaked brim had no shape and only slapped at the water futilely. Throwing it into the drink, he ripped off his goggles, too, cracked and bloody, and threw them into the sea. The aeroplane had begun to tilt dangerously, its tail in the air, as if flying down under the waves. So he reached behind the wicker seat and found the rope. He looped one end around the propeller and the other end around his waist and dove into the sea. Emerging from the waves, he trod water as the cuneiform tail fins rose and the ship began its slow, stoic descent into the sea. As the aeroplane plunged from sight, he turned away and began a steady swim toward England.

As he swam he did not have the impression that he was pulling the aeroplane, but rather that it was swimming after him, following him in some way. Soon he and his machine were tossed by the rising surf onto the sands of a small, secluded beach, nestled in a cove beneath the cliffs. There, standing in the surf, waiting for him, stood the gray-eyed Gastambide with her dark features, shimmering in a dress that was wet from the knees down, her parasol open, white netting over her face. Like a shipwreck, the aeroplane lay half on the beach and half in the breakers, bucked by the waves, while Antoinette sat in the surf and Latham lay, his head reclined on the wet, draping lap of her dress, spread out like a drenched bed over the sand where the waves fell back. She lifted the veil, and her eyes held the most ecstatic, dreaming serenity. It was just as she had prophesied. "I knew you would swim to me," she said. "I just knew you would."

"Where else could I go?"

"I know." She cradled his face in her shy, nervous hands. "I know."

≈≈≈

According to one of the sailors who rescued Latham, he would most likely have drowned had the rescue taken much longer. The navy oarsmen had to pull the semiconscious pilot by the shoulders from the sinking aeroplane, and two other shipmates helped to haul him up into their launch. One of the aviator's goggle lenses was cracked, and though the sea had washed off most of the blood, Latham's coat was soaked a deep rusty red at the shoulder.

The medic's cabin of the *Escopette* was a small, dull room. Latham sat on the surgeon's table with a blanket around his shoulders, fully clothed now in navy issue. He grimaced, squinting up into a surgical lamp, as the ship's doctor saw to the wound above his eye. The glass of antiseptic solution holding the surgical tools trembled, tuned to the shifting pitch of the ship's engine. Nearby, Levavasseur peered out the round portal of the medic's bay, along with Jules Gastambide. Pulling on the gray straw of his beard, Levavasseur repeated in a slow, far-off hush that he could not keep throwing aeroplanes into the sea.

"But we have to."

The ship's surgeon frowned like a photographer whose subject had moved beneath his hands.

"Careful," said Levavasseur.

"Sir," said the surgeon, a sage old ascetic with tangled teeth, much too old to still be in service. On him, the ship's uniform looked oddly religious. His liver-spotted hands moved like an ancient sail maker's. "I nearly stabbed you," he said, and cleared his throat. "Begging your pardon."

He pulled the needle from Latham's brow, and took up the slack of the catgut suture.

"We're just lucky you're even here," said Gastambide. "Another *Antoinette*, pulled from the sea—What if you weren't? What would our publicity be then?"

"Must I remind you that I am also an investor?" Trying not to blink, Latham held his head up steady, peering into the large, round electric lamp. "Nothing could help us more than a successful flight to England."

"Yes, I know, son." Levavasseur paced the cabin and put his hand on Latham's shoulder. "We'll be docking there soon enough."

Still Levavasseur paced and settled himself before the view out the round portal, the glass besmirched by seawater. The ship idled, in and out of gear, waiting for the tug to arrive. Levavasseur and Gastambide could not see their aeromachine, lashed as it was to the rails of the navy ship, but through the dense portal they could get a sense of the sprawling flotilla that by the minute grew—pleasure boats, tenders, yachts, work vessels, rowboats, every kind of boat imaginable. Most of them English. Or all of them, it seemed. The two investors were shocked by the sheer number of boats that had gathered around the aeroplane, which would have sunk long ago had it not been secured to the *Escopette*.

"I can't bear to watch," said Gastambide, who stood fixed before the circular window and did not move.

"There's a tournament coming up," said Levavasseur. "Not a mere challenge accompanied with prize money. But a competition! Pitting plane against plane, all at the same time, on the same airfield. All of the world's best aerocraft, and all of the world's best pilots will be there. Farman, Ferber, the Voisins, the Wrights—"

"And Blériot?" asked Latham.

"Yes, Blériot. Of course, him. *Because* of him." Levavasseur turned again to the small view of the sea out the portal. "It's practically in his honor."

Book V

La Grande Semaine d'Aviation de la Champagne at Reims
August 22 to August 29, 1909

The whole French nation seems to be coming to the quaint and ancient Cathedral City, to which a curious chance has brought the first meeting of flying men in the world's history. A vast multitude will probably witness the most stirring spectacle ever seen—races in the air.

—*New York Times*, August 22, 1909

Attendance was estimated at half a million throughout the course of the week, with 200,000 attending on the Saturday of the Gordon Bennett Cup competition for speed. These numbers reflect only those who paid admission. Many more looked on from the surrounding fields.

—Jacques Molay

56.

AFTER THREE MONTHS ON THE NORTHERN COAST, the Antoinette company put all of its efforts into the approaching aviation competition to be held at Reims. Meanwhile the notion of the birdman as a mythic hero, ushering in the modern day, had taken the country by storm.

Midmorning found me with Simone on a pilgrimage of growing excitement.

This was the first day of the competition, and I was supposed to have arrived at the aerodrome the day before to help ready the aeroplane, but the roads to Neufchâtel were completely overwhelmed. Worse yet, our wagon could travel only as fast as the procession of motors and horse-drawn vehicles would allow. Slowly we approached the town of Reims, its famed gloomy cathedral presiding over it, just as the picture books portrayed. The train station was even more overrun, despite the new *Gare des Voyageurs*, built especially to take passengers to the newly constructed aerodrome. Passengers rode in small open carriages with tent-like tops, looking very much like toy trains, and so full that they had to sit up on the railings and hang on to the bottom of the brightly striped tarps.

Once we'd gotten beyond the town limits, the bicyclists and foot traffic moved yet slower. I thought the vanguards of capitalism and machinery—like the festive mini-trains—would leave the slow-moving inhabitants of the countryside behind. But no, the vast migration of the country folk kept up, slow, awkward, and absurd in their jumble of eccentric costumes. The crowd advanced over a wide, flat plain, broken only by a few tree stumps here or there. People cried out when an ambitious motorist demanded that we clear the way, and when a motor stalled entirely, we revamped the surly catch call "Get a horse!" to *"V'la m'sieur! Faut q'vous achetiez un aéroplane!"* Those who wished to avoid paying admission altogether stopped their wagons on a knoll or lookout along the way. Here the great crowd languished. Sporadic bouts of rain did nothing to curb our expectations. It was here, in the open grounds, that the country folk paid a cheaper admission than those in the covered, many-tiered grandstands.

The aerodrome was a vast, open pastureland. We pushed our way along, careful of where we stepped. Everywhere were fortified encampments, quartered off by campstools, blankets, baskets, opened bottles, and tiny fires, hissing here and there in the rain that never quite began.

The skies threatened though, and the late afternoon winds grew worse. The crowd, not suspecting that the slightest of breezes would cancel out every event on the program, grew restless and mean. Approaching the garages, I saw no sign of any aeroplane, airman, or flight crew. More and more of the irritable spectators left the grandstands and gathered on the aerodrome rails, glaring at the garages. Worse yet were those in the surrounding fields. Barroom chants turned to outbursts of threats and abuse. A shoe filled with dirt came hurling over the fence, along with an effigy of a gentleman with a bird's beak. Empty bottles spun in the air. The threat of riot brought the mounted dragoons out in rank, and beyond the fence they sat atop their horses, protecting the airfield.

Above us a troop of bawdy comedians performed on stilts, with faces of grease paint and shoulders of wings. Adding to the bacchanalia was the carnival barker in his small hot air balloon, not a Charlière filled with gas but one of the originals, a small, decrepit Montgolfière. Compared to the magnificent aeroship of the *Buontemponi*, it was a little circus organ grinder of a ship, and painted like one too, grimy with age, covered in soot, small, listing, and diabolic. To lift it, one had to stoke the fire. The busker's show involved taking his dirty balloon up and dropping some frightened animal over the side, attached to a parachute. At first only the idle and debauched would pay to see a confused dog hanging like a limp croissant as it floated below the parachute. The bearded mutt strangely perceived its own eminence, though, as it descended proudly down upon the crowd. And the longer the winds prevented a demonstration by any aeroplane whatsoever, the larger became the fee that the carnival barker demanded to release his ship. Despite the increasing heft in his assistant's hat, though, the winds soon grounded even this decrepit showman, who quit stoking his flame and, his shrewd, porous face streaked with soot, sadly watched his evil little ship collapse in the wind.

⸎⸎

"Ah yes, the aeroshow in miniature," said Latham, his boyish grin taking on a harsher edge.

We found him outside the aeroplane hangars, off to himself, contemplating the spectacle of the dog falling by parachute in the early evening torchlight. I didn't recognize him at first. He wore his traditional checkered derby cap, now over a tightly wound bandage. The arrangement caused his hat to sit up a little high on his head, producing the overall impression of a turban. His face was still red and swollen in places, altering his features, and his smile seemed especially injured.

Immediately Latham asked Simone how she had arrived. "Not with the same companions who brought you to the coast?"

"No," she said, "with Auguste." She pointed.

Latham's usual composed optimism could not hide his sudden unease. He'd hoped to hear other news, I thought, news that somehow Simone's loose connection with Antoinette had continued.

Simone stood spellbound by the dressing of Latham's wound. Her deafness had given her a strange democracy of spirit; she cared nothing for social standing or fame. She stared openly at his bandages for so long that Latham seemed to feel as though somehow he was being touched. Though she spoke little, she still made slight, involuntary movements with her hands. For Latham the sensation was somewhat like a balm, for she saw him in the way he just then wished to be seen, though only just now did he realize this. He felt both supremely understood and misunderstood at the same time, mostly because he could not understand it himself. He realized how acutely his wound itched when he was tired, how it reacted to a sudden change of temperature, and how it stung when he thought. Not fully formed yet, sensations from the scar radiated not outwardly, like ordinary pain, but inwardly, seeming to absorb elemental changes such as those in the weather.

Latham turned his attention to the mobbing exodus, and especially those who hiked up their skirts and plodded through the soaked field. Still he had not yet seen Antoinette, though he'd known all along she was near.

❧ ❧

The rain grew heavy and soon scattered the crowds, though the cavalry stayed on guard, the rain streaming off their great helmets, until their cloaks were soaked. Once the orders were given, even they dispersed, jangling and splashing through the wallow of mud and trampled grass. But soon enough the cavalry was called upon again, this time to guard the aerodrome café. By firelight the crowd outside had grown hungry, and unruly, and threatened the barriers with horrid flames. Atop their horses, two squads of dragoons stood in idle formation before the grandstand balcony, ordered by the general to protect the wine.

What had merely been sullen protest in the afternoon turned sinister in the glow of the flames. You could not tell where it ended or where it began, stretching back into the crowd, men grumbled unseen near the fires lit here and there in the dark with self-righteous outrage. How much of a threat was the thirst of the mob, against two military detachments on horses? Men with their high-crested helmets of gold, their mounts with streaming manes, the dragoons stood like the imperial Roman guard. The mob, though unarmed, acted like angry Communards, shouting out from behind the barricades in the streets of Paris.

Here the nighttime of humanity revealed itself in all of its sordid possibility. I know not what mysterious force drew us in. Not too far away were the lurid carnival acts, and I sensed a dark pervasive power from the rioters, a power that could turn primitive and violent in an instant, overwhelming the soldiers. A horrible lust for it filled the air. One of the dragoons fired his pistol above his shoulders, and his horse reared, braced for the charge.

57.

MEANWHILE, INSIDE THE CAFÉ, GARLANDS OF electric lights hung like strings of pearls.

Across the long table from Latham sat Antoinette, staring down as if in protest. From the moment Latham took his seat, she'd kept her eyes fixed on the table before her, cluttered with unbussed plates, the linen cloth stained with purple blots of wine and smudges of cigar ash. In a rush of excitement her husband, Charles Chaudberet, introduced the fallen aviator to a good many members of the newly formed aero-locomotion company, his new friends, the visionaries and investors who had organized this very event and who, in their broad-minded wisdom, had chosen to set the competition here, in the Champagne region of France.

"What an enormous bonanza you have provided."

"To the birdman!"

"...The birdman...."

"Yes, I know you can't think of it, while you compete. But think of it."

With an adroit tilt of his spoon, their host the marquis, so long-boned and languid, and also the chief officer of Champagne Pommery, informed their champion that someday all this would become commonplace. Aerodromes such as this! Aeroplanes such as these! And the

bourgeoisie—he put his own curious spurn on the word—will be able
to fly the entire country, at will, from one aerodrome to the next, all as
commonplace as the railroad today. And with this progress, chimed
in Chaudberet, also flies our family investment. Imagine—the glories
of it! And imagine the committee of experts appointed to gather fifty
of the best Parisian chefs, along with one hundred and fifty of the best
Parisian waiters, all railroaded in, along with over three tons of pork,
beef, and lamb, and almost as much plump, plucked game hen, duck,
and rabbit, garages full of wine, yes, more of the specialty?

Chaudberet poured. The bubbling wine fizzed to the top, leaving
Latham's glass frothed with dread. Here was where the investors hoped
to make the real killing. The cases and cases of bottles stored in carts of
ice, beside wheels of cheeses racked eight high, boxes of fruit, crates of
vegetables, vaults of bread, shelves of teas, jams, and marmalade, brick
walls of butter. Yes, all agreed, what a great shame it was that the café
and surrounding dining arrangements could seat only six hundred,
and they cast their eyes out over the smoldering darkness, where so
many campfires burned, as if it were a vast pilgrimage ripe for the
fleecing. From far off, the din of motors and music kept on. And the
marquis tossed his napkin to his plate.

"Next year." He sighed. "Next year. Look! Just look at it, though!
What we have here is merely the beginning. It appears we are embarking
upon the sport of sports."

"Since the beginning," said César, his eyes glistening with inspirational fever, "there has always been the will to fly."

"Exactly."

"And now—" from a few seats away, César raised his glass, "to the
aviator! Our knight in the sky who conquers heaven!"

They toasted, not to Latham himself but to his wound, beneath
the bandage, the eye of Jupiter, the fate etched on his brow, like a typo-
graphical record of events, his inability to reach England, the sum of all
of his shortcomings. Antoinette searched his scar also, relieved by it as
if it were a blessing but also a curse, and she darkly at fault.

After dinner, the board of trustees of the exalted Antoinette
company all stood and sauntered magisterially down the grandstand
stairs and onto the soggy fields below. Restless bystanders jostled
beside the rogue campfires, anxious for something that would never

arrive. Latham was relieved at last to be out in the dark, where he could feel anonymous and seek Antoinette out on his own. But he'd lost sight of her. Everywhere the crowd moved like a foreigner lost in thought, unsure of where to go next, moving but then stopped again before the bouncing string of paper lanterns, the jangling of the out-of-tune guitar, the faces grown grotesque in the firelight. Tires spun. Horses surged. Mud clods flew. But nothing moved. In the shifting beams of light, all manner of gentlemen in soiled cuffs, dismounted cavalrymen, and villagers in their Sunday best helped to push along bogged-down motorcars and wagons. Even Chaudberet. Spectators pooled up everywhere, idling before the wooden planks laid down to cover the mud. Finally catching sight of her, Latham positioned himself to help Antoinette across.

In the far light of the fires, her dark dress seemed all the more dark and vague, with a depth as in a dream, and she like a spirit wrapped within it. She looked down, seeming to wait for something, giving the impression that all of her attention was upon him even while she looked somewhere else. Latham felt tall and light beside her, filled with purpose. He believed that here, in their next meeting—and every meeting hereafter—something definite would occur. Yet he'd felt the same in the villa in the Italian Alps, and the last time he had seen her, that night at the Hôtel Neptune—that what happened on those nights had no effect on her. She moved still in the perfect completeness of her own social eddies, and these kept her immersed. As she stood waiting in silence to cross the plank, an empty, open sensation that nothing had changed between them filled him with turbulence, until he saw her again in a gray agitation. In uneven shadows and flashes of dim light, he remembered how she'd barged into his hotel room, possessed, like some exalted priestess delivering the stuff of prophecy. She'd actually traveled out to the coast to tell him she had dreamed of him in the ocean, and in turn he *had* fallen, and dreamed of her, or so he imagined, though he could not recall the actual experience of falling into the sea a second time, only the sensations that accompanied it. They *had* met, he and she, through dreams in a sea as vast as the eminence of its own truth; it had to be. He had lived out and survived her revelation. All the laws and tides of gravity followed this pull. He loved her as the sun shone and the wind moved over their faces.

Wishing to bring her closer, he asked, "It seems like ages since we've seen each other. How long has it been?"

"Three weeks."

"That's all?"

At first he'd failed to notice her arm, held out to him. When he reached for her, she moved away as in a dance. There was the hint of dark waters and hidden currents when, like a puckish ballerina, holding her parasol out in deft counterbalance, she hopped down. He was reminded of the thin girl in her flopping gray swimsuit, jumping from the rock into the lagoon.

"So, what did you think?" she asked. And he followed her down. "Really, you must tell me." She smiled anxiously in the new privacy that the path afforded. Perplexed, he squinted at her. Perhaps the scar beneath his bandages furrowed too, because that's what she looked at, what she addressed.

"Of the letters?" she said. "You mean you didn't even read them?" She glared, just as a knowing smile crossed her face. "You didn't even read *one* of them, did you?"

"I opened some. I began them—"

She turned on him—angry, resplendent.

"I was too distracted," he said. "I had only one day, and I thought you were going to tell me all over again of another catastrophe, just waiting for me, so I put them back in my pocket."

"Those letters were written so long ago—before any of this."

"I was going to read them," he said, "in England. But I wanted to get there first."

"You believe that whether or not you made it to England should have any effect on how you feel toward me?"

He was breathing hard, with a throbbing in his ears, and a rushing sound of seawater over rock, as the impossible longing from the view of the far-off cliffs clouded over him once more.

"No. I just couldn't read them—the letters, or anything, before I left. Then they got soaked. Entirely. They were beyond reading."

"You mean—" She turned, mollified. "You took them with you when you flew?" Her face opened, softening, as a mother would soften, looking at her child. Resentment fell over him like a cloud. She'd matured beyond him, and she pitied him.

"I read them," he said. "I did. As much as I could. It made me think we should have run away. Way back when, when we could have. Though it would have ruined us."

"It ruined us anyway."

She looked at him with a distant, remote warmth, as if she realized they shared sentiments that would most likely remain unshared, that they must endure this portion of their hearts lost forever to the deep, silent and inexpressible.

"Where are the letters now?"

"In the ocean," he said. "Some of them. I suppose. Most are unreadable, a large wad of papier-mâché."

"My dearest Hubert. Had something happened to you—"

"Reading them would have been one of the first things I did in England."

Moving with the crowd, they approached each other on the railway platform.

"When you and I are in England, then," she said, and from her mantilla, she extended a hand. "Yes, something like that: when we are in England someday, or some other precious place, though I'll never be able to remember it all—all that happened—all I felt—it was in those letters." She took his hand. "*Mon cher*, my love. I must go now."

In his heart he knew that the next time he saw her, it would be that somewhere else, and they would be together again as they were meant to be, or else why would he feel this way? Her hand slipped from his, and she wove through the crowd, joining the loosely scattered Gastambides along the platform. The train's idling engine steamed, its vapory plumes eerily lit. She turned around once more to see him, and boarded.

58.

ALL THAT NIGHT LATHAM SLEPT POORLY. Waking dreams of a vague troubling matter plagued him. Meanwhile the late-night celebration outside the hotel kept on, followed by the relentless chirp of house sparrows in the dead of night, kept awake by the fires. The noise narrowed down to one dull bird with its shrill repetition—thin, one-noted, and stupidly urgent, interrupted again by some lost reveler, fading off into his own slurry. There seemed to Latham, while he lay awake, some force or will in life much stronger than his own. If ever there was a supernatural presence, it appeared to him most vividly when he tried to force himself into one of life's elemental roles that seemed forever beyond him. But the more he sought out this simple state of grace, the further away and more mysterious it became, until he was seized with a personal enmity toward this impertinent force.

All of the delays to his flight across the sea to England, beyond those of the weather, had created what looked like a pattern of outside meddling, something Latham refused to entertain, even now. There'd been the leaky radiator, the missing accumulators, the suspicion that those sympathetic to the moneyed interests of the Wrights had wanted to create more time for the Comte de Lambert and his two Wright Fliers. How could anyone have overlooked the topping off of the fuel tank, and instead found it empty? But the most difficult clue to explain away was the piece of wire found in the motor after Latham's first fall into the sea. Could it be a secret partisan of Blériot's? But no, Latham did not believe in any of those petty conspiracies normally accused of bringing about certain outcomes. This thing—this thing that crossed him—it was more dignified than some comic rendering of a devil. It was less malevolent than that, more vast and gently indifferent to his plight, like the outgoing tide of the sea.

☙❧

With the morning's sun, though, Latham's optimism returned. The early light spread above the hills, bearing the promise of the long, hot days of summer. He walked around the silent aeroplane tents and hangars, not yet come to life. In the fields beyond the aerodrome, a crowd was already gathered, having camped out nearby. The sparrows that had kept him awake all night now chattered around broken clumps of horse dung, and when a motorcar approached, the birds flew off to the eaves of the garages.

In the gathering heat, the acrid fumes of petrol rose from the fueling station's only pump. Boys, proud of their grease-stained shirts, toted milk pails of the gasoline back to the hangars. One by one, the hangar curtains were drawn aside, like stages of so many theaters set one next to the other, and the workers like competing choruses, advancing earnestly, sending out instructions in an undertone. The workers of the English team were the most impressive, in their long white work coats, like pharmacists. And you could not tell who Blériot's crew was, for all the other fellows wishing to walk alongside the aeroplane. The crowd cried out in unified patriotic fervor upon seeing the machine of historic record. But there was also Blériot's newer, larger number XII. Big. Very big. A bustling monster of a ship. And with a powerful engine, too, situated directly above the pilot. Not an Antoinette engine, nor an Anzani for that matter, but a prototype eight-cylinder, sixty-horse-power, water-cooled ENV, weighing 287 pounds—the same engine that would power him through the speed competition, and the same one that, earlier, had burned his leg so badly. Still Latham could not help but notice the terse, forced air of the other pilots. Even if one of them took every award on the program, none could outdo Blériot. And unless one of them lost his life wholesale in a crash, none could prove more battle-weary than himself.

⁓⁓

Waiting for Latham, the Welféringers were too clean, idle below the upstretched wings in the hangar, both the IV and the VII, both of the models flown so tragically into the sea. Still we thought our chances, set beside any of the other aeroplanes from America and France, were excellent, especially when you considered the skill and unrequited ambition of our pilot. Immediately I felt a stirring of pride. Having seen all the other flying machines, I realized how superior our own beloved aeroship was, by far the most beautiful and birdlike, the most like flight itself, a vessel of imagination and dreams.

Even so, one could not help but marvel at the varied shapes of the other contraptions, wheeled out wing-to-wing, ready for flight. Some, of course, looked like flying ships, while others were altogether odder, like food stands, or fences with sails. The Voisins, and Farman's modified Voisin, were the most numerous, with their deep, double-decked rows of sails, some with sails like those of a sailboat tilted upward. On their bicycle wheels, the overall effect of these creations was of a regatta ready to set sail.

Having eyed his rivals, Levavasseur walked near. "Ah, yes, our good friend. The Potato."

The inventor cast a weary glance at me and then at Simone.

"Which way does the wind blow?" he asked—and all he asked—as he put a gentle paw on my shoulder, staring far off into the approaching conflict.

"From the southeast, sir."

But Levavasseur had already walked out from underneath the wings of his aeroplanes, never expecting an answer, nor did he hear one.

⁓⁓

Before the gathering crowds, the mounted dragoons, so apt at defending the Grand Buffet the evening before, rode out into the airfield. They were joined by the Musical Corps of the Fifty-Fourth Infantry, the local police, seventy-eight of Champagne's Forest Guard, and members of the Bethany Volunteer Fire Brigade. At last came France's favorite: a detachment on bicycles—the Lyonese Eighty-Fourth, with their smart black pompoms on eighteenth-century caps, struggling to pedal through the brownish dust kicked up by the horses, their large Egyptian bandannas protecting them from the dust and the sun beginning to glare.

Then the bugle. The rattling of drums. *Salut!*

The cavalry came, hooves pounding, the artillery dragged into place. Orders were barked, howitzers loaded. The blanks echoed with their dull, muted thunder. Again the bugle and the thumping of horses, encircling the infantry in dust.

With the planes and other pilots, Latham took in the vast, awful array that swarmed the grandstands and outlying fields. Presiding from the box suite above, sat the eighth President of the Third French Republic, besashed and bull-bearded, old Nebuchadnezzar himself. In the breeze the gunpowder lingered like an ancient incense, blackish with fire, sweet and blackish with sulfuric smoke.

≈◦≈

The rattle of an unmuffled engine started up. It clacked like musketry over the field and sped up to an angry little drone. The hushed crowd pressed in around the miles of fence. There was a snort, a burst, a stream of dust. The aeroplane took off. Just as it leveled into the periphery, another motor burst into life. Then another. Just as one plane leveled off toward the humming outskirts, another was wheeled out into the field.

Always a variety of aeroplanes were in the air, circling above the vast, distracted crowd, competing in some mysterious capacity, and trying in too many cases to avoid collision. They landed and took off in staggered starts, allowing the prevailing winds to favor one aviator over the next, especially in the contests of speed. Even before Latham's first flight, the crashes had begun.

Hardly airborne, one ship sailed precariously like a quail above wheat, hovering between one yard up and two, until it flopped down and collapsed where it landed. The aviator, freeing himself from the firemen, emerged—victorious! The crowd burst out, euphoric, buoying him up and sweeping him along—the survival of our man, complete! In the same wind, the next flight, the same results. Henri Farman's modified Voisin came hurling down so near the first wreck, the downed pilot had to dash to avoid it, the impact twisting Farnan's rudder. The propeller cracked in two. But the undercarriage held. And the soldiers and workmen were able to right the ship and push it on its wheels back to the hangar, Farman walking behind, now a champion, thrust into vivid focus. And for what? For waving his hat to his admirers. At the café the gypsy band swooned out the "Marseillaise" for the triumph, however fleeting, of the fallen athlete of the air, still waving his hat to the well-wishers as he followed his brave, tragic, broken machine off the field.

All day, all week, more crashes. No matter what the competition—the fastest, the farthest, the highest—planes fell from the sky.

After the first day, the gypsy musicians no longer had to compete with the military's marching band and now the "Marseillaise" played only when a world record was broken. New benchmarks in flight were toppled within the hour, within the heat, it seemed.

Of course Mlle. de Dauphinois christened Latham's first flight, pinning the accustomed flower to his lapel and demurely fading back into the crowd, where a dark Parisian man received her.

Latham took off.

Above the aerodrome, he heard the roar of the crowd follow him in waves, willing him to be greater than his aeroplane could ever be. A small flock of rooks flew across his path. There was an explosion of feathers. The air boiled and dropped out from beneath him as he passed over the "graveyard," where no less than eight aeroplanes lay in varying states of char and ruin. He flew swiftly, but he would not beat the time of the frontrunner, the American, Glenn Curtiss, he thought. He'd barely qualified to represent France for the Gordon Bennett Cup. In the duration contest, however, Latham prevailed. He sailed in monotonous circles over the aerodrome until the day came to a close. Dark, towering thunderclouds threatened, and still he flew, through a squall, and then on, long after there was no other plane in the sky. The spectators, those who remained, watched on in silence as he flew, hardly visible through the gray curtain of rain. When he finally landed in the dark wet gloaming, he'd been up nearly two hours, far and away the best.

⁓ ⁓

His triumph did not endure past the following afternoon, when Henri Farman made the winning time in altogether fairer weather. Despite the judges' sympathy for Latham's superior piloting in worse conditions, they concluded that Farman had met every criteria of the competition, and ruled reluctantly in Farman's favor.

Latham plunged once again into the depths. No matter what he did, no matter how hard he tried, a great gray element closed in, a gray sea of despair.

But he had one last chance.

In the late afternoon of the last day of competition, his run at the altitude competition was called. All week the attention of the vast sea of people had dissipated and gathered by turns. Under the constant distraction of the buzzing contraptions of the sky, his muse—Mlle. de Dauphinois—did not neglect her duties. As a patriot of the heart, of passion and theater and all that was true, she stepped through the wandering crowd with her open parasol before her breast. Reaching out to him, the urgent actress lowered the parasol to reveal one clipped rose in her hand. The dark curls that fell from beneath her netting veil shone as if dipped in oil. She affixed the rose to his lapel. This was her last call. She would follow him no more.

"In flight, as in love."

Her two hands lingered over his lapels, as if she would pull him toward her once more, but she stopped with a strange pity and turned a significant glance to the grandstands, like Latham, searching out a familiar face. And Latham kept searching that face out, from the sea of others, even as his aeroplane took off. Every time he flew over the grandstands, he wondered which one was she.

57.

It was César's intention to take his two friends from the farm—his two apples of the earth—up in the aeroship of the *Buontemponi*, to get as close a view as possible of Latham's attempt at a new world record, which he was positive Latham would achieve.

The three of us walked well past the aerodrome and into a clearing beyond the fences, where only the most disinterested and vagrant of spectators wandered. We came to the area reserved for "captive" balloons, where presently a half dozen balloons were tethered by their guide ropes at varying heights. There the silver aeroship floated with a gentle, passive sway, at about twice the treetops' height, among other balloons not nearly so noble, the giant orbs forming a village of sorts.

César stood completely at ease below his large, docile neighbors. "Let's escape the madness, shall we?" He beckoned like Jack of the Beanstalk, putting his hands to his face, bullhorn fashion, and calling Marcus down.

⤳⤳

The three of us stepped into the balloon.

César then handed Marcus—now standing on the ground—a sandbag. And just as I remembered it, there was the very stillness of the air, the curious elation of motion with no movement, no effort, no sound, we rose. Slowly at first, for it seemed we merely hovered above the lawn. Simone, naturally a bit wobbly, clung to my sleeve, looking down at the gentle turning of the grandstands—the sporadic crowd against the fences, the slanted roofs, the far-off cathedral. We saw the hills spread out in all directions. Everything took on a cool, faraway hush as we drifted through the different layers of breeze and temperature, and as the reactions of the crowd grew distant, the aeroplanes too took on the distant feel of history, growing small below our balloon.

There was a loafing ease to our neighbors in the sky, rafting in their small wicker frames. As the silver aeroship of the *Buontemponi* rose to meet them, César waved in greeting, and like friendly picnickers the other balloonists waved back, some of them raising their glasses, and it reminded me of the time we rowed the *Little Turtle* to the mouth of the harbor.

When our aeroship came to the end of its rope, there was a slow and delayed knocking to the line, recoiling all the way to the stakes in the ground, as if it were a long elastic. With a tug and gentle rap, our ship kept reaching the end of its tether. The wind strained against the rope. With the other balloons leaning so near, I felt we were all a fleet of ships that might take off all together, as if we were on the verge of some great exploration. All that was left was to let go. Day was turning to dusk, and a nearly full moon rose through the harvest haze of the hills, above an atmosphere now warmed by the fragrant fields spread out below. Now and then an approaching aeroplane interrupted with its miniature mechanical fury, before fading back to some far corner of the sky. Then the dense sound of the earth would return, like dust settling over all of the land.

The coming of evening inspired César. Here, in the Olympic heights, he told us tales of sailing, of the perils of the aerial sea. Simone's serene understanding brought him even closer to an elemental truth he was just then trying to explain. I would always remember him like this, shrouded in saintly speculation. Again, as in former days, César spoke through me, and I worked my hands in the air for Simone. Curious, so curious, when she understood something, she laughed. Understanding was a pure pleasure to her. Though a bit glum that he could not truly join us in on our precise silent language, César caught her pleasure, even if it was a measured joy. As is often the case with generous sentiments, he could only express them so far, so sadly, they remained private.

Still he used elaborate hand gestures of his own. Simone had many questions. Had they ever sailed at night? How far was the farthest? How high the highest? César told her what it was like to sail across the English Channel, and to look down upon the blazing lights of the capital city at night. More than once, a cluster of thunderclouds had kept the aeronauts captive in the sky until well past midnight. To land in the dark was impossible, so they had to sail above the rumbling storm clouds until morning. How the darkness all around would suddenly light up in the shape of rolling clouds, only to disappear back into darkness . . . César reached out towards Simone's shoulder. The electric charge of the clouds makes your hair stand on end. You can smell it in the very air. The thunder, so close, makes your gut rumble. A constellation of lights burns in a town far below, radiating out in ragged lines, signifying roads that lead out to other towns. Don't forget your passport. A necessity. Oh yes, because you truly are explorers—of a dark sea more vast than continents or dreams. What language will they speak, the inhabitants of the morning, when you land? Flemish? Dutch? Basque? One time the constable arrested them and kept them prisoner in the police station until well past noon. In the morning they were spies, but by nightfall they were ambassadors once again of good times, laughing over aperitifs and cigars.

Then Latham's *Antoinette* appeared, heading straight for our ship. While climbing in circles over the sunset, before reaching the pinnacle, the highest an aviator had ever flown. Latham took the time to fly close enough to the stationary balloons to wave hello. He doffed his cap, bit down on his cigarette holder, and peppered the countryside with his feisty aura.

One double-decker Voisin made the first attempt for the altitude prize, plowing by with a steadfastness that drew the usual murmur, though much of the crowd was already slowly drifting away. The aviator kept his front elevator wing aimed high into the stiff climb before him as he flew in long, slow, ascending circles. As he passed the aeroship of the *Buontemponi*, the broad uprights of his wings rippled like the sails of a ship.

Then another aeroplane separated itself from the circling fleet. It was Latham in his *Antoinette VII*. To record his elevation, he was told he had to hold the barograph in between his knees, so he monitored his altitude in a stooped position. In this way he ascended, staring down at his instrument. I was surprised at how, from up here, the piloting of an aeroplane seemed completely unremarkable, as if the aviator were a disinterested office clerk riding upon a desk. I had the impression that Latham was riding his writing desk far into the nighttime sky.

Hubert Latham set a new world record for altitude that day at Reims, with a flight of 505 feet, which was the limit the judges would allow. His barograph could not calibrate any height greater. Though many reputable observers claimed he had flown much higher, the next highest flight was 165 feet below his official mark.

After Latham came Farman, Rougier, and Bunau-Varilla—all in his trail. In widening circles, each aviator made his own attempt to rise above the others. The crowd, sensing one last rush to be had, paused involuntarily before the exits, gazing up into the approaching night. The white shellacked canvas of their crafts gave the fliers a sheen of unreality, as ghosts against the gloom.

One by one, the other aeroplanes reached their limits and turned back, flying the same wide circles in descent. But still Latham climbed. The sound of his engine faded and then disappeared altogether. On soundless wings he rose, far above the sea of upturned faces, which in turn grew silent. Long after Latham had clearly won, he kept climbing, and climbing. The crowd found its voice again, unified in one long, rousing cheer of approval, of amazement. But Latham heard none of it. The gothic, canvas-covered swan floated through the darkness, a much darker and thinner medium up there perhaps. For a moment his craft was silhouetted against the moon's pale-lit face. And silently, as it grew difficult to make out his shape, he bore off into the tranquil nighttime sea.

There, in the balloon, César went on to speculate that, while sailing the vast expanses, be it in a ship, or especially a ship adrift in the loneliness of the sea, when two vessels cross each other's path, the occupants, being entirely isolated from one another, make a most special effort to wave and say hello. They either fight, immediately, and with a vehemence, or the isolation makes them fast, immediate friends. But listen. César tried to give a sense to Simone of the distant, echoing voices of the crowd following the birdman. He wrote down his more urgent thoughts on a notepad, that they—he and his friend of the *Buontemponi*—had both sailed this very ship from England. That they'd flown over oceans. Landed in foreign countries.

Then César looked on with that gentle, far-off optimism of his at our gesturing hands. "I dare say, you two have invented something so intriguing, and marvelous, without even trying. A language all your own."

As César talked on, Simone and I leaned out over the rails of the world. We saw the far-reaching hills of the horizon, and the hills beyond those hills, and how the earth rose gently into the fantails of the dissolving clouds, beyond whatever could be seen.

Acknowledgements

I AM BLESSED TO BE ABLE TO THANK THE FOLLOWING PEOPLE FOR THE hope, expertise, and help of all kinds during the 15 years of writing this story. Without them, the spirit of the work would have perished long ago.

Special thanks to Erin Wilson and Chris Moulin for their help with the French language and to Lu-Devine Tekapy for the geography of France. My thanks to the following for reading all or portions of the manuscript, or helping me talk through aspects of it, or, who truly are muses to me, in whatever form: John Marsh, Dave Downing, Caleb Powell, Sarah Powell, Britton Steele, Scott Driscoll, Nick O'Connell, Jason Emmons, Bill Thompson, Kelly Brown, John Toelle, Karen Rooker, Ed Trumbule, Andrea Hayes, Larry Swanson, Misha Van de Veire, George Corrigan, Jean Fee. Jeanine Cummins, Carolyn Turgeon, Scott B.F. Bailey, Vinnie Sarroco, Krista Mirhosieni, Phyllis Lutjens, Ben Jacklet, Toddie Downs, Anne Mini, Matt Setter, Christi Dicker-hofe, Doug Siepp, Tracy from Canada, Angela Wheeless. Safiye Senturk, Isabelle Franklin, Irene Franklin, and Wendy, Brian, Mike and Carrie Maheu, and Lisa and Rich Meyers. Frank and Allie and Spencer Fee. To my mom, once the fastest knitter in all of Oregon! Thank you. To my son Sam for his constant encouragement and the endless inspiration of his music.

My gratitude to the staff at the Boeing Flight Museum, curator John Little, curator emeritus Dennis Parks, and to Chris Stanton, for assisting me with my research, and for talking out historical specula-tions. It is an inspiration to talk with people for whom history is a living, breathing thing.

To Jeff Kleinman of Folio Lit for his dedication in developing early drafts, and to the generous guidance of Fred Ramey at Unbridled Books.

My amazed gratitude to Miranda Ottewell for her careful, artful editing. And to Cindy Willis for having read so many drafts and bringing the breath of life to the story.

Especially to my publishers at Chatwin Books: the editors, Annie Brule, Megan Gray, Molly Silvestrini, and Phil Bevis, for the patient, heartfelt support over the years, and the help with the very shaping of things till it no longer seemed like fiction, and the belief it takes to bring out a book.